VENETIAN RHAPSODY

Katherine Shaw arrives in Venice, the most romantic city in the world, to be governess with the aristocratic Voccheroni family. Twenty years of age and from a quiet English upbringing, Katherine suddenly finds herself plunged into a gay whirl of fashion, riches and romance.

VENETIAN RHAPSODY

Venetian Rhapsody

by

Denise Robins

Magna Large Print Books
Long Preston, North Yorkshire,
BD23 4ND, England.

British Library Cataloguing in Publication Data.

Robins, Denise
  Venetian rhapsody.

  A catalogue record of this book is
  available from the British Library

  ISBN   0-7505-2437-5

First published in Great Britain in 1954
by Hutchinson & Co. (Publishers) Ltd.

Copyright © 1954 Denise Robins

Cover illustration © John Hancock by arrangement with
P.W.A. International

The moral right of the author has been asserted

Published in Large Print 2005 by arrangement with
Patricia Clark for executors of Denise Robins' Estate

Magna Large Print is an imprint of Library Magna Books Ltd.

Printed and bound in Great Britain by
T.J. (International) Ltd., Cornwall, PL28 8RW

1

Katherine leaned across the breakfast-table and looked at her family with eyes that were brilliant with excitement. Out of the big envelope which the postman had just delivered to her, had tumbled a fascinating assortment of pamphlets, blue, red, and yellow. Katherine's voice, warm and low-pitched, was a tone higher as she read aloud:

'And this one is from the *Ufficio Turismo* – that means Official Tourist. It says: *"Venice, a unique city of world-wide fame ... of marble palaces, churches, Byzantine, Renaissance, lacework of windows and colonnades ... matchless and authentic marble and..."'*

She was interrupted by an exclamation from her schoolboy brother:

'Oh, golly!' he said, and giggled.

But Katherine's mother bit her lip and felt an absurd inclination to cry.

'It does sound wonderful, doesn't it, Kath? I've always longed to see Venice, but your father' – she gave a polite little cough and glanced at the grey-haired, mild-looking man who was half-buried behind the morning paper – 'never cared to go abroad. He said that England was good enough for him.'

Mr Shaw had heard. His bespectacled eyes twinkled over the rim of the paper.

'And I still think so, my dear. You can keep your Venice and all the glorious ruins. Take a look out of this window. Isn't that good enough for you?'

'Dear old British die-hard Daddy!' laughed Katherine, but her cheeks remained pink with excitement as she sorted through the literature sent to her by the London Travel Agency. She knew that view from the window so well. It was a wonderful one. But wonders can fade a little through habit and custom. She had lived here all her life. It was splendid enough. Towering cliffs, rocks glistening with wet, blue mussels, a long line of creamy Atlantic rollers breaking on the superb yellow sands. Dear little Mawgan Porth! Her father had worked in St Columb as a doctor for many long years. He was still struggling, in his late fifties. And her mother, ten years younger, had worn herself out in the effort to bring up her children. There was Peter, aged fourteen, and David, twelve, and the youngest, barely ten, a girl named Veryan after the Cornish village in which her mother had been born.

Life in this little stucco red-roofed house on the cliffs had been a struggle for as long as Katherine could remember. Worse when Daddy had been in the R.A.M.C during the war and Mummy had had to carry on alone.

And for the last two years Mrs Shaw had not been at all well, which worried Dr Shaw and distressed Katherine. It was especially unfortunate because Katherine was not really domesticated. She was a scholar by nature. She had more of her father in her and was always to be found with her head buried in a book. She had also inherited from him those rather weak, but beautiful, grey eyes; needing glasses for close work. She had a particular passion for learning. As was to be expected, at school she had been what she herself called a 'wash-out' at games, but carried off all the prizes for history and English.

She had set her heart on a career. But now at twenty – she was still helping with the endless chores. Dr Shaw was too busy and harassed to give much thought to Katherine's personal ambitions. But the mother was not unaware of the many sacrifices her eldest girl had made; her unselfishness, her devotion to them all. She had lately become sharply aware that Katherine was undergoing a spiritual struggle – a longing to spread her wings and use that fine brain of hers which showed itself in all kinds of new ways. Sudden irritation with the younger children ... fits of impatience ... all the outward signs of an inner secret rebellion. But Constance Shaw had been rebelling too, in her quiet way. Determined that this quiet, clever, and thoroughly nice daughter of hers should not waste all her youth and gifts in Mawgan Porth. When she took pains with her appearance, who could be lovelier than their Katherine? Tall, like her father, with long straight legs and his fine-cut features, and her mother's thick, burnt-gold hair with a deep wave in it. It was generally tied back severely with a ribbon to keep it out of her eyes. But she could look really wonderful when she tried. Veryan wasn't going to be nearly as pretty. The boys were good-looking and, thank God, strong. Constance and Steven Shaw had a wonderful family.

Now, at last, Katherine's big chance had come. Mrs Shaw, as she heard the girl talking about Venice, rejoiced that she had never lost touch with her old school friend, Beatrice Crichton.

Constance and Beatrice had been at the same boarding school. They had shared bedrooms, studies, pastimes, and struck up a friendship which was destined to last. Somewhat an incongruous one really, because Beatrice was the only child of wealthy parents, brought up by an ambitious mother to believe that the only thing that mattered was that she should make a brilliant marriage. The young Beatrice had been rather a haughty little girl, disliked by her companions. Constance, the antithesis; warm-hearted and cheerful, easy to get on with. And she had been quick to find there was a nice side to Beatrice, and befriended her. Long after Beatrice went abroad and made her 'brilliant marriage' she continued to write to her less-fortunate friend who had married a poor doctor.

Connie remained in Cornwall, Beatrice had become the Marchesa di Voccheroni, having netted one of the most illustrious titles in Italy. Whether or not she had found real happiness, Constance Shaw did not know. Beatrice had been too discontented by nature – ever seeking for more than she had. But she had sent her old friend, Connie, photographs of her magnificent *Palazzo* on the Grand Canal in Venice. And long letters describing the wonders of her handsome son, Renato, and her daughter, Bianca, who was Connie's god-child.

Naturally as the years went by, correspondence grew less frequent between the old school friends. And during the war it stopped altogether. Then started again, in order to let Constance know that Beatrice and her family were reinstated in Venice, having spent the war years safe and sound in America.

After that came only spasmodic news. The latest news, a year ago, was that the old Marchese had died. Renato, the son and heir, who had been educated at Eton and Oxford, appeared to be leading the gay life of a typical wealthy Italian boy. Bianca was at a finishing school in Paris.

Then a wildly thrilling letter had come from Beatrice suggesting that Connie's girl should go out to Venice and live with the family for awhile.

My Bianca's English is so poor, Beatrice wrote. *I want her taught properly. She is at an awkward age, seventeen. Too grown up for the school-room, yet not as old as I wish her to be when she takes her place in society here. As you may know we lead a very* mondaine *life and I am always enormously busy entertaining for Renato and his friends. He will, of course, make a brilliant marriage. But I want Bianca to have a companion and tutor for a year. If I remember right, your girl Katherine must be nearly of age. You've always said in all your letters that she is a good linguist and a nice clever girl. Send her to us, and I will of course pay all her expenses. Apart from her work here she will have a good time. She will relieve me of the tedious responsibility of amusing my teen-age Bianca and help to keep her out of mischief.*

How Connie had smiled over that letter. Particularly the familiar words *'brilliant marriage'*. So like the old Beatrice. As ambitious for her son as her own parents had been for *her*.

12

At first Katherine had gone crazy with excitement over this letter, then shaken her head. She couldn't go. She couldn't leave Mummy and the family.

But this time Connie Shaw put down her foot. This was Katherine's big chance. *She was to take it.* With what was perhaps the most superb gesture of her life, Constance proceeded to send a telegram accepting her old school friend's offer.

And after that it didn't take long to make Katherine agree. The girl was longing to go.

Winter still held Europe in the grip of ice and snow, but the Marchesa had said in her letter that Venice was quite lovely at this time of year. They had central heating in the palace – every modern comfort. As for clothes, the Marchesa could help Katherine in that respect. She must go to Venice as soon as she could. The Marchesa had a full social programme ahead of her and was longing to get Bianca settled. The real crux of the matter was the fact that Bianca had not been at all well lately. The poor child suffered from *migraine* and the doctor had advised that she should not return to her studies in Paris, but lead a less strenuous life in her own home.

Now all was settled. This was Saturday. On Monday Katherine was to fly to Milan; thence to Venice. In her imperious and not ungenerous fashion, Beatrice had already sent a cheque on her London bank to cover all the girl's expenses. There had been a wild rush to the Newquay shops to get together a modest wardrobe for Katherine. She had nothing but 'rags' her mother had declared. She must not go out to the Voccheronis looking so shabby. This was where a little of the money that Dr Shaw had put by for a rainy day should be drawn upon – for Katherine.

Katherine had sent for all these pamphlets from the tourist agency because she wanted to read all that she could get about the golden city of canals.

But now, suddenly, the keen scholar, and would-be traveller, was replaced by the affectionate young girl who had just adored her parents and home.

'Oh, darlings!' she exclaimed, and her underlip quivered. 'I'm going to send a wire and say I can't go.'

Mrs Shaw moved to her daughter's side and put an arm around the slim, straight figure and smiled at the earnest, charming young face through the mist of her own tears.

'Stop talking nonsense, darling, and slip upstairs and get on with your sorting and packing,' she said.

Katherine flung her arms around her mother's neck speechlessly, kissed her – and went.

14

2

At ten forty-five on the Monday morning, Katherine sat in the waiting-room at London Airport. Last night she had stayed with a cousin who had a flat in Kensington. The B.E.A. bus had brought her from the Terminus. There was a slight fog this November morning – enough to delay the take-off just a little. Over the tannoy it had just been announced that there would be no departures for another half an hour.

Katherine did not mind. And she had no nerves about flying, and fog. It was to be her first flight. She was inwardly seething with excitement. She listened enthralled as loudspeakers sonorously called each glamorous name:

'*Milan ... Holland ... Cairo...*'

It seemed a long cry now from Mawgan Porth.

Katherine looked unusually well-groomed in her new tweed suit and the nicest, most expensive Jaegar overcoat she had ever had in her life. She had taken a little more care with her hair.

Two young men who were standing by the bookstall, lighting cigarettes, glanced in her direction. They had just driven up to the airport in an Aston Martin. It belonged to Richard Kerr-West, the elder of the two. He was saying:

'She runs like a bird, doesn't she, old boy? Sleekest thing I've had for years.'

'Well, using the word "sleek" – what about those legs?'

Kerr-West looked at Katherine and shook his head.

'Incurable, my dear Renato. I admit that she's got beautiful legs. But the rest is not up to your standard.'

Thoughtfully, Renato di Voccheroni surveyed the young girl who seemed so engrossed in a book. She had no chic, of course, as compared with the exquisitely-dressed women of Italian society. The girl in the corner was English – a trifle *bourgeois*. But those legs *were* poems! Now, suddenly, as though a sixth sense told her that she was being criticized, Katherine raised her head.

'Schoolmarm with glasses,' whispered Richard. 'You're slipping, my lad.'

Katherine removed her glasses. Richard changed his mind, and Renato raised his brows. He was near enough to her to see the length of her eye-lashes and the extraordinary purity of her skin. The two men turned away.

'Think again, buddy,' said Renato lightly; 'she's "got something".' He spoke with a slight American drawl, and with no trace of an Italian accent.

'I'll hand it to you,' said his friend, 'and I see *Venice* on the label. You're always lucky. Never without a companion. Is any girl safe with you?'

'Mind you, I like them to be beautiful and responsive,' laughed Renato.

'And with a good bank balance,' his friend reminded him. They laughed together.

Katherine listened to the laughter and looked at the backs of the two young men indifferently. They seemed to be sharing a good joke. The tall dark one with the bag was obviously the traveller being seen off by the one of shorter, sturdier build. He was extremely handsome, although not strictly Katherine's type. If she had an ideal, she reflected, he would be essentially English, perhaps fair, and, of course, studious. As fond of books, of art, as herself.

The tall man looked anything but studious. And she didn't much care for those brown suède shoes or that beautiful silk scarf – a little *too* beautiful, she decided. He also looked rather conceited, and had actually turned to glance back at her. Katherine primly lowered her gaze. But she was flattered, nevertheless.

Renato walked out to watch his friend drive off. He was devoted to old Dick. They had been at Oxford together. Dick had since become a barrister and was already working in London. Renato di Voccheroni had never known what it was to work, except to get his degree. But he had little ambition for a career. He was too fond of life as it could be lived by a rich young man – who, at the age of twenty-four, was head of an illustrious Venetian family.

He rode well to hounds. He was a skilled fencer. But his English blood frequently warred with the Italian strain in him.

Life so far for Renato had been merely a gay pursuit of pleasure. He was genuinely proud of his magnificent ancestral home. In Venice he had his own motor-boat. He owned a racing car. He could hunt and ride and shoot in Tuscany where they owned a delightful country house. He could come to England and behave like an Englishman when the fancy took him.

In spite of too much money and soft living he was fundamentally unspoiled. He had been exceedingly generous to Richard, whose people were unable to give him more than a meagre allowance. Now Richard had come into money – and was making it, but he could never forget Renato's warm-hearted munificence. He really had an awfully nice side.

Richard was a bit worried at the moment because Renato's English mother was as extravagant as her son, and the di Voccheroni fortune was dwindling rapidly. Renato had told Dick that it was essential that he should 'marry money'. Richard himself, had every intention of marrying for love.

He knew that Renato was returning home to try and get himself into the frame of mind to propose marriage to one of the girls his mother had selected for him. The Contessa Violantè Chiago, the young and beautiful widow of one of the wealthiest industrialists in Italy, and an American girl, Hilary Drumann, were Renato's latest girl-friends. But somehow Richard could not visualize him as the husband of a spoiled Roman beauty or as son-in-law of a corned-beef king.

Affectionately, Richard bade Renato goodbye and added with a mischievous twinkle:

'Have a good flight – happy landings and all that, and I'll lay ten to one you'll be taking the little schoolmarm with the lovely legs out to dinner in Venice tonight.'

Renato laughed heartily and gripped his friend's hand.

'I accept the bet. You can pay me when you see me. Now I'll see how quickly I can remove the horn-rimmed spectacles and bring a smile to the lovely lips. So long, old boy.'

Katherine looked up sharply from her book. She had heard her flight number being called over the tannoy.

Excitedly she sprang to her feet.

An attractive-looking air hostess piloted her

19

to a window-seat. The rest of the seats filled up rapidly. Then, somewhat to her embarrassment, the tall young man wearing the expensive clothes, whom she had mentally labelled 'film star', dropped into the chair beside her.

The take-off thrilled Katherine so much that she took no further interest in him. She saw roof-tops below her at one moment, blank space the next. Then up, up, up, rocking through the clouds.

A pleasant voice from beside her said:

'Well, that's *that*. I'm always thankful once we're airborne, aren't you?'

Katherine turned now to her companion. At close quarters she saw that he had fine eyes, as grey as her own, and superb teeth that seemed very white in the tanned face. He looked as though he must have found some sunshine this winter.

He smiled at her with such a disarming friendliness that she had to smile back.

'It's my first flight,' she said.

How amusing, thought Renato di Voccheroni. His shoulders touched hers. There wasn't much room between these chairs. His gaze, so critical of feminine charm, could find no fault with her flawless skin.

Renato constituted himself her instructor – told her that she could now unfasten her safety-belt and offered her a cigarette which she refused. So she didn't even smoke, he smiled to himself. And she asked for coffee when he suggested a stronger drink.

'What, no vices?'

'Oh yes, if I could afford it, I think travelling would be a vice with me. It's so exciting.'

Renato, who had done too much of it, envied her.

Katherine did not really know how to stand up to all the charm that Renato so deliberately put over. During the three hours of that flight he seemed to take complete charge of her, whether she wanted it or not.

'We must meet,' said Renato gaily; 'you must give me your address and, perhaps, allow me to show you Venice. I know it well enough. It is my home.'

This surprised her. What was an Englishman doing living in Venice?

She took off her glasses and regarded him a trifle severely. She decided that he wanted snubbing – he was much too self-confident. She was quite certain that he expected her to drop like a ripe plum into his lap and say: 'Oh, how *thrilling* – I'd *love* you to show me Venice.'

But she said nothing. She would much rather visit all the places of interest in Venice alone, she decided, with her little handbook of information to help her.

Eventually Renato Voccheroni lapsed into silence. He was being forced, incredible

though it seemed, to realize that he was getting nowhere with this grey-eyed, funny little
thing in her awful suit. (What a laugh for
Dick!) It was certainly not a walkover. He
was a long way yet from taking her out to
dinner.

She had returned to that book of hers.
Renato had the most primitive desire to
remove her glasses and kiss her on that
beautifully-moulded, disapproving young
mouth; he was positively intrigued. Why, she
wouldn't even give him her name.

He made one or two further attempts to
engage her attention and failed, so buried
himself moodily in a magazine. Just before
they landed, he tried another line. Perhaps
her violent interest in the countryside would
conquer her. He heard her indrawn breath
of delight when they first came down, broke
through the clouds and she could discern
the mighty city of Milan unfolding itself
beneath her.

'Oh, I believe I can see the cathedral!' she
exclaimed. He saw the colour sweep her
face and throat and he thought:

'This girl's *got something*. I'd like to see her
blush because of *me*. The cathedral, indeed!
No girl with legs like her should go haywire
at the sight of a *cathedral* – and scowl at me.
It isn't natural.'

He began to tell her about Milan. But she
was still not taking much notice of him

when they landed. She rejected his offer to drive her to Venice. She was going on by plane as arranged, she said.

Renato found himself reduced to an humiliating attempt to interest her in his car, since she made no response to *him*. He pointed to the big, powerful, yellow Alfa-Romeo beside which a green-liveried chauffeur with smart black gaiters stood waiting.

'Won't that tempt you? Do come along with me. I can show you the countryside.'

'It's terribly nice of you but I shall keep to my schedule, thanks,' she said, and then gave quite a pleasant smile because she thought she was being rather too unfriendly. He had really been very nice to her and well … he *was* a heart-throb to look at!

Renato said: 'Oh, well, as you wish. I'd like awfully to see you again, though. What about that address you promised me?'

'Did I?' Now her lips trembled into a smile and Renato Voccheroni, who had been 'the great lover' ever since he left Oxford, found himself absurdly elated because the ice had momentarily thawed.

'Come on – tell!' he pleaded.

She thought there could be no harm in letting him know her address. After all, he lived in Venice.

'I am going to the Palazzo Voccheroni,' she said.

Renato was staring at her incredulously.

'The Palazzo di Voccheroni?' he repeated. 'But why ... what for...?' he broke off stupidly.

'Why not?' asked Katherine indignantly. 'It happens to be my home.'

'*Your home?*' It was Katherine's turn to look stupid. She put her hand to her lips. 'Oh, lord,' she added, 'you're not *Renato* by any chance?'

'I am, at your service,' he bowed. 'And you–?'

Katherine did not answer for an instant. She took off her glasses and began to laugh, helplessly.

3

In the diary which Katherine had brought with her and decided to keep as a faithful record of her life in Venice she wrote:

I was absolutely flabbergasted to find that the conceited and handsome young man who was trying so hard to 'get off with me' during my flight, was the son of Mummy's old friend. It was really rather funny. He seemed a bit annoyed. I think he lost his sense of humour when he heard who I was. Mummy warned me that the di Voccheronis might be snobbish; I expect the great Renato wasn't too pleased to find that he had been shooting such a line with his sister's English teacher-companion. I must say he was very courteous, and did everything he could to help me. We got through the Customs without a hitch and it was nice to have someone with me who spoke fluent Italian, and was so well known, and once I knew who he was I couldn't go on refusing to let him drive me to Venice. And I did so want to see the countryside.

Renato is autocratic. He likes getting his own way. He put a phone call through to his mother and I heard him explaining that he had met up with me and would be bringing me along.

Milan is a huge, noisy, bewildering city. Unfortunately I didn't have time to catch more than a glimpse of the magnificent cathedral. We drove so quickly through it. Renato took the wheel with me beside him; the chauffeur at the back. I still can't get over the fact that he is half Italian. I suppose it is his English education that made him seem so very English. We raced at rather a terrifying speed down the autostrada – bound for Venice. We had three hundred kilometres to do – that is about one hundred and eighty miles. It was a terrific thrill and Renato was most interesting and slowed down at the places of interest. He said we had four hours' drive in front of us, and we couldn't make Venice before dark which was disappointing, but at least I saw some amazing country. The wind blew coldly down from the snow-capped mountains. It was most exhilarating. But on the plains it was mild compared with winter at home. I adored the picturesque little villages, the olive groves, the old churches on the hills among the cypresses. We drove down narrow little streets, passed ruined towers, dark belts of forest and saw peasants leading their donkeys along streets as we flashed by in the gorgeous Alfa-Romeo. We reached Brescia and then skirted the end of Lake Garda which is so lovely that I longed to stay there. Oh! that heavenly emerald water – green snow water fed by the melting snow from the Alps; the exquisite white villages on the shore! But we had to press on to Verona (remembering my Shakespeare) through Padua and, at last, in the gathering darkness came to the end of the mainland, the Piazzale Roma, where the chauffeur parked the car, and Renato's motor-boat was waiting to take us across the canal.

'Sorry you won't see Venice for the first time in the daylight, but it has its compensations at night,' *he said to me.*

He was friendly, yet somehow not as gay as he had been before he learned who I was; perhaps the knowledge that I was going to be his sister's paid companion had subdued him. I felt a bit awkward. It appears I must have been very frigid and unfriendly to him in the plane, because talking about his sister Bianca for a moment he gave me a queer smile and said: 'My young sister is far too sentimental and does a lot of weeping and copying out sad poems. She's at the sloppy age of course. But you'll soon cure her of that.' *When I asked him why, he answered:* 'Well, you're not given to weeping or reading sad poems, I am sure, my dear Katherine.' *That flummoxed me; but when I asked him if he thought I was hardboiled, he said not exactly but that I was too reserved and that he would be quite intrigued to find out if I had a heart. That embarrassed me so that I didn't answer, and anyhow I was much too excited about Venice to listen to Renato's nonsense. Of COURSE I've got a heart and it beat much too fast when I slipped as I got into*

27

the motor-launch, and he caught me in his arms for a moment. I nearly died of embarrassment but I just won't let Renato number me among his conquests. I remember quite plainly now that the Marchesa said in one of her letters to Mummy that her son 'had his pick of the flower of Italy'! Anyhow, he would not take any notice of me in future.

How shall I write of Venice? The Venice I saw first in the purple dusk of that winter's night, under a sky of radiant stars. Stars mirrored in numberless little canals, silvered the charming humped bridges and turned the marble statues and carved stone buildings into something out of a dream. We passed mysterious narrow houses with shutters of faded blue and peach and rose. I saw the gondolas as I had always imagined them, the gondoliers calling out 'Ohé' – that note of warning – as they round the corners under the arches.

We came to the Palazzo that was his home. It had a noble façade of pillars, of wrought-iron, and carved stone. Two great lamps burned outside the massive studded doors which were thrown open as Renato helped me up the stone steps. I found myself in a wonderful hall full of fine Florentine tapestries and had a confused glimpse of flowers on a long black marble table: carved chairs with old velvet seats; an unfamiliar odour of burning wood and wine and scent and very old things. A wide, curved staircase leading up to a gallery filled with *paintings; burgundy-coloured velvet curtains drawn across immensely high windows. Then I became aware of a bevy of servants, all wearing dark green livery. Incredible to think that they still exist in rich Italian households. Then I heard Renato say:* 'Here's Mother.' *Down the stairs came Beatrice di Voccheroni. Tall, thin and handsome. The sophisticated life she has led makes her look years older than Mummy, I thought. She was very lined, terrifically chic. She had silver-grey hair, a pale skin and discontented lips, faintly rouged. She appears to live on her nerves. But I could see that she adored Renato. She gave me a warm welcome and said nice things about Mummy and how my fair hair reminded her of 'dear Connie's' at school.*

Then Bianca appeared. Thin, sallow, with huge dark eyes and dark curly hair. She said ''Ello' and gave me a limp hand. She looks scared and rather furtive, poor thing. She can only speak English with an awful accent. It appears that she wasn't with her mother and brother in America during the war. She was always so ill as a child, they left her with an aunt in some safe, remote place up in the Italian Alps and collected her again after the war.

I've a pretty shrewd suspicion that the Marchesa is all for her handsome son and can't be bothered with poor little Bianca. I can also see that it isn't Renato's fault if he is vain. They all worship him here.

The Marchesa told me at once that my main job would be to make Bianca talk good English. She told me a lot of other things which I hardly remember as I was too confused and excited. But I gathered that Bianca and I were to make ourselves scarce as a rule. Tonight we were to join the little dinner-party that she had speedily organized to welcome Renato. She appears to be amazed that he had flown with me and had not expected him until next week. Although she put an arm around my shoulder and looked at me kindly – I got the impression that the Marchesa is not kind at heart, but a supreme egotist, charming only when she gets her own way. I wonder if mother and son ever clash? Poor Bianca is certainly the odd one out in this family. She hardly mentions her mother but can't stop talking about her wonderful brother. The man seems to get under one's skin, despite oneself...

It was here that Katherine stopped writing. It would be fun to keep this diary, and send it home bit by bit, perhaps for Mummy to read to the family. But no, on second thoughts Katherine decided she would keep it locked up.

She gazed round the bedroom. It was sumptuous. There were never-ending signs of luxury here. Her bedroom had three tall windows, *jalousies* opening out on to the balcony. Thick white rugs on the polished floor;

thick curtains of green and gold Florentine silk. There was a fine old carved oak cupboard for her clothes; a typically Italian writing-bureau on curved spindly legs. Then a luxurious bathroom with black and white rubber floor and black glass walls and ceiling. She was to share this with Bianca.

Katherine glanced at her wrist-watch and jumped. She must have a bath and change. It was eight o'clock. Luisa, the maid, had told her they did not dine in the *Palazzo* until half-past nine. She would have to get used to such late hours. Why at half-past nine at home Mummy and Daddy were already thinking of bed!

While she changed (the Marchesa had told her to wear a short dress) Katherine received a visit from Bianca. The young girl wore a simple, dark velvet dress with lace collar and cuffs. She looked young for her seventeen years and was obviously being 'kept young' by her mother. She seemed pathetically anxious to make friends with Katherine and her sallow face blushed for pleasure when Katherine suggested that she had drawn her black, rather greasy, hair too tightly back from her face, and should loosen it a little.

'Tank you, I want very mooch look *bella* – beautiful–' she said, wistfully.

'Why, you do, I've never seen such long eye-lashes,' said Katherine smiling, and felt as though she was going to add another young sister to her own family. She remembered what Renato had said about Bianca being sentimental. Little wonder; for she seemed to lead a very repressed lonely life, and it was a shame she should suffer so from these dreadful headaches. She needed some love and individual attention. Katherine began to brush her own hair. Bianca touched it reverently.

'It is gold,' she said admiringly, 'and you are *multa bella* – beautiful wizout your glasses.'

Katherine laughed.

'I don't always wear them, you know, only for close work.'

'I am glad you have come here, I am always by myself. Mamma is so busy.'

'I am glad I'm here,' said Katherine. 'We'll do lots of things together, Bianca. You must show me Venice tomorrow.'

'I am sick of Venice,' said Bianca grimacing.

'You can't be!' exclaimed Katherine. 'It's too beautiful for words.'

'Did my brother make love to you?' asked Bianca abruptly.

Katherine went crimson.

'My *dear* Bianca–!'

Bianca suddenly giggled. This made her seem more homely to Katherine who was on the verge of feeling homesick. It would be nice to laugh and relax with Bianca.

'Renato makes love to most women; zey fall at ze feet of Renato. He is wonderful, is he not?' Bianca added.

'I think he is attractive, but I have by no means fallen at his feet,' said Katherine drily.

'I tink you will,' said Bianca.

'Nothing of the kind,' said Katherine in a shocked voice.

Really it was detestable the way this family circled around the young man of the house.

During dinner there was so much for Katherine to take in, she did not know where to begin. Everything in the massive dining-room gave her the impression of magnificence – the fast-fading splendour of the Renaissance coupled with modern comforts.

The Contessa Violantè Chiago wore tonight a brown velvet dinner suit, collars and cuffs encrusted with gold embroidery. Her hair which was a dark red was brushed smoothly back from the white forehead, showing ears completely hidden by gold and ruby ear-rings. She was heavily made-up like so many of the smart Italian women, and had a large red sensuous mouth and a black beauty spot at one corner. She did not speak English. Except for saying. ''Ow do you do' to Katherine when they were first introduced, she afterwards ignored her. She chattered in Italian like a vivacious magpie, for the most part to Renato on whose right hand she was sitting. It seemed to Katherine that she coquetted with him outrageously, giving him the full benefit of those huge eyes with their blackened lashes. Katherine was fascinated too, to hear the flow of Italian which poured from Renato in response. He looked less English now than when they had first met. The young Contessa was obviously madly in love with him.

Now and again Renato addressed himself to Katherine. He did not refer to their journey but mentioned a particular exhibition of paintings, and a *film première*, both to be seen in Venice tomorrow. He wondered if Katherine was interested.

Katherine answered rather shyly. She was a trifle over-awed by this dinner party, and felt, especially, the cool critical gaze of the Marchesa always upon her.

Had she but known it, Beatrice di Voccheroni was none too pleased to find the daughter of her old friend such an attractive looking girl. The candles burning in the huge gilt candelabra cast a pearly lustre on Katherine's wonderful fair hair and healthy skin. Her black dress, with white collar and velvet bow, was obviously 'off the peg' – atrocious the Marchesa decided. Dressed properly the girl would be a beauty, and Beatrice made up her mind then and there that Renato must not see too much of young Katherine. She would have to talk to him seriously about money-matters. There were far too many bills mounting in his desk and her own. And she had a very uncomfortable hour yesterday with the manager of their Bank. World affairs had affected the di Voccheroni resources considerably. It was high time Renato settled down and married money. He *must*. He ought to be sensible and propose to Violantè whose husband had left her a fortune. She talked too much and was a little self-centred and *exigeant* but she was lovely, and would make a spectacular wife for Renato.

Beatrice watched her son gloomily. He was flirting with the Contessa but only because it was second nature for him to do so. She knew it. Now and again his mother caught him looking through his lashes at Katherine.

In fact Renato had by no means recovered from the surprise of learning who Katherine was. A pity, he decided, that she was not as well off as Violantè. Being what she was – a paid companion – she could never enter the orbit of his serious thoughts. On the other hand she intrigued him. He had a normally gay, facile disposition, and was used to being a success with women. She had made him feel altogether unsuccessful and he resented it. He wasn't going to be snubbed by a little schoolmarm (yes, that was what Dick had called her at the Airport). Added to which he found her a challenge and in a curious way attractive to him. He respected her intelligence; she wasn't just a girl 'with lovely legs'; she had something much more worthy of a chap's notice.

Then the Marchesa broke the sudden silence that had fallen.

'Renato, darling, wake up – Violantè has just asked you to meet her for coffee at Florian's tomorrow morning.'

Suddenly Renato's deep grey eyes took on a stubborn expression. Continuing to look at Katherine he spoke to Violantè.

'My apologies, Violantè, but I have already arranged to show some of the glories of Venice to our English guest.'

Katherine gasped. The Contessa who did not understand English, smiled gaily. The Marchesa who never showed emotion also smiled. But her hands clenched in her lap.

'I'm afraid dear Katherine will be busy with Bianca,' she said.

Before Katherine could answer for herself, Renato spoke again with a cool deliberation.

'Oh, you must give her one day of freedom, *Mamma mia*. She will have plenty of time for trailing after Bianca. Tomorrow I intend to take her around and be her guide. It's all arranged, isn't it, Katherine?'

4

Katherine by nature was truthful almost to the point of bluntness. But on this occasion she was floored. She could not drop a bomb-shell by openly accusing the young master of the house of being a liar. *'All arranged'*, indeed! It certainly hadn't been. But what *could* she say? She looked so confused and unhappy that Bianca, young though she was, felt sorry for the English girl and saved an awkward moment by breaking into a flood of Italian which she translated for Katherine.

'I tell my mother, I no want to work tomorrow. Too hot. My brother and I both show you Venice.'

Katherine breathed again. The atmosphere cleared. But she was quite sure the Marchesa did not approve. How nervous she was! Her long thin fingers, sparkling with gems, kept clenching and unclenching. She continually pressed her embroidered table-napkin to her lips, and a deep frown puckered her high white forehead. Only the Contessa continued to smile and talk, quite believing that her invitation had been accepted. She took it for granted.

As soon as her elderly husband died,

Violantè had transferred her attentions to the handsome di Voccheroni boy. He was two years younger than herself, but what mattered? Everybody in Venice was aware that the di Voccheronis were hard up. The Chiago fortune would undoubtedly be welcome. The two families had known each other for some time and Renato had always flirted with her and once told her that she was the most beautiful woman in Venice. It did not even enter her stupid, vain little head to imagine that he could be interested in the quiet English girl. The Contessa did not like Englishmen as a rule. But she suffered them when they fell in love with her enormous eyes, the entrancing way she had of tilting her head on one side and pouting her red lips; the exquisite petiteness of her figure, and her fabulous clothes. She wore absurd, *outré* hats, too. She was a legend in Venetian society. She was scornful of this English *mees*. What an ugly black dress; so badly cut! Nothing *élégante* about Mees Shaw – no finesse – just suitable for her job – companion-teacher to Bianca.

So Violantè's thoughts ran on. And Renato sat and finished his lemon-ice and was pleased because, as usual, he had got his own way. As for Bianca coming with them tomorrow – oh no! he would soon settle *her*. She should have one of her 'migraines'. She always did what he asked her. He would make certain that Katherine saw Venice through *his* eyes – and his alone.

Katherine was glad when the meal ended. As they rose, the Marchesa asked her if she played Canasta. She said she did not. The Marchesa smiled graciously and excused her, but thought:

'Of course – poor Connie; they would hardly have heard of the game that all smart Europe is playing.'

What a dull life she must lead in her Cornish retreat. Yet she wrote happily enough about her doctor and her 'brood'. One could not understand such people.

The Marchesa was quite pleased when Katherine said she would like to retire instead of joining them for coffee and liqueurs in the *salon*.

When she said good night to Renato, she felt far less calm and assured of herself than she had done during their journey. She even blushed as she held out her hand to him. He saw the high colour and inwardly exalted. So the little 'schoolmarm' was not so negative, neither did she lack sensibility. He smiled at her and said gaily:

'After breakfast, tomorrow – I'll have the motor-boat ready and we'll make a tour of the canals and I'll show you the sort of things I'm sure you'll want to see; museums, churches, galleries – I haven't seen them myself for so long, it will do me good. You are going to influence me to turn my thoughts to culture.'

'That would be a nice change, Renato,' put in his mother drily. But after Katherine had vanished, she added – still speaking English so that the Contessa could not understand– 'It's very naughty of you, *caro mia*. Violantè was counting on seeing you tomorrow.'

Renato lit a cigar.

'My dear Mamma,' he said, as he puffed blue smoke into the air, then examined the lighted end of the cigar. 'Violantè has countless admirers who will take her to Florian's. I thought it would be hospitable of me to put myself at our English guest's disposal.'

'She is hardly a *guest,* dear,' said the Marchesa with some impatience. 'She has come as Bianca's companion-governess.'

'But she is still the daughter of your old school-friend; the famous Connie we have always heard about, who was your slave at school.'

'Certainly, and I hope always to be loyal to Connie. She helped to make life tolerable for me at a place where I was atrociously unhappy. Katherine seems a sweet child, but you must *not* spoil her, Renato. You know how attractive you are to women.'

He laughed outright.

'Dearest Mamma – you flatter me. But I assure you that Katherine doesn't find *me* attractive. She snubbed me unmercifully – as only an English girl can do – in the plane.'

Violantè now felt that she had been ignored too long; she walked up to Renato and lifted her brilliant face to his.

'I think you must teach me English, Renato. I find it very difficult and ugly,' she said in her own liquid language. 'But you would like to hear me speak it – yes?'

He smiled as he would have done at a pretty, spoiled child.

'You have no need to study. You are a lovely picture. It is enough. One needs only to look at you,' he said.

This was the sort of language Violantè understood very well indeed. She was delighted. He switched on the radio. The *salon* was filled with the stirring sound of the love-duet from *Madame Butterfly* coming from the Opera House in Milan.

The Marchesa sipped her coffee and watched them, her brows still knitted and her thoughts none too happy. She adored her son but knew that it meant nothing when he paid compliments to beautiful women. He had been doing that since he left Eton. She began to regret that his father had died so early and that Renato had never been encouraged to work. But of course none of them had anticipated the collapse in Europe and such a change in their fortunes. Beatrice

41

was regretting, also, her own besetting vice – gambling. Renato, knew, of course, that she was a gambler, never happier than at the gaming-tables in places like San Remo, Monte Carlo, or Cannes. She had lost heavily last summer and then – using her gambling instincts in another direction – been foolishly persuaded to take a lot of her private means out of the sensible shares which had been paying small and regular dividends, and buy new stock. She had backed a certain oil concern which had gone crash during that recent trouble in Persia.

Only a small portion of the di Voccheroni money was tied up for Renato, but the Marchese had left his wife in control of the greater part of it. She had never said 'no' to Renato. She had indulged all his wild caprices as well as her own. As for Bianca – she was a thorn in her flesh. She had never really wanted a daughter; or a second child. And she was annoyed because the girl had turned out to be plain and sickly, and never likely to make a brilliant, helpful match. One of her reasons for wanting Bianca to perfect her English (and, incidentally, for bringing Katherine Shaw over here) was a plan to get Bianca out of the way next Spring; perhaps even send her to England when Katherine went home. She might live with the Shaw family for awhile. Beatrice couldn't be bothered to chaperone Bianca for another year or even two. She planned to shut the *Palazzo* and herself go down to the South of France as soon as she had settled the finances. But first she *must* ensure Renato's co-operation. If he couldn't come up to scratch with Violantè, then he must propose to Hilary Drumann.

Hilary and her parents were staying at the Royal Danielli – had been there for a couple of months. Not because they liked Venice at this time of the year, but because Mrs Drumann had contracted typhoid fever and was still confined to her bedroom, with two nurses in attendance. The Drumanns were typical of the wealthy American whom the Marchesa found boring, and slightly vulgar. But the girl was well educated, extremely good looking, and madly in love with Renato. If he took her as a wife, he would also get all the dollars the di Voccheronis needed. Old Drumann, with his corned-beef factories all over the U.S.A, was a millionaire.

Later that evening, Renato took the Contessa home in his motor-boat – the Chiago residence was only a short distance away. He broke the news to her that he would be too occupied in the morning to idle away an hour at Florian's with her. She was disappointed, and piqued.

'Then we will arrange something for the evening.'

With his easy grace he raised her hands to his lips and murmured:

'Thank you, I'll telephone you. Good night, *cara mia*. A thousand thanks, too, for dining with us – it was a delightful welcome home.'

But as the motor-boat speeded across the dark, dimpled waters of the Grand Canal, he forgot that Violantè existed. He was thinking of the flush that overspread Katherine's fresh, intelligent face as she said good night to him; of her utter lack of response to his blandishments. He felt suddenly restless. He knew that had he suggested it, Violantè would gladly have stayed for another hour with him out here on the Canal, under the glittering stars. But he wished he could knock on Katherine's door and make *her* come down and look at him – with temptation in her eyes, like the beautiful Italian widow. Life was queer, he reflected, that so much beauty coupled with riches should leave him stone-cold, whilst he found a distinct challenge in a cool, inexperienced English girl.

He knew that his mother wanted to talk to him. He was not anxious for a 'show-down' with her tonight. He was devoted to her but she could be too possessive and dictatorial at times, and so nervy that she was apt to put his own nerves on edge. He couldn't do with all her scheming and worrying and

44

match-making. He wanted life to flow along leisurely and smoothly for himself – to enjoy it in his own way – and for others to enjoy it with him.

He avoided the heart-to-heart talk which the Marchesa coveted and told her that he had to go out again at once to call on an old friend of his, Jacques de Grenoble, a Frenchman who was staying in Venice and wanted urgently to see him.

In the magnificence of her vast bedroom Katherine closed her shutters and, with a sigh, slipped into bed and drifted into sleep.

She awoke to find Luisa, Bianca's personal maid, opening the *jalousies*. The big bedroom was flooded with golden sunshine. Katherine sat up in bed with a gasp. Luisa said:

'*Buon giorno, Signorina,*' and placed at her side a tray bearing coffee, rolls, a big pat of yellow butter, and a jar of honey. Katherine blinked. Breakfast in bed! What luxury!

The coffee was strong and she was not sure that she fancied the burnt Continental flavour. But, in time, she was to grow to like it very much.

Before beginning her meal, she got out of bed, and with a dressing-gown around her shoulders, stepped on to the balcony and looked eagerly up and down at the canal. This was her first *real* sight of Venice, never to be forgotten. That pure golden light. The sheer radiance of it. The clear blue of the sky.

Even at this time of the year, the sun was quite warm. Last night Venice had seemed a fairyland of lights glittering in the water. This morning it was an enchanted city of amber, blue and rose and emerald. The water looked fantastically green.

Then Bianca came in. Katherine turned and was about to say how wonderful it all seemed to her, when she saw that the girl looked white and dejected and was holding her hands against her ears.

'Oh, Bianca dear, are you ill?' began Katherine.

Bianca shook her head.

It was nothing to worry about, she answered. Just the usual wretched *migraine*. But as for going out she could not *possibly*. She must be excused. She must go to bed for the whole day.

'Then, of course,' said Katherine, '*I* shall not go out either.'

Then from Bianca came a stream of protest, ending with:

'You *must* go. Renato would be so angry.'

Katherine sniffed.

'That can't be helped.'

Bianca looked at her almost with horror.

'But you must not upset Renato!'

'I've never heard of such a thing,' said Katherine. 'If you're not well, I shouldn't dream of leaving you.'

Bianca began to snivel. Katherine *must* go or she, Bianca, would have to drag herself out to appease Renato. Renato *wished* to show Venice to Katherine.

Katherine began to feel bewildered.

'Surely,' she said, 'Renato will not care two hoots whether I go or not. He has only offered to accompany me out of kindness.'

But Bianca continued to press the point that unless Katherine would keep the appointment, Bianca would have to stagger out with them, in spite of her poor head.

Katherine was nonplussed. She could not begin to understand. But the poor child seemed so upset and wept so copiously that finally Katherine had to give in. She would go out with Renato, provided, she added, that Bianca's mother also wished it.

Bianca shrugged her shoulders as though this did not concern her. Katherine retired to the bathroom. Outside in the corridor, the younger girl speedily dried her tears and with a smile ran to her brother's door and knocked on it.

Renato appeared, wearing grey flannels and a pullover; dressed casually like an English sportsman rather than as last night with the studied elegance of an Italian nobleman.

'Well – have you worked it?' he asked his sister.

Bianca giggled.

'She didn't want to but I tell her I am mooch too ill to go, so she say "yes". *You* must arrange with *Mamma.*'

'Good child,' said Renato. 'I'll reward you. I'll take seats for the opera and you shall come with Katherine and me – next week.'

'Oh, how lovely,' Bianca exclaimed and gazed at him with adoring eyes. Her splendid, handsome brother! Katherine was lucky to be going out with him alone. Bianca didn't quite see why he should be so keen although Katherine was awfully nice, of course. But she hadn't questioned it, when he asked her to *'have a migraine'* and drop out. Anything that Renato did was right. He didn't like 'trios' he said, and didn't want to trail round Venice with two women. Bianca wished she could ask a real favour in return – ask Renato, for instance, to suggest to their mother that she should be allowed to begin violin lessons again. But she dared not mention this *even to him.* He was always sweet and good to her but he knew nothing about that episode of last summer. He had been away in France when it took place and Bianca had got into such awful trouble with Mamma. But she had implored Mamma not to tell Renato and be disgraced in his eyes. So Mamma had said that as long as Bianca kept *her* promise, which was never to see Benito Usilli again, she would let the matter drop.

48

No, Bianca dared not mention it to darling Renato. Anyhow, he, like Mamma, would disapprove.

This particular episode – the first budding romance in the life of the adolescent girl – had been short-lived. Benito Usilli used to come to the *Palazzo* to teach her the violin. She had fallen desperately in love with him, although he was nearly forty, and a married man. But he was poetic and handsome – in a plump, dark Italian way – and he had played the violin exquisitely. Played to *her* ... actually composed a little song for her. And whereas everybody else thought her a stupid schoolgirl, he had told her she was beautiful and talented and would soon grow into a fascinating woman. When she had told him that it was her birthday he had lost his head and kissed her. Never could she forget that kiss – that moment of awakening passion; and all the wonder of unfolding love.

After that they began to exchange notes. There had been a servant in the *Palazzo* then who had become a willing accomplice; even helped Bianca on one occasion to meet Benito when the family was out.

Then Mamma had discovered it. The servant had been dismissed and Benito Usilli soundly admonished. Mamma had threatened to expose him and ruin his reputation as a teacher in Venice, but had refrained because she wished to avoid a scandal in which her daughter would be involved. Never would Bianca forget her mother's ice-cold anger and scorn.

'You little fool! You – a di Voccheroni – to stoop to a violin teacher – to be flattered by the adulation from a common creature like that – a paid tutor! If you ever repeat such folly I shall lock you up and treat you as though you were out of your mind.'

Bianca had wept for a week and had one *migraine* after another. But she had never been allowed to see Benito again.

This morning, as Bianca went back to her room to seek her bed (where she must stay for the rest of the morning if she was to fall in with her brother's wishes and excuse herself from the tour of Venice), she felt a sly pleasure in the fact that she had managed to get the better of her mother. For although she had not spoken to Benito since the awful discovery – they *had* communicated. He had found another ally in a certain gondolier who was a friend of his. While Bianca was leaning over her balcony one morning, she had seen him passing. He had looked up at her and whispered that he had a message for her. She had rushed down and received the precious note: a message of love and longing from her Benito. After this the gondola came at regular intervals with letters from Benito. She sent hers back to him. Benito seemed undeterred by the Marchesa's wrath and anxious to meet her again. The sentimental girl was only awaiting an opportunity. So far, her mother had been a close gaoler and when she was not with her, personally, had the girl watched by Thérèse the elderly French woman who was the Marchesa's personal maid. Bianca loathed Thérèse. She was an ill-tempered and unsympathetic person but perhaps, Bianca thought, Katherine would help her now. Life would be easier with Katherine for a chaperone. Anyhow, Bianca felt it was worth while to please both Katherine and Renato. She was by nature as scheming and subtle as her mother – if that lady had but realized it.

Today was the day that *the* gondolier from Benito came by the *Palazzo*. Under cover of taking a photograph with her little camera, or talking to a friend who passed in the boat, she could usually slip the note for Benito into their ally's hand.

Feverishly she began to write. She always enclosed a poem. Her mother treated her as a schoolgirl, but she was like so many Italians of her age, ripe for passion. And Benito had been the worst person in the world to educate her. An egotist, without scruples. She began to tell him about the new English companion and how sweet she was and how she, Bianca, hoped to win her sympathy – in time.

While she was in the middle of this letter, Katherine suddenly walked into the room. Bianca, with a crimson flush, hastily concealed her note under a piece of blotting-paper.

Katherine said nothing. She did not feel that it was her place to do so. But it was her first intimation that Bianca had a secret which she wished to keep from the rest of the world. And it worried Katherine a little.

5

'And this,' said Renato, 'is St Marc's.'

Katherine opened her guide-book and began to examine it. Renato, mildly amused, took the book away from her.

'I find that insulting. I am sufficient as a tutor for you. Put that book away.'

She gave a rather nervous little laugh. Renato was so masterful. There was no arguing with him. But during the last hour he had proved himself an interesting and charming guide. She could have no complaints.

She gazed in rapt silence at the beautiful Basilica. There were such endless palaces and churches to admire in Venice. Each piece of marble or stone seemed a work of art. It was almost too rich a diet for her.

'Oh, it's all so old – so wonderful!' she broke out.

'You're a strange girl,' he observed. 'You haven't yet asked to see a single shop or wanted to buy a hat. I can't believe it!'

She laughed.

'You can get hats anywhere in the world. But you can't always see Venice.'

'Yes, that is true,' said Renato. He took her

arm and led her through the great arched doorway of the cathedral. Inside, the strong sunlight was shut out. Katherine peered through the shadows at jewelled lights burning dimly, at exquisite holy paintings, at delicate tracery of carved wood, mosaics, and fluted stone ... endless wonders made visible as her eyes grew accustomed to the dimness. There had just been a service. The tall candles were even now being extinguished by a white-robed acolyte. The air was full of the rich smell of incense.

'Oh – it's all *gorgeous!*' whispered Katherine.

Renato continued to look at her, rather than the interior of the Basilica. He could feel her trembling. It was quite astonishing to him that Katherine, with her cool, even prim, exterior, could become a veritable flame of enthusiasm for culture and art. He found a new, deep pleasure in her company that he had never known with women like Violantè, or the gay, talkative American girl, Hilary. Katherine seemed completely oblivious of him except when she whispered a question. Later, as they came out of the Basilica and into the sunshine again, she blinked and drew a long breath.

'Oh, I'm in a daze! But oughtn't we to be getting home?' she asked.

'Certainly not,' he said, 'I told my mother we would not be back for lunch. It is part of your education that you should eat prawns caught in the Adriatic, on the terrace of Danielli's – that is the Royal Danielli Hotel – once one of the most superb palaces in Venice.'

Her pulses thrilled.

'It sounds great. But Bianca...'

'Bianca is all right. She'll stay and doze in her room – if I know what her heads are like,' he said, and refused to feel guilty because of the white lie.

Now Katherine turned her thoughts from Venice, to look a trifle dubiously at Renato. She had been enjoying every moment of this 'tour' with him. But she had set out feeling awkward. The Marchesa had graciously permitted her to go – but even whilst smiling, she had said:

'I think it's a great pity Renato had to choose a day when Bianca couldn't go too. Ah well! run along,' and she had waved a white languid hand to dismiss Katherine. But the voice and manner intimated that she was not pleased.

There was a devil lurking in Renato's handsome eyes, too, which made Katherine wonder – well – wonder if Bianca really had a *migraine,* or if the whole thing had been manoeuvred by *him.* Yet it seemed conceited to imagine that he *wanted* to be alone with her.

But Renato was not easily rejected. He

had made up his mind to take this girl out today. Tomorrow she could be 'imprisoned' with Bianca, if his mother so wished.

'Come along – don't waste time wondering whether you ought to go home or not,' he said with a faintly humorous laugh; 'I promise you won't get into trouble with Mamma. I'll see to that.'

So she gave in. She wanted to, so much. And they continued the fascinating tour of inspection.

Sitting on the terrace of the loveliest hotel in Venice, she accepted the *aperitif* that Renato ordered for her, and found herself telling him about her own home life. He seemed to want to know. He could not have been more charming. She noticed how all the smartly-dressed women (some of whom recognized and acknowledged him) always looked at him twice. He was certainly interesting to the opposite sex, she decided. She was lucky to be spending this wonderful day in his company.

The hours sped by.

'Thanks for today, Katherine; I haven't enjoyed myself so much for years,' he said when finally they returned to the *Palazzo*.

He spoke so sincerely that her heart warmed to him.

'I'm *terribly* grateful for all you've done for me,' she said. 'It's been a revelation.'

'Oh, there's still much more to be seen.

We'll repeat the tour quite soon,' he said, and lifted her hand to his lips.

She had not yet grown used to this touch of Continental gallantry. With hot cheeks and an increase in the ratio of her heart-beats, she turned from him and ran up the stairs to Bianca's room. She was still feeling guilty about it all.

In the little *salon*, Beatrice di Voccheroni faced her son. She had watched the two come in. Under her delicate rouge her face was white with anger. She looked at her son in a way he had never before seen her look at him. He lifted his brows.

'You are annoyed?' he asked.

'Annoyed!' she repeated the word through clenched teeth. 'More than that. I am *furious*. You have behaved abominably.'

Renato was normally of a sunny easy-going disposition, but her tone of voice chilled him. He stiffened and spoke to his mother with a frigidity to match her own.

'May I ask why?'

She glanced at her jewelled wrist-watch.

'You've been out with that girl since ten o'clock. It's now nearly five.'

Light dawned on him. So that was it. He gave a short laugh and, pulling a cigarette from his gold case, lit it.

'*Mamma mia*, you must learn that I am no longer an undergraduate to be dictated to, or "gated" because I've broken the rules.

Besides – what rule can there be against me showing Venice to the daughter of one of your oldest friends?'

'Under ordinary conditions – none. Although I think you were very ill-advised to flatter Katherine by insisting on taking her out alone today.'

'Katherine is not easily flattered and Bianca was not well enough to come with us.'

'We have already been over that.'

'But I must add,' Renato went on, 'that it takes more than a few hours to show the wonders of Venice to a stranger.'

Suddenly the Marchesa flushed an ugly red. Her long thin fingers tore at the chiffon handkerchief she carried. She was in one of her nervous and excitable states, having just spent a most unattractive half-hour with the director of the biggest stores in Venice where her account had remained unpaid for a year.

'Renato, you are a fool – a thoughtless fool!' she said violently. 'You offended Violantè by taking Katherine out instead of meeting *her* this morning, and now I suppose you've forgotten that you were asked to lunch at the Danielli with Hilary and her father, in order to meet Hilary's aunt who has just flown from America and who, incidentally, is leaving Hilary a great deal of money. I didn't know anything about it until Hilary phoned me to say that she had written to you when you were in England to tell you that she especially wanted you for this lunch-party, and that you wrote back and said that you would certainly attend it if you got back to Venice in time.'

'Oh, lord!' muttered Renato, and changed colour. The appointment had gone completely out of his head. He had to admit it.

'They saw you two lunching at the Danielli. But Hilary said she didn't disturb you because you seemed so occupied.'

Renato's colour deepened.

'Then she's an idiot. Why on earth didn't she come over and talk to us.'

'She may have thought that she was being tactful *not* to do so. She's a very sweet girl. Didn't you *see* the Drumanns there?'

Renato said that he did not. Possibly, because he and Katherine had had an early lunch, and the Drumanns rarely ate before two o'clock, by which time he and Katherine had returned to their sightseeing.

His mother's anger descended upon him again.

'Apart from being ill-mannered, you have chosen to offend the two most important women in Venice, for whom you should be putting yourself out. And what for? To try and turn the head of a girl who has come to our house as – well – practically as an employee, and who hasn't a penny-piece.'

Renato grew angry now.

'Is it something against her that she hasn't got any money? I admit I made a *faux pas* about the Drumanns, but Hilary should have come over and talked to me. And I have *not* turned Katherine's head!'

'I don't mind Katherine not having any money. I like the girl from what I have seen of her. And I was devoted to her mother. But Katherine was not brought to Venice as a companion for you.'

'My dear mother – do control yourself. I have no wish to appropriate all Katherine's time. What does *one day* matter?'

'It doesn't really. What matters is that neither Violantè nor Hilary will ever speak to you again.'

Now Renato gave a lazy laugh.

'Don't be silly, darling, you know that they will.'

'You're a vain, stupid boy!' the Marchesa stormed at him, refusing to allow his charm to mollify her. 'Don't you understand that you've got to propose to *one* of those girls, and that it has *got* to be announced in Venice very soon, or we are ruined.'

'Isn't that exaggerating?' Renato drawled the question, but he frowned uneasily. He had rarely seen his mother quite so upset.

'No,' said the Marchesa, 'I'm not exaggerating. And if you like to come to my boudoir, I will show you a few figures which might prove to you that it is high time you settled down to this marriage, or you'll find yourself having to do a paid job of work instead of drifting around Venice with your sister's companion.'

6

The hour that Renato spent with his mother was filled with staggering and unpleasant surprises for him.

It became clear that unless he sent a cheque or gave some substantial proof that he could pay his bills in the future, the di Voccheroni accounts would be closed.

'Look here, *Mamma mia,* we're spending a fantastic amount keeping up this house in the old style. Surely–'

'I refuse to allow a deterioration to enter our mode of living,' she cut in sharply. 'There are many other things that can be "cut down" first.'

'My wines, my cigars, and my women–' he suggested and laughed.

'Don't be coarse, darling,' said the Marchesa, coldly.

'Sorry! But why don't we commence this economy campaign in the home?'

'Because at my age I do not care suddenly to become poor and made to look small in the eyes of my friends. No – I am too old for that!'

He leaned forward and patted one of his mother's thin, beautiful hands.

'Never old, *Mamma mia*. Eternally young and beautiful.'

She flushed with pleasure but snatched the hand away.

'I won't be flattered. I insist on you talking sense. It is because you rely so much on your charm, my dear Renato, that you are so careless. There is no need for economy either on your part or mine if you will marry well.'

He scowled at the end of his cigar.

'*Dio mio*,' he groaned, 'how degrading it is when everything has to be brought down to a question of *lira*.'

The Marchesa moved her silver head impatiently.

'Be sensible, please, Renato. This is all my fault because I've spoilt you shamefully and you have never given a thought to your wild extravagance.'

'And what of yours, darling?' he asked without rancour, still charming.

'Oh, I admit I have been foolish, too. All the more reason why you must bring off an important wedding.'

So the conversation went on, and on, until it was drummed deep into Renato's brain that he could no longer regard the subject of money as 'degrading' but must face hard facts. He just could not retain his delightful freedom. He must try to fall in love with a rich woman. As his mother pointed out, the

63

announcement of an engagement to some-body like Violantè with her vast industrial fortune behind her, would satisfy their creditors that they need not panic.

'I'll try to do what you ask, Mamma,' he said gloomily.

Delighted, she embraced him.

'You have such a good choice, Toto' – it was the name she used to call him when he was a very little boy. 'Personally I suggest Violantè. She is more of our world. Al-though, of course, Hilary is a sweet girl and that garrulous old father of hers could buy a dozen *palazzos* in Venice if he wished.'

'One appears to be enough,' muttered Renato.

'One last word, *caro. Please* do not waste your time with girls who do not matter.'

He made no reply. But as he kicked off his shoes and rang for his valet to run the bath he uttered a very English *'damn'* under his breath.

In his heart of hearts he knew that he wanted something better out of life than a crazy pursuit of pleasure and easy-living. He had always wanted more, but been too lazy to pursue any ideal. And above all he wished to choose a wife for himself. Now, Violantè Chiago was most attractive. Hilary, too. He had flirted with them both. Either choice would be good. But it was degrading to have to marry money.

As for his mother's parting shot 'about girls who do not matter', he knew perfectly well of whom she had been thinking. And he, too, was thinking about that same girl whom he had piloted around Venice today. Penniless Katherine might be, but there was something about her that made a fellow *think*, not merely *feel*. That was new for Renato di Voccheroni. In his luxurious bathroom – it had a dark purple sunken bath of the old Roman style – Renato scrubbed his brown back vigorously and tried to forget Katherine and concentrate on the choice between Violantè and Hilary. He weighed it up.

Violantè was a beauty, voluptuous, sophisticated, and a widow. But she was also inclined to be self-opinionated. He was quite sure that once she recovered from the first flush of passion she would be as dictatorial as his mother. And much as Renato loved the latter, he really did not want to spend the rest of his life being 'managed'. Now, for Hilary – well, she might be more reasonable and easily managed than Violantè. He liked her rather boyish elegance, her smart New York clothes and amusing slang. The way she had of saying with her sing-song drawl: 'Oh, Ren-at-*o!*' The way she called a tomato 'a tomayter'. All her funny little habits; they made him smile. But she had no real sensibility – no great depth. She might even turn out to be frigid, although she had shown him clearly that she was in love with him. The last time they had gone out together, she had murmured, '*Say*, I'm crazy about you, Ren-at-*o!* and your cute Venice!'

But did he want a wife who thought Venice *cute?* He had shuddered at the time.

Oh, to *hell* with all the millions of *lira* that either of those two girls could bring to the Palazzo Voccheroni! And to the grim memory of tax demands. Old Richard had been saying in London that English income-tax was heavy. But *per dio* – here in modern Italy, there were huge taxes on one's property, one's income, even one's children!

Later, dressed, and combing back his damp dark curls, Renato told himself that he had better put a heavy foot on any inclination he might feel to show Katherine Shaw more of Venice. He also took a vow to consider his and Mamma's and Bianca's comforts seriously.

As he passed his sister's door he was sorely tempted to look in for a chat and perhaps catch a glimpse of Katherine. His mother had already told him that Katherine would not be coming down to dinner tonight. They were entertaining his father's oldest friend, the Barone de Mallighi. It was obvious to Renato that little Katherine was not to be allowed to meet the important people. Alvise de Mallighi, a grand old man with a white imperial and monocle and the courtly manners of the eighteenth century, had been in love with Renato's mother for years. As far back as Renato could remember. The dear old boy never came here without a bouquet of carnations. Red carnations and just one white in the bunch which he said was for her, alone. He was full of charming ideas. She might have married him if he had had more money. But his title carried little these days and he had lived in seclusion in one of the smaller hotels on the Lido since the war. But he was important to Beatrice di Voccheroni because he knew all the right people. He had brought many distinguished guests to the di Voccheroni parties.

With his new resolutions fresh in his mind, Renato avoided his sister's sitting-room and went down to join his mother.

In the little room which used to be Bianca's schoolroom and now had become her boudoir the two girls sat eating their evening meal.

Bianca called it 'supper'. It was more simple than the complicated dinner that would later be served below. But to Katherine it was rich, heavy food compared with the simple 'high teas' at home. Besides, she had not really recovered from her vast lunch at the Danielli.

Bianca, however, seemed to have recovered with a completeness that made Katherine once more suspicious about that *migraine.* The girl was full of good spirits this evening. She chattered so fast in her atrocious English, interspersed with Italian, that Katherine now and again had to ask her to wait. Bianca wanted to know everything about Katherine's day out with her brother. Having heard about it, she fixed her gaze on the English girl and gave her a somewhat knowing smile.

'Churches and museums. *Alora!* And then–?'

'What do you mean – *and then?*' asked Katherine, rather irritably.

Bianca shook her head and giggled. Katherine went scarlet. Bianca giggled still more and pointed at her.

'*Alora!* You are ve-r-y red.'

Katherine felt a positive distaste for Bianca although she had come back full of compunction because she had left the 'poor girl alone so long'. But here was Bianca – smirking, inferring that the outing with Renato had '*meant* something'.

'You really are stupid, Bianca,' said Katherine icily.

Undaunted, Bianca giggled again. She was enjoying herself at Katherine's expense. Katherine could only suppose that the young girl had suffered so much from lack of companionship, that now – having somebody only a few years older than herself to associate with – went to her head. It was all this sickly sentimental twaddle in which she seemed to indulge. Bluntly, Katherine said:

'Look here, my dear, if you think your brother and I wasted our time holding hands or something, you're dead wrong. There *is* such a thing as friendship between men and women, you know. It needn't always be a question of romance.'

'It is as a rule,' said Bianca and turned her thoughts to her own affair which was going quite well. She had decided on a big plan of action for meeting Benito – and very soon. Mamma would be going away, no doubt. She always made trips to Rome or Milan for 'fittings' and stayed away several days. Generally she asked some ghastly old woman-friend to come and stay in the *Palazzo* to chaperone Bianca. But this time, Bianca reflected, she would be left alone with Katherine, and Katherine was going to be a sport, Bianca was sure.

However, she could see that her companion did not seem to like this teasing about Renato. In Bianca's over-ripe imagination, Renato was already desperately in love with Katherine and *she* was surely ready to die for him. But Katherine avoided discussing him.

'After supper, I think we'll read an English book together. You *must* try to improve your accent, Bianca,' Katherine said.

Pouting, Bianca consented. Katherine,

while she conducted the first lesson, thought it as well that Bianca did not know how often her memory strayed to those hours in Renato's company seeing the wonder and glory of Venice. And to the thought of him tonight downstairs with his mother and their guests. The American heiress, Miss Drumann, was making up the fourth, Bianca had said. She also told Katherine how cross Mamma had been because Renato had forgotten his lunch date with Hilary.

'And there he was lunching with *you* in the same hotel – isn't he too vague for words?' Bianca had laughed.

But it didn't seem very laughable to Katherine. How could Renato have made such a *faux pas*. And how furious the Marchesa would be. Renato was obviously as irresponsible as he was charming. She would have to watch her step in this house and 'keep her place' as a companion-governess.

Much later, after Bianca had grown tired of her English book and embarked on some embroidery which she did rather well, Katherine sat down to write a letter home.

Suddenly the sound of music drifted up from below. Not warm, beautiful Italian music, but American dance tunes being played on a piano extremely well.

It almost hurt Katherine to hear it.

'Somebody's playing most professionally, but it sounds all wrong in this house,' she smiled at Bianca.

Bianca shrugged her shoulders. The English *mees* was more artistic than the half-Italian Bianca who enjoyed hearing the negro music. She grinned.

'It is *Mees* Drumann. She play very well. *Magnifico.*'

Katherine raised her brows. Yes, certainly Hilary Drumann played extremely well. Did Renato like it? She could not imagine that the Marchesa did.

In fact, Beatrice di Voccheroni had retired to the library for a *tête-à-tête* with her old admirer, the Barone, and discreetly left her son alone with the American girl. Renato and Hilary had wandered into the big magnificent *salon* which was illuminated by great crystal chandeliers. Renato had not particularly wanted to leave the fireside in the small *salon,* but making Hilary play was always a good way of entertaining her and he admired her technique. He whistled some of the engaging tunes as she played them.

She had quite forgiven him – just as he knew she would – for his slip-up earlier today. When he had started to make profuse apologies she had grinned in that boyish way she had and drawled:

'Say! I'm not Nelson. I don't expect people to do their dooty.'

'But I assure you it wasn't a duty – I wanted to lunch with you – but I just forgot,' he had grinned back at her.

She had waved it aside. She 'couldn't care less' she said. She would much rather lunch with him alone than with her 'ant', and so on – making it easy for him. Yes – she was a nice girl. Violantè would have made a scene.

Almost regretfully Renato watched Hilary as she sat playing the big concert grand which was rarely opened except when his mother gave a musical *soirée*. If only he could fall in love with Hilary! She was about twenty-four – tall and straight with long American legs, long thin feet. Her chestnut hair, short-cropped, was swept up. She wore one spray of diamonds and rubies on a severely cut grey velvet dinner dress. He wondered how much both dress and spray had cost. Possibly enough to pay a number of those bills upstairs (oh, *hades!* how he loathed this enforced mercenariness. He wasn't really built that way and he was beginning to realize it.)

Hilary turned bright grey-green eyes on him and started to croon a tune from *South Pacific*. She had a husky voice with quite a lot of appeal in it.

'I'm gonna wash that man right out of my hair–'

She broke off and shot a remark at him mischievously.

'I've a good mind to wash you out of mine, Ren-a-*to.*'

'Don't do that,' he begged mechanically.

'Okay – I won't,' she murmured.

He knew that she was all his for the asking. He wished he could force himself to go up and put his arms around her, bend back her head and kiss her on that big laughing mouth; ruffle the short crisp hair.

Why *couldn't* he? Why was he seeing, continually, in his mind's eye the serious face of Katherine Shaw? The ardent pleasure she had exhibited for the old stones and bricks of Venice; not for *him.* Was it just being perverse – and that a man always wanted what he couldn't get easily? Katherine would be hard to get – his thoughts broke off abruptly. Hilary had stopped playing and sauntered towards him.

'Let's take the launch and go have a drink some place,' she suggested.

'Excellent idea,' he said.

But it was without enthusiasm that he ran up the staircase to his room to fetch his pocket-book.

As luck would have it, he ran straight into Katherine. She was walking out of Bianca's bathroom. She carried a towel and wore a most unglamorous dressing-gown, which made her look like a schoolgirl – a blue flannelly sort of thing which bred the most curious feeling of tenderness in Renato as he gazed down at her. Her face was scrubbed clean. Her fair hair fell almost to her waist. She really did not look more than thirteen or fourteen, he decided. The most incredible blush overspread her face as she stared speechlessly up at him.

'Oh, g-good night,' she stammered.

'Good night, Katherine,' he answered.

But as she was about to retire hastily into her bedroom, he called her back.

'Katherine–'

'Yes?'

She turned her head, and flinging the towel over her shoulders, began to plait her hair nervously. She had not anticipated that she might run into the *Signore Marchese*. Across the canal came the boom of a great church clock. Eleven o'clock. How late it was! But surely too early for *him* to be going to bed? He seemed to read her thoughts.

'I'm just going out – you are up late, Katherine. By the way, I missed you at dinner.'

'Oh, thank you,' she said confusedly.

'You *are* a funny little thing. What are you thanking me for?'

'I don't know...' (What a ridiculous conversation she thought. It meant nothing.) She hastily explained that she had been writing a long letter home and hadn't noticed the time passing.

He pulled at his ear, frowning. What was it

that made him want to stay and talk to her – when downstairs, Hilary Drumann, wearing a fabulous blue mink coat, waited for him to take her on the canal – *waited for him to ask her to marry him.*

Katherine, completely embarrassed, now darted into her room and shut the door.

And for the first time in his life, Renato Voccheroni cursed the thought of money while he went slowly downstairs, to join Hilary.

7

By the end of another fortnight there was quite an addition in Katherine's diary. She wrote bits whenever she could find time in what had begun to be a busy life.

It seems a very great deal more than three weeks since I left Mawgan Porth. I am already another Katherine, leading the life of a Venetian. No longer the little Cornish girl whose existence was once so narrow, so limited. I have grown used to Continental ways. I even prefer coffee to tea, which makes me laugh when I think of the endless 'cuppas' Mummy and I used to have at home. I am also picking up a smattering of Italian and can find my way about the shops. But I don't buy much because everything is madly expensive and the exchange for the English so poor. The Marchesa sent for me soon after I first got here and said that I need never want for anything but just ask her when my own supply of lira ran out. I told her that I wouldn't accept anything for nothing so I am to get a salary for the work I do for Bianca. High-class servants here get about fifteen pounds a month and I'm to get twenty, which seems very generous. The present rate of exchange is about one thousand seven hundred lira *to the pound. Oh, how filthy Italian notes are – all shapes and sizes – all very muddling at first.*

I really like the Italian people – the way they show their lovely white teeth and smile and say 'Buon giorno, Signorina'. *They're so polite, and all so gay. There is always music in Venice. I haven't yet got over the thrill of hearing the bells, the music and the singing that floats across the water every night. It's too romantic for words.*

I hardly ever see the Marchesa except when she wants to give an order or comes into Bianca's boudoir to see her. She is a strange and highly-strung woman and always seems to be in a state of nervous irritation. How different from Mummy who works so hard and takes real trouble so calmly! The Marchesa seems to work hard doing nothing. All her rich friends are the same.

Just how rich the Marchesa is, I'm not at all sure. I hate servants' gossip, but that cross French maid of hers, Thérèse, was gossiping the other day and would insist on dropping dark hints that the Signora Marchesa had lost a lot of money and that the Signore *– Renato – was squandering the family fortunes. All very dramatic. They seem to steep themselves in drama in this country and I think it is a pity that Renato, in particular, takes that side from his father. He dramatizes himself a lot and is so spoiled – by everybody! He appears to be quite*

77

stunned when I am too busy to talk to him or won't fall in with his plans. I've absolutely refused to go out with him again since that first day. Not because I didn't enjoy it – I haven't forgotten it yet – but it has been made so plain to me that the Marchesa frowns on any familiarity between me and her son. I think she wants us only to be on nodding terms when we meet in the Palazzo.

But Renato does come up to see his sister and talks to me and I always enjoy it. I can't deny it. He can be so incredibly charming. But I try not to let him know that I think so, and I won't give Bianca a chance to pull my leg about it any more.

I don't really like Bianca. I go on being sorry for her because she gets all the wrong treatment here. But she is deceitful. I'm always finding her out in stupid little lies. The other day I saw her talking to a gondolier and I swear she put something in his hand. I wonder if she is up to any mischief? I'm in the sort of 'older sister' light to her now, and I feel a bit anxious. But she hasn't confided in me so far. I know she needs affection and a bit more gaiety and would be all right if she got it. She was perfectly sweet last week when Renato kept that promise to take us all to a concert, when the Marchesa was out on some party. His French friend, Jacques de Grenoble, made up the fourth. I don't know how Renato squared his mother because she is all against Bianca 'coming out'. Bianca, of course, inferred that he did so because he wanted to take me – *but that's too ridiculous. However, off we all went to a concert at the Doge's Palace. They have concerts there every Sunday evening. It was* wonderful. *Apart from the magnificence of the place the music was superb. I heard one of the greatest living Italian tenors sing. I think Bianca enjoyed it too and kept saying, poor kid, that she wished her mother would allow her to go on with her violin lessons. I did mention it to the Marchesa afterwards but she looked rather oddly at me and refused point blank.*

Well, during the concert, Renato was most attentive. I do wish I did not blush so easily. I went scarlet when he tried to take my hand in the middle of one of the songs and whispered: 'What a deep impression art has upon you, little Katherine. Those grey eyes of yours look quite dark. The pupils have grown so big...' *I took my hand away and hurriedly put on my glasses. He does notice things about one so and it's most embarrassing.*

I promised the Marchesa faithfully that I would get Bianca home immediately after the concert and not go on to supper, although Renato tried hard to make me say I would go back and join him and his friend at the Colomba. That is one of the smart restaurants. But I wouldn't. I just can't have any nonsense, I know I'd regret it if I did, but it's awfully hard to say 'No' when you want to go out and dine with a man like Renato. What girl wouldn't?

79

It has never been so cold again as it was that first night when I arrived here. I do love the blueness of the skies, and the sunshine. Renato told me to watch the almonds, and the peach trees – they call them pesca *out here. They will be the first to come out in blossom he says. I shall see them early in March, when Venice begins to be warm and heavenly. I do so look forward to it. But I wish that Renato–*

The diary broke off here as though Katherine had been interrupted, which indeed she had. And later, when she started to write again, she felt slightly ashamed of what she had 'wished'. In a moment of romantic tenderness she had wished that Bianca's brother were not the wealthy (or *soi-distant* wealthy) master of the Palazzo Voccheroni. She wished that he were just an ordinary young man whom she had met and could go on meeting outside this house without complications. Although she could not admire him, and often felt that she wanted to 'rag' him in the good old English way about his enormous conceit – she *had* to like him. Even to miss him when he was not here. And he was away from home a good deal. Bianca told her one evening that Mamma was furious because he would not pin himself down to an engagement. Mamma was terrified, too, because the Contessa Chiago had a new admirer in Venice – a Milanese like her first husband, with high political ambitions. If Renato did not act swiftly – the rich and charming Violantè would be out of his reach.

In a curious detached way, Katherine was glad that Renato did not seem so anxious to 'sell himself'. She found this idea of him – or anybody else – marrying for money, beneath contempt.

She had been interrupted when she began to write, *'I wish'* – by Renato, himself.

They had dined that evening *en famille*, including Katherine and Bianca. The Marchesa had been in unusually good humour. But Renato hardly opened his mouth. His handsome face looked sullen all through the meal.

When he knocked on the door of his sister's sitting-room, Katherine hastily closed her diary and stood up to greet him.

'Do you want to see Bianca?' she began, 'she's just going to bed. I think she'll have to have glasses like me, because her eyes get so tired and we did rather a lot of reading this morning and–'

'Don't call her. I don't want to see Bianca,' he interrupted.

Katherine sat down again. He, too, took a chair and stared at her. The fair hair was neat and shining in the lamp light, coiled at the nape of her neck. She wore a dark woollen dress, with an Italian studded yellow leather belt which the Marchesa had given her.

81

When she thought about it, the Marchesa often gave odd gifts to what she called 'poor Connie's girl'. Renato looked into Katherine's grave eyes and sighed. He could not honestly say that he found Katherine exciting – or seductive in a purely feminine fashion – like so many of the lovely women in his life had been. And during the month that she had lived here they had one dispute after another. She seemed positively hostile towards him at times. Even when she said nothing, he fancied he could read scornful indifference on that cool young face. Yet he could not keep away from her. It was as though he had become possessed of an incredible desire to make her change her opinion of him. She hadn't a good one. For all his vanity, he was sure of that. At times he laughed about it and thought that the best place for Katherine Shaw was the schoolroom – with Bianca. Yet he wanted to change that. *He couldn't keep away.*

Suddenly he kicked the fender in front of the fireplace before which they were sitting, and muttered something in Italian under his breath. Katherine looked up and blinked.

'What's wrong with you tonight, Renato? I'm sure it's a good thing I don't understand what you said just then.'

'Yes – it is a good thing,' he said sulkily.

'Aren't you going out tonight? You generally do.'

'Do you object to me being up here with you?'

That hot blush which never failed to amaze him, stained her face.

'Don't be absurd – of course I don't,' she said.

'There are moments when I think you positively dislike me.'

She bit her lip and remembered that sentence which she had just been about to write, and added, 'I don't at all but–'

'But you think I'm lazy, and a cad–'

'I've no proof of the last word.'

Renato eyed her suspiciously. Was she laughing at him? There was a dimple at the corner of her mouth. Those fresh lips were the most provocative feature in her face. He wasn't really sure how to tackle her. She was so utterly different from Violantè or Hilary. He knew what to say to women who melted under his merest gaze. But Katherine...

'All right, I'm lazy,' he barked out furiously. 'We'll leave it at that and I don't like to work. So I'm going to get married and let my wife's father supply my money.'

It was curious how that last statement worried her. She didn't really believe he was so heartless and mercenary. She looked at him.

'You are engaged?' she asked.

He stood up and with hands in his pockets began to walk up and down the quiet room.

From outside there came the *swish-swish* of a passing gondola. The faint lilt of a tenor voice singing: *'Pagliacci'*.

Then he swung round and glared at her. She found him in that moment extraordinarily like her young brother David, who, when he had done something wrong used to glare at her as though *she* were to blame.

'You despise me, don't you, Katherine?' Renato broke out.

'Really, Renato,' she said in a shocked voice, 'I don't know what's bitten you tonight. What you do is not my business.'

'You mean you're not concerned?'

'Why should I be?' she asked confusedly.

'All right, you're not. So it won't concern you when I tell you that my mother is giving a ball in the middle of December – that's in a fortnight's time, and a very splendid affair it will be, my dear. During the evening, I am to announce my engagement.'

Her lips drooped. She was astonished to find how fast her heart was beating. She said:

'I hope you will be very happy. Will you tell me the name of your future wife?'

8

He did not answer that question at once, for in his heart of hearts he had not really decided. He had merely given his word to his mother that he would announce the engagement to *one* of those two – Violantè or Hilary. But as far as he was concerned, he could quote the old hackneyed lines: *'How happy I could be with either...'* (Or how *un*happy!)

Abruptly he turned away from Katherine's tranquil gaze, which had far from a tranquillizing effect upon Renato – it dived into hitherto unplumbed depths within his very being. He said:

'You'll know soon enough.'

'I see,' said Katherine.

'Don't you think it will be a good thing? Don't I strike you as a man who wants steadying up, or sobering down?'

She knew that he was being sarcastic. In one way, so transparent in his vanity and ruthless egotism. In another way so baffling to her. She bit her lips as she replied:

'I don't know why you ask me these things? As though my opinion mattered?'

'Perhaps it does.'

'Oh, I can't believe that,' said Katherine with a little laugh.

'We are friends – aren't we?' he demanded.

Katherine was confused by his persistent attempts to sound her. In a way it was flattering and yet ... why did he do it? Why *should* her opinion be of any value to the great Marchese di Voccheroni?

'Yes, of course, we are friends,' she stammered, and added: 'I hope.'

His moody eyes surveyed her for a moment.

'There are moments when I doubt it.'

'I really don't understand you, Renato.'

'Never mind. But just as one friend to another, tell me if *you* think I *ought* to take a wife?'

Now she coloured and laughed in an embarrassed fashion; laid down her diary and crossed to the window. Parting the curtains she stood looking out a moment at the glittering lights on the Canal. From the Campanile came the deep musical sound of the great clock tolling the hour. And she thought what fun it had been looking up at that fabulous clock and seeing all the sights with Renato. And for a brief crazy second, allowed herself to wonder what it would be like to be the girl of his choice – always to have that brilliant charming companion at her side. *To be loved by him.* Then as if afraid of such ideas, she hastily said:

86

'Oh, I'm sure it is right for you to get married, Renato.'

'You believe in early marriages?'

She turned and faced him, hot and pink in the cheeks.

'You're submitting me to a terrific cross-examination this evening.'

'Go on – tell me,' he urged, as though it were really important to him to discover what lay in the mind of this curiously untouched, intelligent young girl who had come to live under his roof.

'I haven't had much experience but I do believe that it's a good thing to marry young if you happen to meet the right person,' she said.

'And supposing it's the wrong person?'

'I really can't speak from any experience, can I? And I haven't seen much of married life even amongst my own friends. My own people were terribly happy, of course. A perfect example of what married life should be. But my father always said he knew the first moment he saw Mummy that she was the one he wanted, and that there could never have been anybody else.'

Renato half closed his eyes.

'How simple! No inner confliction, no doubts, just plain sailing.'

'Well, it *should* be like that.'

'Then you don't think love can develop later on. You believe that it must always be at first sight.'

'Oh – n-not at all,' she stammered, 'I mean – it *can* develop, can't it?'

'And do you think it might do so *after* marriage – this great romantic love you advocate?'

She refused to be annoyed by his sarcasm.

'No, I don't think I believe that,' she answered after a moment of reflection. She guessed that he was referring to his own state of indecision about the two women in his life. Bianca had so often discussed those two – the Contessa and the American.

'Why not?' he rapped out the words.

'Oh, really!' protested Katherine, 'this is awful. You're not giving me any notice of these weighty problems. I just feel that two people ought to *know* their own minds before they get permanently tied up.'

'Need it be permanent?'

'Of course,' said Katherine simply.

'Oh, my dear, what an idealist you are,' he said, fresh respect dawning in his heart for her. 'You are the sort who would never break a vow or go back on a bargain, aren't you?'

'Well, if I married the wrong man, I would blame myself for making the wrong choice. But I think it might be fatal to start out on a marriage as a sort of trial run. It isn't like a play that can be taken off just because it's a failure.'

'Yet how many curtains ring down on that particular play a thousand times a year and more all over the world.'

'Well, that doesn't prove it's right,' said Katherine earnestly.

He began to walk up and down the room again, his brows drawn together.

'H'm – life isn't always as correct and conventional as you make it out to be, Katherine. It can quite easily be a mere sequence of romantic episodes.'

'I could never regard marriage merely as a "romantic episode".'

'So you expect you will be lucky and make the dead-right choice first go off.'

'When the time comes, I hope so,' she said and went hot and pink again.

He felt a morbid desire to tell her a few more unpleasant facts about his own enforced choice of a wife. How she would despise him because he had to marry for money, and trust to luck about the love. Suddenly he said:

'How strange it is to think that your mother and mine were friends at school when they were both children and ignorant of the tortuous paths life can take! Your mother married for love and has been happy, despite her poverty. Mine has always been restless and dissatisfied, although she had money and a title. I ought to benefit from their experience and rush to love and bread and cheese in the cottage without further ado. And yet I should hate to be poor for many reasons.'

'It's not so bad. But then I've never been rich, so I'm no good judge,' said Katherine with that swift smile which he found so charming because it was so rare. He turned from her. He felt that he had no more to say at the moment. He left her with an abrupt *'Good night, Katherine'*. And he felt much more discontented with life and more apprehensive about the future than he had been before he talked to her.

After he had gone, Katherine's mind started spinning with thoughts – not only about Renato – but herself, that quiet life which had lacked experience.

She felt oddly sorry for Renato. He had neither looked nor sounded as happy as the young man she had first met.

She sat down at the table to write in her diary. And she crossed out the last five words she had previously written. She no longer knew what she *'wished'* about Renato. Instead she put:

Things are obviously about to come to a head. The Marchesa is going to push poor Renato into an engagement. Why should I pity him? He has put himself into a contemptible position. How stubborn he was, shooting all those difficult questions at me! I felt most awkward. I think I shall be rather glad when the night of the Ball comes and we all know what he is going to do. It is producing such a tense atmosphere. Thérèse says that the Marchesa's nerves are frightful, and she has to take all these pills to make herself sleep at night. She does seem irritable. I've been brought up to believe that money can't make you happy and my goodness I've discovered that for myself, in this gorgeous Palazzo. *The more they get, the more they want. Simple things pass them by. But I don't care a hang how many* lira *I've got, or whether my dress is off the peg, or made by Biki. It would be nice to have a dress made by Biki, but what really interests me is when I shall see the first almond blossom – and Venice in the spring.*

Then she put away the diary, and scribbled a quick note to her mother. She also addressed one or two of those lovely glossy postcards – photographs of St Marc's Square – to her friends in Newquay; and a pretty photograph of an Italian peasant child riding a donkey to little Veryan.

Before going to bed, Katherine looked in on Bianca. The light under the door showed her that the younger girl was still awake.

She found her sitting up in bed staring at something on her knees that Katherine could not quite see at first. Bianca was disgracefully untidy and the room was in its usual state of disorder. It was not furnished quite as elegantly as the rest of the house. Some of the painted furniture looked quite shabby but it had a homely look with its pictures and books and pieces of pottery including a collection of glass animals that Bianca adored – and various other evidences that the owner of the room had not quite passed the adolescent age. Bianca was mad about the films – she had been allowed to go to one or two of the Film Festivals and had pinned a huge framed photograph of a famous actress and her Italian husband over the fire-place. Bianca had recently confided in Katherine that although she knew that her religion discouraged divorce, she thought these two had been very courageous over their love-affair. She had made a heroine of the film star. But Katherine privately disagreed. She had no respect for a mother who could leave her young dependent daughter. But Katherine had already found that Bianca entertained no ideals. She generally seemed to want to make a heroine out of the wrong type.

Poor Bianca, with her warped, secretive nature! It was sad, thought Katherine, when one remembered that she was barely eighteen.

'I've just come to say good night, Bianca–' Katherine began. Then she stopped. To her surprise Bianca looked as terrified as though she had been caught in the act of committing a crime. She made a nervous movement of her hands and a photograph slid from them on to the floor. Katherine stooped to pick it up. Bianca gave a cry and held out her twitching fingers.

'Give to me–'

'What on earth's the matter?' Katherine began again, and was again interrupted by a flood of words from the girl – Italian interspersed with bad English.

'Give to me that picture – *per favore* – if you please – it is mine–'

The girl's wild stammering mystified Katherine.

'What on earth's wrong, Bianca? Of course it is yours.'

She handed back the photograph. A swift glimpse showed her the head and shoulders of a typical Italian, dark-browed, full-lipped, fleshily handsome, although the type of man did not appeal to Katherine in the least.

Bianca seized the photograph and thrust it under her pillow. Then, with a nervous laugh, she said:

'Do not tell Mama you have seen, *please.*'

Katherine sat on the edge of the bed. Once or twice she had wondered if this girl had a secret admirer. Now she had no further doubts. All those mysterious letters she wrote – her attempts to conceal them – probably that gondolier the other day, had something to do with it. Perhaps Bianca was *in love with the gondolier,* Katherine hazarded a wild guess.

Bianca stared at her with her big sullen eyes.

'You no understand.'

'I think I do,' said Katherine drily, 'but you needn't be afraid I shall carry tales, because I'm not like that.'

'What you mean – carry tales?'

'Well – tell your mother. But you have a boy-friend, haven't you, Bianca? That's *him.*'

Bianca gave a shrill laugh.

'No – no. *Niente di simile* – nothing of the sort–'

Katherine felt as she did when she questioned one of her brothers who was being mischievously secretive.

'Come clean, Bianca – why deny it? Why not tell me about your friend?'

Bianca maintained a sulky silence. In a way she *wanted* to tell Katherine about Benito, in fact, the whole story. How she had managed to hide this photograph from Mamma; how she looked at it every night before going to sleep. She needed a confidante and ally. But not just yet – she was not too sure she could altogether rely on Katherine. The English *Mees's* morals and principles were not as lax as Bianca had hoped they would be. However, there was plenty of time. She could afford to wait. She tried to put Katherine off the scent.

'Is nothing – just someone *mia* Mamma doesn't like. *Scusi* – I have nothing to tell you about "boy-friends". Just *my* photograph, so please not to tell Mamma.'

Katherine shrugged her shoulders. She could hardly insist on the girl making a confidence. But she was disappointed. She must go on watching Bianca. She was such an unformed child in so many ways. She needed protecting.

Katherine went to her own room after assuring Bianca that she would not tell the Marchesa about the mysterious photo. She grimaced at her own thoughts. It was a case of 'the blind leading the lame', she decided. For what experience had *she* of men, of life, of love? Renato would say, none at all!

It was a long time before Katherine could get to sleep that night. Her mind would keep reverting to the conversation about marriage which she had had with Renato.

9

December 10th was a crisp cool night with a full moon gleaming over the canals and lagoons of Venice, making silver magic for the guests who came by gondola or motor-boat to the Palazzo Voccheroni for the Ball of the season.

It used to be a regular event twice a year for the Marchesa to entertain Venice in her lovely home; it was usually a masque in the summer, and a more formal dance before Christmas.

For Katherine, still so unused to magnificence, it was a momentous occasion. For days now the big staff had been cleaning and polishing. The *Palazzo* reeked of beeswax and turpentine. The wonderful floors looked like glass. Everything sparkled. Flowers, beautiful beyond description, had been arriving all morning. Katherine usually arranged them, but this time a famous Venetian florist came in person to decorate the *Palazzo*. There were huge gilt baskets, tall jars, gilded tubs in every room filled with artistic sprays of roses, carnations, or lilies, set off by feathery green leaves. The gloom in some of those vast halls was dispelled by lights flashing from gilded wall-brackets and huge Venetian glass chandeliers that shimmered like diamonds. A red carpet covered the old stone steps leading down from the terrace to the water. The entrance hall looked mysterious and romantic with fat wax candles burning in giant candelabra. Every available servant including two footmen wearing powdered wigs, spruce and smart in the green uniform with the di Voccheroni crest on their lapels, rushed around, working at fever heat. Enormous logs burned in wrought-iron baskets in all the big open fireplaces. In the great flower-filled *salon* an orchestra played softly. Champagne started to flow from the time that the party started.

Beatrice di Voccheroni was at her best on a night like this; she made a superb hostess, standing at the head of the beautiful marble staircase to receive the long line of guests. She was wearing a Schuberth model in black velvet, of an exquisite simplicity, cut low to show her still beautiful shoulders. She wore with it a dog-collar of pearls and emeralds which had been a wedding-present from the late Marchese; long drop ear-rings, and long black gloves embroidered with seed pearls. Beside her stood Renato in 'white tie and tails'. Mother and son made a distinguished couple.

Earlier in the day, the Marchesa had

graciously told Katherine that she and Bianca could stay up to see the guests arrive, then they must disappear. Bianca was not of an age to join the supper-party. Katherine thought this rather absurd, but as Bianca was forbidden to attend the 'feast', she, too, would 'vanish' with her young companion.

She was young enough to regret it. All the same she knew she could not hope to hold her own among the cream of Italian society with their magnificent jewels and fabulous dresses. So she and Bianca watched from the library door, both having done little more than change into short dark dresses.

One elderly Duchessa – so-called friend of the family – caught sight of Bianca's thin pale monkey-like face with the dark eyes and furtive expression and whispered to her husband:

'That's Beatrice's daughter. *Alora* – she is excessively plain! But Beatrice is naughty – she keeps her down and won't let her appear yet in society. Anybody would think this was the year eighteen-something-or-other and that she needs to be kept from wicked men. The girl hasn't a chance–'

'Who is the lovely fair-haired child beside her?' asked the Duc, who had noticed Katherine and not Bianca.

His wife could not enlighten him. They passed on.

Bianca whispered to her companion:

'Are they not dull – these so-old people?'

'Oh, many of them are young, and the dresses are fantastic!' exclaimed Katherine, who watched the scene wide-eyed in honest amazement.

She was seeing some of the loveliest girls in Venice tonight, accompanied by their good-looking, well-bred escorts. Many of these young men in the diplomatic service came from Rome or Milan. The fabulous toilettes of the women entranced Katherine – rich satins, velvets, and brocades of every colour and design. Priceless furs – sable, mink, ermine, wonderful silver foxes. She saw the last word in hair-styles; the most expensive bags and tiny, jewelled shoes. It was, she wrote home in her next letter, as good as a fashion-display. The guests walked up the wide staircase and shook hands first with the Marchesa, then her son. Katherine now fixed her attention entirely upon Renato – watching with absorption how he bent over each gloved hand extended to him, kissed it, and paid some light, graceful compliment to the owner, showing his white teeth in the usual gay wide smile. 'Piling on the charm', as Katherine called it. Yet she could not altogether deride him tonight; she felt peculiarly disturbed. She *knew* that for him this might be a fateful night on which he must announce his choice of a wife to Venetian society. She, herself, was extraordinarily anxious to hear who he had decided to select. Even Bianca, full of her usual chit-chat did not know. Mamma had been cross all day, she said, and Renato had snapped her head off, earlier – obviously troubled and ill-at-ease. And he had sent floral sprays to both Violantè and Hilary; dear, diplomatic Renato! Bianca had heard him ordering the flowers over the telephone.

Katherine, from her strategic position half-hidden behind the library door, craned her neck to watch the two 'special' girls come in.

Hilary Drumann and her parents were first to arrive; Hilary was perfectly groomed in pale maize-coloured satin, with which she wore marvellous rubies – necklace, bracelet, and ear-rings to match. With her shining hair and a blue mink stole over her shoulders, she looked chic and self-confident. There were huge purple orchids pinned to the fur – Katherine presumed they were from Renato.

With a humorous twist of her lips, Katherine murmured:

'Enter Contestant Number One.'

Bianca did not understand (which was as well).

Many lovely women walked up those stairs. But Violantè Chiago's arrival was as she liked it to be – a sensation. Her small petite figure was certainly spectacular in the crinoline dress she had chosen and had made for tonight in Milan. She, too, wore satin; dead-white, corsage and hem gorgeously embroidered with rhinestones. The skirt spread out so widely on her hips that it made her tiny waist look fabulously small. A satin jewel-encrusted cap sat on the back of her dark red head. A white ermine jacket with huge cuffs completed a toilette that Katherine reckoned must have cost the Chiago estate many millions of *lira*. Pale pink orchids were pinned to a bag she carried in her white-gloved hands. A collar of diamonds encircled her long throat and bracelets glittered half-way up one arm.

Katherine drew in her breath. This was a bit too theatrical for her taste, but she was well aware by now that the Contessa was happy only when creating an 'effect'. With curious intentness Katherine watched Renato as he kissed the hand of this small, glittering figure behind which lay so vast a fortune.

But Renato gave Violantè no more than the set smile and charming word he extended to everyone. Katherine sighed and turned back into the library. She stood a moment in the room, watching the wood fire, which burned fragrantly and filled the room with flickering shadows. There was only dim lamplight here in the quiet world of books. A relief after the heat, the chatter, the glitter in that extreme world just outside the library door.

'Would I *like* that world if I had it offered to me?' Katherine asked herself, and dubiously remembered her own home-life – the kitchen-sink, the perpetual 'chores'; washing-up with Mummy; the high-teas, the saving of the pennies, the struggle for existence which was made easy only by virtue of the fact that it could be led in an atmosphere of real abiding love.

Was there nothing deep and sincere in Renato to *want* abiding love rather than its counterfeit, *passion* ... and power? Or would he find *both* tonight? Wouldn't it be easy for a man to love either of those attractive women who carried his flowers?

Katherine turned to speak to Bianca and found her gone.

Thérèse came in with a tray on which there was a selection of rich dishes.

'The *Signorina's* supper,' she said.

'And the *Signorina* Bianca's, too?' asked Katherine, taking the tray.

'No; she has said to tell you she has a *migraine* and has gone to bed. Not to be disturbed.'

Katherine raised her brows. How odd! Bianca hadn't said a word about a headache. What was afoot? Katherine was apt to mistrust Bianca's *migraines*.

She thanked Thérèse for the lovely-looking supper. The Frenchwoman's sour face creased into her best smile. She had a soft spot in her heart for the English *Mees.*

She jerked a thumb over her shoulder to indicate the noise and the music beyond the door.

'Huh! The cr-e-a-m of Venice – selfish, vain lot! It is a pity *Mees* Katherine has not a so-beautiful dress and can dance with one of the so-handsome young gentlemen.'

Katherine laughed.

'I assure you I don't particularly want to dance with any of them.'

Thérèse bent down and whispered with the air of one who adores a mystery:

'You have heard – is it not? The young Marchese is to be affianced this evening?'

'Yes, I have heard it, Thérèse.'

'It is time,' said Thérèse with a meaning nod of her head, and without explaining these cryptic words, walked out of the room.

'Was it *time?*' Katherine asked herself. Was Thérèse right? Or would tonight merely be the beginning of much unhappiness for the gay, charming, irresponsible Renato? Strange, how kindly she felt towards him tonight, despite his failings.

The supper was cold and could be left. She had no inclination to eat just now. She walked out of the library, slipped through the crowded, brilliantly lighted hall un-noticed, and descended the steps under the

103

archway, reaching to the edge of the dark lapping water. She looked up and down the Canal.

The last gondola bringing the final guests had just arrived. Lights glittered on the water and from the distance came the inevitable lilt of a dulcet tenor voice singing an amorous song. Suddenly Katherine's attention was drawn to a gondola moving quickly away from the house. A girl's figure had just vanished into the tent-like seclusion behind drawn curtains. But not before Katherine's quick eye had noted and recognized her shape.

Bianca. She could hardly believe her own sight, but it *was* Bianca. So that is where the girl is at this moment – not in bed with the *migraine.* Just, Katherine thought, as she had imagined. The young girl with her sly summing-up of the situation had seized the opportunity to steal away to a secret *rendez-vous* with her admirer while her mother and brother were engrossed in the party.

This was where Katherine had to act promptly, because she knew it was her duty to do so. She did not even wait to fetch a coat. Fortunately she was warmly dressed in a dark red wool dress which had a fringed shawl-cape. The December night was crisp but not too cold. In some anxiety, Katherine hailed a passing gondola. In the few words of Italian which she had picked, she bade him follow that other gondola as quickly as possible.

The gondolier – a slender, dreamy-eyed young man – smiled admiringly at the beautiful fair-haired English girl. He began to sing. He was a little hurt when Katherine said: 'Shush.' She would have liked the song normally, but not in the mood just now. Someone had to find out what young Bianca was up to – that was her main consideration.

She followed the first gondola as far as St Marc's Square, where it stopped and the girl in it alighted. Now, with the bright lights full upon her, she was revealed to Katherine beyond all doubt as Bianca. A thick-set man wearing a black suit and hat met her. Leaning out from her own gondola, Katherine saw him pick up Bianca's hands and kiss them passionately. Katherine's cheeks went pink. She recognized this man. He was the flashily handsome creature whose photograph she had seen in Bianca's bedroom.

So she was right! Bianca, poor, silly child, was having a secret love-affair and her choice was old enough to be her father! Who was he? How had Bianca met him? She was so strictly guarded, it was a mystery. Then Katherine remembered that she had rushed out without her bag. She turned to the gondolier who continued to smile at her respectfully, admiringly. She told him that she could not pay him now, but wished to be taken back to the *Palazzo* if he would wait. He made a grand flourish of the hand to indicate that he did not mind. '*Grazie, Signorina,*' he said, doffing his cap.

And now, thought Katherine, for the peroration. It was going to be both awkward and unpleasant.

Bianca and her escort, arm-in-arm, were hurrying across the square. Katherine followed. Before they could enter the café outside which they stopped, Katherine touched Bianca's arm and with fast-beating heart, she said:

'Bianca – wait a moment, please.'

The girl swung round. Her sallow face went scarlet, then livid. She looked startled out of her wits.

'Katherine!' she gasped.

Katherine, who had never had an unpleasant scene with anybody in her life before, began to wish she had not come. The Italian stared at her angrily. She said:

'Yes. You see – I saw you go. I got your message about the *migraine.* I suppose you didn't want me to know about this.'

'No, I did not – you spy on me – you are like the rest – a spy!' burst out Bianca, tears of rage and chagrin filling her eyes.

The man beside her shot a few rapid questions in Italian at Bianca which she answered. Katherine did not quite under-

106

stand, but gathered that Bianca was explaining who she was.

The man bowed to Katherine and said:

'I speeka English. Benito Usilli. Gooda evening, *Signorina*.'

Before Katherine could answer, Bianca cut in.

'Yes. Now you know. Benito was teaching me the violin. We fall in love. That is why Mamma forbid violin lessons.'

Light dawned on Katherine.

'I see,' she said. Her eyes suddenly caught the flash of a gold ring on Benito's marriage finger. Bianca followed the gaze and in a sullen voice, she said:

'Yes, he has wife – very bad wife – not happy. I make him very happy. Do I not, Benito?'

He answered warmly in the affirmative, seized her hand and kissed it several times.

Katherine felt slightly nauseated. She liked a romance, but this middle-aged married man who was obviously ill-bred and utterly unmindful of Bianca's extreme youth and position, repelled her. Of course, she could see why Bianca had been taken in by him. She was a mere schoolgirl responding to the first man who made love to her and who offered some of the adulation and affection which she lacked under her own roof. With all her heart she pitied poor little Bianca, and could find it easy to excuse this deception but she had to go on with what she had set herself out to do. Ignoring Benito, she spoke again to Bianca:

'Don't you think it would be better if you came home with me at once?'

'No, I not!' Bianca was crying now. 'I not go home. I stay with Benito. He love me.'

'*Si, si!*' said Benito, showing all his teeth.

'All the same, I think you had better come, darling,' said Katherine quietly. 'You'll only get into terrible trouble if your mother finds out.'

'I no care!' The girl was sobbing now, clinging on to Benito's arm.

'Bianca, dear, I *must* drag you away for your own sake. I'm responsible for you,' protested Katherine, feeling hot and embarrassed.

Now a three-handed argument began. Bianca weeping and imploring Katherine to let her stay with Benito; the man imploring her to act as an ally. In the end, Katherine had to use the only weapon that she had. She informed them both that if Bianca did not immediately return with her, she would tell the Marchesa everything. Benito Usilli was not anxious to have that happen. Already he had lost many pupils because of the Marchesa, whose wrath had descended upon him when she first found him out. He whispered to Bianca that he would find some other method of contacting her and that she had better go with the English *Mees* now.

Bianca, snuffling into her handkerchief, at last consented.

'I come,' she said and then followed these words by a cry of consternation, *'Dio mio! Renato!'*

Katherine swung round. Her own relief over her victory was short-lived. It was, indeed, Renato – hatless – a spectacular figure in his impeccable evening clothes, moving swiftly towards them. She could only suppose that he had, unknown to them, been watching and seen them leave the *Palazzo*.

Benito hastily kissed Bianca's hand and beat a hasty retreat. He was not at all anxious to come in contact with the hot-tempered brother of his former pupil.

Renato reached the two girls.

He looked at both of them unsmilingly, anger darkening his handsome eyes.

'What the devil are you both doing here?' he demanded.

Katherine, completely floored and not at all anxious to betray the wretched Bianca, could not for a moment find a suitable reply.

'I saw you go out – I *thought* alone,' Renato went on, addressing Katherine, 'but I see you have Bianca with you. We do not allow Bianca out in St Marc's Square without a male escort so late at night. Surely you knew that? It is not right for you to be here, either. Bianca–' He turned to his sister. 'Have you anything to do with this? Are you up to some mischief?'

Before Katherine could put in a word, Bianca, who looked sick with fear, revealed herself as a cowardly little traitor. Nervously she clutched her brother's arm and broke into a stream of Italian. Renato listened and then turned to Katherine. She could see that his anger was mounting. In a scornful voice he said:

'Well, I must say I *am* surprised. I did not think it of you, Katherine. Bianca tells me that you have a secret admirer. That you came out here to meet him. What you do is your own business, my dear, but you have no right to drag my young sister into it.'

10

Renato spoke with anger because he was in no mood to be tolerant. As everybody had noticed, he had been in a state of acute irritation all day. The nearer he came to the hour when he felt he must do as his mother wished in order to prop up the crumbling structure within which their sheltered lives had been led – the worse he felt.

Tonight he had suddenly felt that he did not really find either one of the two girls who wished to present him with 'all their worldly goods' the smallest temptation. He positively disliked them. He was at war with himself and the world. And now he disliked Katherine. He had built up a kind of boyish ideal about her. She had become to him a symbol of the perfect girl. But here he was faced with disillusion. His distorted fancy led him to think that behind her strength lay normal pitiful weakness. Behind the façade of virtue and honour was little but an ordinary young woman who wanted a man to flatter and amuse her. He knew that Katherine had no friends in Venice. So presumably she had 'found somebody'. It was astonishing how furious he felt – more because she had shattered his illusion in her than because of her paltry little love-affair. He saw no reason to disbelieve his sister. Her story was that Katherine had made friends with an Italian and often came here to meet him. His mother would not approve, to say the least of it. But Renato was not going to allow little Bianca to be drawn into Katherine's nocturnal assignations.

It was only by mere chance that he had left his mother's side after they had received the last guests. He had strolled out for a breath of fresh air before beginning the host's arduous duties on the dance floor, and had caught sight of Katherine moving away in the gondola. Quickly he had taken his motor-boat and followed.

At first he had not been disturbed, but thought it best to tell Katherine it was not wise for a young pretty girl to wander alone in Venice at night. Then he had found Bianca with her.

'Come along quickly, both of you,' he said.

Katherine opened her mouth as though to retort and defend herself, but Renato walked on ahead towards the Canal. Bianca seized Katherine's arm.

'Please – *per favore* – *mia cara* Katherine – do not give me away.'

'What have you just told your brother?' Katherine demanded furiously.

Bianca added lie to lie. 'Nothing much –

112

only that you came to meet a friend.'

Katherine, who was red with annoyance and indignation at the way Renato had addressed her, muttered:

'I don't believe you!'

'*Si! Si!* It is true. Oh, please not tell him about Benito. He not know. Mamma never tell him because I promise to be good. I do not want Renato to think badly of me. Mamma will lock me up in a convent if she know tonight – this–' Bianca broke off hysterically. Her eyes were glazed with fright. Katherine felt slightly sick. The whole episode nauseated her. Renato called them from the motor-boat:

'Come on – please.'

In silence the two girls stepped into the launch. Renato started up the engine. They moved swiftly down the Canal away from the glittering magnificence of St Marc's Square.

As a rule the waterways of Venice under the stars held unfailing fascination for Katherine. But this time she was conscious only of her injured feelings and some considerable doubt as to how she should act. She wondered what the deceitful Bianca *had* told her brother. She did not see why she should take the blame. On the other hand, she did not wish the wretched child to get into a frightful row. Most of Bianca's present troubles were due to the fact that the Marchesa had such little sympathy for her adolescent yearnings. Further punishment and deprivation of affection might drive the girl to do something desperate. So Katherine kept her mouth shut and waited events.

As soon as they were back in the *Palazzo*, Bianca rushed straight up to her room. The one thing she wanted to avoid was a cross-examination by her shrewd and unsympathetic mother.

But with her wily nature, she was quick enough to kiss Renato good night and thank him for bringing her home and to add, cunningly:

'Do not be too cross with Katherine, as I love her very much and do not want her to be sent away by Mamma. She can have a boy-friend, can't she, Toto?'

'She can do what the hell she likes,' was Renato's curt reply. But he tweaked Bianca's ear quite kindly and bade her run along. He had no quarrel with her.

He had no real quarrel with Katherine either, except for the fact that she had taken Bianca out on the jaunt with her.

A waltz was now being played in the grand *salon*. The Ball had begun. The Marchesa had just been led out on to the floor by her old admirer, the Barone. The great *Palazzo* was warm and bright. But Renato's hands felt cold and his head throbbed with nerves.

He had inherited a tendency to nerves from his mother. In England, as a boy at school, and later at Oxford, a normal healthy life had done much to conquer and improve this state. But in Italy – and especially with the daily contact with the Marchesa, who had a devastating and devitalizing effect upon everybody – Renato was subject to these nervous attacks, and a slight melancholy – heritage of his southern blood. His was a mercurial temperament – up one moment and down the next.

Katherine had not spoken one word to him since his verbal attack upon her in the Square. Now, as she followed Bianca, that slim, straight young figure in the red wool dress disappeared round a curve in the staircase – and he felt an irresistible desire to follow and make her talk to him.

'Katherine!' he called her name just as she reached her own doorway.

She swung round. 'Yes, what is it?'

He reached her side. 'Katherine, I – I was a little hasty just now, perhaps – even rude to you. But–'

She broke in:

'Please don't bother to apologize. I couldn't care less.'

It was her turn to be rude, she thought, still furious because of the way he had looked at her and accused her in front of Bianca.

He bit his lips and made a nervous movement of his head. What kept him here, anyhow? Why did he bother with Bianca's companion-governess, when the most beautiful women in Italy waited for him, below? He knew that if he did not soon make an appearance, the Marchesa would notice his absence and come in search of him. And if he were found up here like this – there would only be a scene. He was sick of Mamma's scenes.

Yet he lingered. 'Mind you, Katherine – it's none of my business who you meet outside this house as I said before,' he began lamely.

'No – it is *not* your business,' she agreed, and had an inclination to laugh only it wasn't really fun that *she* should be thought the flirtatious young thing who had stolen out to keep a common, sordid little 'date'.

'I only want to warn you,' he continued, 'that you had better be careful. This isn't Cornwall. Over there you can stroll around and look at your fishermen quite safely, but you can't do it with our Venetians. They're a hot-blooded lot.'

Her eyes flashed at him. He was quite astonished to see how brilliant with feeling they could grow – those cool, critical eyes of Katherine's. Certainly, she was not the little icicle he had sometimes imagined. And she looked wonderful with that hot, pink colour and those smouldering eyes. It was quite *something* to have roused her.

She, on the other hand, felt a deep distress because she had allowed herself to be roused. She had felt hurt rather than indifferent when he had taunted her about the intrigue.

'Oh, do go downstairs and get on with the fun and games,' she said, and was quite aghast at herself for being so horrid. She added: 'And good luck to the wonderful girl you're going to marry. She'll need some patience – I should think you must want a lot of putting up with!'

This rather childish attack astonished Renato. It piqued his vanity, too, beyond endurance. No girl had ever spoken to him like that before and he was not going to take it from Katherine.

'You are impertinent,' he said, his face colourless.

'You, too,' Katherine retorted, 'and I don't intend to be insulted. I don't want anything whatsoever to do with you. I'm here for Bianca. *You* go away.'

Renato lost control. He flung at her:

'And a fine way you take care of her – it's no good you putting yourself up on a pinnacle of virtue, my dear!'

That was the last straw. Katherine drew in her breath. And now she spoke in an ominously quiet voice:

'Anything more?'

He looked down at the young, proud face, into the wide, angry eyes. His heated brain spun with pictures of Katherine smiling at some greasy-haired tenor-voiced Venetian youth – perhaps even permitting him to hold her hand or kiss her. For some inexplicable reason the mere idea roused the strongest repugnance in Renato. He knew to his own humiliation that he was positively jealous of the man she had gone out to meet; the boy who could induce her to accept him as an admirer whereas she had done nothing from the start but show hostility towards himself.

Katherine had turned her back on him and started to open her door. Before he could restrain the impulse, Renato seized her by the shoulders and swung her round to face him.

'Yes, there *is* something more I want to say. You've been pretty keen on making me feel that my way of life is wrong and that yours is right. You've even ignored me. I accepted it because I thought it was the way you were built, but I can see it isn't so. You're just the same as any other woman only less honest about it. Isn't that so?' He shook her.

Katherine gasped. She could feel his strong fingers bruising her flesh. She was so astonished by this unexpected physical contact with him that she could not for a moment find words in self-defence.

Then he swept her into his arms.

'You drive me crazy – there's a devil in you, Katherine,' he muttered.

'There's a devil in *you*–' she began, but her retaliation was smothered as his lips took toll of hers.

It was not an idle kiss. It was deep and passionate, and shook Katherine to the depths of her being. She had never been kissed like that in her life before. Only for a breathless instant she surrendered. So that kiss went on – deeper, deeper – until it seemed to burn away all remembrance of the cool, calm Katherine who had once believed herself invulnerable; who had always thought that she could never be swept off her feet.

Then Renato made his greatest mistake. He let her go and taunted her.

'Thanks. That was charming. You may be inexperienced in love, but you are delightfully responsive, and not at all the frigid Katherine she likes to pretend to be.'

Katherine drew in a sharp breath. She was trembling from head to foot; out of her depth. Narrowing her eyes, she said:

'That's put paid to *our* friendship. I think you're the most despicable man I have ever met. I don't envy your wife.'

'I haven't got one yet–' he began, and felt

the most absurd inclination to draw her back into his arms and kiss her again – wipe every trace of cold hostility from her face. For he was ready to swear that she had *wanted* him to make love to her just now. He had never in his life known a girl so provocative.

But Katherine had turned and rushed into her bedroom and shut the door in his face.

Renato drew aback, smoothed down his hair, straightened his tie and went quickly down the staircase. He needed a strong drink. And as the fever in him cooled down he began to feel genuinely remorseful for that stolen embrace. It had 'put paid to their friendship', Katherine had said. That was the last thing he wanted.

In her bedroom, Katherine had not even switched on the light. Shaken by a storm of weeping she lay face downwards on her bed. She cried as she had not done since she was a little girl. But there was nothing of the child about her now. She was all woman – outraged – burning with indignation – horrified to think that her defences had been so attacked and that she had for an instant gloried in the very conquest of herself.

She loved Renato di Voccheroni. She was madly and desperately in love with him. That long devastating kiss had shown her just how much she cared. If a portion of that love was made up of hatred – if she found him and his attitude towards life despicable – it made no difference, she still loved him and that was what love was like. It had all the ingredients of insanity, Katherine decided with an hysterical laugh that became a sob. It could send you just right off your head. She had been off *hers* to allow Renato to kiss her that way and to allow herself to feel such delight in it. But it had been *wonderful.* And *he* was wonderful. There was no denying that fact, no need to be surprised because the little world of women circling around him were all crazy about Renato.

She could call him contemptible – vain – heartless. It might be true. But he was so handsome, so charming. He could be so serious and intelligent, too – and he had so much to offer a woman!

Obviously, after the lies Bianca had told him, he had thought her fair game. She ought to blame Bianca and not Renato. But it was Renato against whom most of her anger was directed. His passionate embrace had led her to the discovery of herself. The real Katherine was awake at last. For that, alone, she could not forgive him. For at this very moment, as she lay there drenched with tears, she imagined him to be on his way downstairs to announce his engagement. To Violantè – or to Hilary? She didn't care which it was– But, yes, *she did care.* And she was never going to be able to look at him again without remembering *tonight.* If she knew herself, she was never going to recover from this first tumultuous love which he had so ruthlessly forced into being.

'Damn you, Renato – oh, damn you!' she sobbed the words into her pillow.

She could not recover a sense of balance. She was both physically and psychologically so disturbed.

She was glad that Bianca did not come in. That girl was responsible for all this. If she started to stutter explanations, Katherine felt that she would want to slap that deceitful little face of hers.

Thérèse knocked on the door, and called out that the *Signorina's* supper was still waiting; and would she like a glass of champagne? Katherine controlled herself sufficiently to answer that she wanted nothing, and that if she did, later, she would go downstairs and fetch it.

She went into the bathroom, bathed her swollen eyes, grimaced at her distorted face in the mirror, and flung open the *jalousies,* letting a breath of the cool night air into the warm room.

Through blurred eyes she stared at the crystalline stars and listened a moment to the enchanting sound of bells. But the

122

beauty of Venice only made her heart ache more intolerably. She had been transformed from a happy, ordinary girl into a mature woman who had just passed through a cyclonic emotional disturbance.

Katherine shut the *jalousies* and turned back into her room.

She took up her pen and diary and began to write, her body still convulsed with little convulsive sobs.

This is the most awful night of my life.

She scratched that out – it seemed too 'young' and exaggerated. She did so want to avoid exaggeration and to be rational about this thing. But her heartbeats were still rapid and irregular and her lips still sore from the violent pressure of Renato's kiss. It had been without tenderness. Violent passion could be like that, she supposed. But if he had loved her – if things had been different – what utter heaven!

She drew her hand across her eyes and began to write again. And as though she could not control her pen, even though she wanted so much to be sensible and to hate Renato di Voccheroni – the words flowed in a hot stream – pouring from her heart:

I love him. *I know that I do. Whatever he is like and whatever he has done. When I was in his arms just now, I wanted to die of happiness. It was awful realizing that it meant nothing to him and that he only kissed me out of a kind of devilment. I realize that there is something about me that makes him* want *to defeat me. It is because I am not easily conquered. But for a moment he succeeded. I gave my whole heart and soul to him back in my kiss. But I was right when I told him that we could never again be friends. And that's terrible. I know now why everybody spoils him. He sheds such a complete glamour – it almost destroys one like a flame. Oh, I didn't want this to happen! And I've only myself to blame because I know that I am nothing to him and that he will marry one of those other girls.*

I hope he goes away soon and that I don't have to see him any more. And I feel that it is wrong that I should let Bianca get away with her lies. I ought to clear myself with Renato. On the other hand, what does it matter? I don't belong here. One day I shall go away and never see any of them again. Let Renato think what he wants about me. It means more to Bianca to keep her brother's respect. I suppose I've lost it. That does *hurt, although I oughtn't to care* what *he thinks, but I do, I do, I* do...

Katherine flung down her pen, hid her face in her hands and began to cry again.

11

Shortly after midnight, Beatrice di Voccheroni passed through the crowded *salon,* gracefully acknowledging smiles and greetings from her guests. She was looking for her son.

Supper was over. A magnificent banquet washed down by the finest champagne frothing in exquisite gossamer-like Venetian goblets. It had been a splendid ball. Reporters were already busily writing up their 'gossip columns'. The Marchesa need have no doubts about her success as a hostess.

But she had seen little of Renato and what she *had* seen caused her some anxiety. He looked so unlike himself; thoroughly unhappy even when he was dancing with some of his most glamorous partners. And Renato danced well and had always loved it, and he had done his duty as master of the *Palazzo;* had partnered the Contessa Chiago in a tango and two waltzes. And drawn a ripple of laughter from an amused Continental audience when, with Hilary Drumann in his arms, he showed them how to execute the *paso double.* But his mother saw that something had upset him. And he had not yet kept his promise to bring one of those girls to her and say: *'Mamma – Violantè (or Hilary) is going to marry me.'*

Where was he now, the wretched boy? Time was getting on. Beatrice came upon the Barone di Mallighi and appealed to him.

'Alvise – *per favore* – find Renato and remind him.'

'Of what?'

Beatrice bit at her lips nervously.

'He will know. Just say his mother *reminds* him.'

The Barone made a courtly bow and touched her hand with his lips. To him she was not a middle-aged harassed, nervously-exhausted woman with a mercenary nature. She was still the handsome intelligent girl he had loved so madly and lost to Ferdinand di Renato. But out of his deathless passion for her, he had forgiven her for preferring money and position to his love. He said:

'You are worried, Beatrice? About the boy?'

'You know our position,' she said in a low voice. 'Renato cannot afford to play around any longer.'

The Barone sighed. His romantic soul detested the way money crept like a poisonous viper into the exquisite nest of beauty and intellect. It was perpetually destructive to mankind's spiritual development. But he said:

126

'*Puo contare su di me*. Depend on me.'

And fixing his monocle in his eye, moved on, searching for Beatrice's son.

When he finally tracked Renato down, he found him under somewhat embarrassing circumstances. At the back of the *Palazzo* there was a long room composed almost entirely of windows – a sort of greenhouse, super-heated, filled with marvellous delicate flowering creepers and forced flowers. Gilded basket-chairs and tables had been placed here for the dancers to 'sit out'. The Barone, hidden by a tall palm, caught sight of a woman's shimmering dress and recognized Hilary Drumann – the American girl who was supposed to be one of Beatrice's chief 'hopes' for Renato. The boy was with her. The Barone heard his voice and it was what he was saying that made the old Italian nobleman stop and became a somewhat reluctant yet interested eavesdropper.

'It's no use, Hilary – I can't do it. I've tried. I want to propose marriage to you. But now I'm going to be absolutely honest for once in my life. I don't love you. Oh, yes, you are charming and gay and we get on well – but I don't love you as you should be loved. You're much too nice. I can't bring myself to ask you just to – pay the di Voccheroni bills. That is why my mother wishes me to marry. Now – you know the blunt, despicable facts and you won't want to see me again.'

'*Per dio,*' the Barone whispered to himself. 'What courage – to say such words to a lovely woman.'

Hilary's young confident voice betrayed no particular emotion when she answered Renato. She was, the listener supposed, typical of her race: practical – in control of her emotions. Sentimental – yes! But shrewd and almost masculine in her outlook on life and love.

'Say, I didn't know things were so tough in the old homestead, Ren-at-*o*. But you've no need to look so sick. Three-quarters of Europe is bankrupt and the di Voccheronis seem to have weathered the storm mighty well, considering. You don't have to be ashamed because you need cash, honey. And I call it mighty decent of you to be so candid with me. As for not loving me, why I'm no fool, dear. I've gathered that. And you can't help it. It's the Contessa, isn't it?'

The Barone held his breath. Now perhaps Renato would give an answer that he, Alvise, could take to his beloved Beatrice and relieve her from anxiety. But the reply was disconcerting even to the Barone.

'Violantè–?' Renato gave a curt laugh. 'Lord, no. I don't love her either. In fact I couldn't even talk to her in the friendly way I've done to you. You're a darling, Hilary, and you've been an angel about this – but–'

'But you're in love with someone altogether

different, I guess,' came Hilary's wistful voice.

An instant's silence betrayed to the experienced old Barone, the truth. There *was* someone else. Renato dissembled.

'No – at the moment I don't really want to get married at all.'

'That's okay, Ren-at-*o*. I'm crazy about you, and you know it, honey. But give it a rest. I'm going back to California after Christmas. My grandmother wants us all home for Noo Year. But I guess I can always fly over to Europe – and to Venice – if you change your mind.'

'I don't deserve such generosity,' came from Renato in a low voice.

The Barone frowned. His monocle dropped.

What was wrong with the foolish youth? Why turn down a charming girl with a fortune behind her? *Whom had he in mind?*

Hilary was asking Renato now what he intended to do about the financial crisis in the family. Renato's answer was 'frankly nothing'.

'We must find some other way of warding off our creditors,' he said.

And Hilary said, sadly now:

'So little Hilary skips back to the U.S.A and leaves the field clear for the Contessa who has eyes big enough to eat little bad Rena-t-*o* right up.'

The Barone left them laughing together. But he guessed that neither of them displayed the real distress they were both feeling.

A little mystified – upset for his Beatrice – the old man strolled back into the glittery *salon* to convey his news to her. When she heard it, the Marchesa's long fingers clenched convulsively over the lovely black ostrich-feather fan she was holding. The old frail handle snapped. Alvise gave an exclamation:

'Ah! What a pity–'

Beatrice di Voccheroni, pale under her rouge, muttered:

'Alvise, Alvise, *checosa devo fare?* (What am I to do?)'

With deep concern he looked down at her, smoothing his snowy pointed beard.

'If only I could help.'

'There is still Violantè... But you say he said he would not marry *her.*'

'*Si, si.* It is so. Candidly the boy led me to believe he has somebody else in mind. Yet he said nothing definite to confirm this.'

The Marchesa's eyes narrowed. She thought with agony of those piles of letters demanding payment; of her fast-vanishing hopes of going to San Remo in the Spring when the Casino reopened, to try her luck and replenish her own purse.

'Someone else. In the name of heaven –

who?' she muttered.

'There are other wealthy women besides the two of your choice, *cara mia.*'

'I must speak to him at once.'

The Barone held up a hand as pale and fine as the ivory she had just smashed. He warned her not to drive Renato too far. The boy was half-Italian – excitable – also stubborn. He liked luxury – he would not easily get rid of his Alfa-Romeo – his motor-boat – his flights to Paris and London. But she must not push him too precipitously into a marriage he was ill-disposed to make. It might be disastrous. Let him alone; let the threat of being 'sold-up' work on him inwardly until he, himself, decided to go in search of desperate measures. He had sent the American girl away – but not Violantè. As for Violantè marrying somebody else – never while Renato remained eligible. She was mad about him. All Venice knew it.

'Leave him alone for a few more weeks and be sympathetic rather than threatening. I know that I am right, *mia cara Beatrice,*' the Barone declared.

The Marchesa wiped her lips with her handkerchief. A tiny spot of red dyed the chiffon. In the violence of her own feelings, she had bitten her underlip. But she was controlled and she was ready to admit the wisdom of what Alvise said. Often in her life she had taken his advice – and found it to be right. Besides, it was so true – Renato had lately shown definite signs of rebelling utterly against her wishes.

'Meanwhile – we face ruin,' she said bitterly.

'Not quite,' the Barone smiled benignly at his old *amorata*. 'The di Voccheronis still have something left and we will put our heads together in the morning and concoct a brilliant letter which you can send to all the creditors – *si, si!* – we will find a method of temporising – they will wait. And before long, you will see – Renato will come to heel.'

'And what of this secret love you think he is hiding from me?'

'I may be wrong.'

'You may be right,' said the Marchesa in a sinister voice, and for one dreadful moment remembered how charmingly Renato always behaved to Connie's penniless girl. *If she thought for one moment that Renato had become really interested in Katherine...* Here her thoughts stopped abruptly. She derided them. It wasn't possible. That was just crazy. Renato was her son – he would never indulge a romantic passion and accept total ruin socially and financially as its consequence.

But as she moved back to the centre of her party – a gracious smile on her lips – swallowing her bitter disappointment, she decided that she would keep a watchful eye on both Renato – and Katherine.

12

Katherine did not see Renato that next morning. But a note from him was pushed under her bedroom door just as she finished dressing, and she read it, her pulses jerking.

I must have either been crazy with worry or had too much champagne last night, but I owe you an apology so here it is, whether you want it or not. I behaved like a brute. Forgive me, please. I value your friendship. And I had no right at all to be so annoyed about your 'date'. I only hope, whoever he may be, that he is worth your attention. It IS a 'thing' with my mother about Bianca being out late at night. Just remember that. I wish you the best of luck and when I tell you I have never needed your friendship more, I mean it.

I am just off to Milan on business. I hope to raise a loan for the impoverished family without handing over my cherished Alfa!

Till we meet again – arrivederci,
Renato.

Katherine swallowed nervously once or twice as she read and re-read this letter. She was generous-hearted enough to appreciate his having written it. It must have cost the proud, spoiled Renato quite a lot to make a full apology. It must also be accepted that he flattered her by making it so plain that he wished to keep her friendship.

Should she accept the olive branch? Those words *'I have never needed your friendship more'* ... troubled her. *Why* should he need it? *What* had she to give him? She, the penniless companion-governess. She neither understood him – nor herself. For last night she had shed tears more bitter than she had thought possible. She was shocked by her own newly-discovered capacity for pain. And she toyed with the idea of asking her mother to send a wire saying that she was needed back at home – so that she could leave Venice immediately, with justification. And nobody need know the truth – in Venice, anyhow.

Now Renato's letter reduced her to a state of doubt and confusion again. There were parts of it that hurt badly. That bit about him hoping *'that the mysterious "he" was worthy of her attention'* – roused her indignation.

She sat down on the edge of her bed and began to laugh. Really, it was funny. But the laughter trailed into a sob. Her heart ached with love for Renato and she shrank from the thought that he imagined her capable of a sordid affair with an Italian stranger.

She walked on to the balcony. Two of the staff were rolling up the red strips of carpet, removing the wilting flowers and plants and other evidences of last night's entertainment. The strong sunlight hurt Katherine's sore eyes and made her blink. But the sky was a canopy of sheerest blue and the morning fresh and beautiful. Across the gleaming water, the cupolas and towers in St Marc's Square were touched with pure gold. She felt her spirits lift at the sight.

Then she saw, below, the grey-flannelled figure of Renato stepping into his cherished motor-boat. The slim, elegant white craft, with its polished wood and gleaming brass. A servant placed a suitcase beside him. Renato's voice drifted up to Katherine:

'Grazie!...'

She stepped back. She did not want him to see her. But she watched until the boat turned under the arch and moved out of sight, chug-chugging swiftly over the sparkling water.

He had gone. To 'raise a loan', he said. Perhaps he would be successful. The di Voccheronis had so many wealthy connections. But what did that mean ... except that he had *not* proposed to either of those two girls who might have bolstered up the family fortunes.

Katherine felt a queer tinge of excitement warm a heart that had been beating sluggishly and miserably since she woke up.

Why hadn't Renato brought off this brilliant match, desired by his mother? *Or*

135

had he? But wouldn't he have mentioned the fact in his note?

Bianca came into the room. She averted her gaze as Katherine said 'good morning'. She looked so ashamed and wretched that the older girl had to feel sorry for her.

'Have you one of your bad heads, Bianca?'

Bianca muttered 'no, no', then burst into tears, wrung her hands and began to implore Katherine's pardon.

'I did wrong – I say *you* meet a man last night. I am wicked – oh, so wicked!' she wailed.

Katherine felt complete reluctance to indulge in an emotional scene of this kind. She patted Bianca on the shoulder and tried to stop her crying.

'It's all forgiven and forgotten, *mia cara*,' she said.

'No, no – I am wicked!' persisted Bianca rolling her eyes dramatically.

Katherine managed a smile.

'Okay, you're wicked. And now what?' she said drily.

'I could not let Renato think it is me,' continued Bianca. 'Oh, Katherine, I am so loving my handsome brother – I not wish him to find out about Benito.'

Katherine sighed. She wondered what Bianca would have said, had she told her that *she,* the calm, supposedly well-behaved companion, also loved the 'handsome

136

brother'. But in a very different way. She tried to comfort the young girl.

'We won't let him know. We won't tell anybody about it, darling. I'm sure you're very miserable, but you *must* stop crying and eat your breakfast. It's such a lovely morning. Let's sit on the balcony for our English reading session, shall we?'

Bianca was not yet to be diverted from her personal griefs. And now she began to give Katherine a garbled version of what had taken place in the past; how marvellous Benito could be; how cruel Mamma had been to send him away.

Katherine listened. In vain she tried to impress it upon Bianca that Benito Usilli could not be all that 'wonderful'. He might attract her physically, or play a violin divinely – but he could not be a good character. He was forty and married – more than twenty years older than Bianca and with a sacred duty to his wife and three children. It was iniquitous of him to take advantage of a schoolgirl's youth and innocence.

Bianca defended her Benito hotly. His wife was a shrew. His children disturbed him. He was composing a violin concerto that would shake the world when it was performed.

'Who said so – Benito?' asked Katherine sarcastically, and with her tongue in her cheek.

She was astonished at herself. How fast she was 'growing up'; changing from the unsophisticated Katherine of Mawgan Porth into a young woman of the world. Why, Mummy would not know her! She had never been very self-confident in the past. And after all – the difference between hers and Bianca's ages was slight. Yet here she was talking to Bianca like a 'mother'.

She might as well have saved her breath, she came to the despondent conclusion. The young girl remained pathetically if annoying loyal to the plump, flashy, horrid violin-teacher. He had certainly taken a firm hold on her imagination. Bianca continued to moan that she adored Benito and that she alone could make him happy.

'But you can't marry him. Besides – you have only just left school – it will be years before you will be allowed to choose a husband,' argued Katherine.

'Then let me see him sometimes – oh, I beg you – just a leetle hour for tea or to talk,' pleaded Bianca, her eyes streaming.

Katherine felt that all her efforts to make the silly girl see how silly she was were futile. So she was forced to threaten Bianca.

'Do try to be sensible and decent about it. If you go behind my back and meet him again I shall have to tell your people,' she ended, with a grim memory of herself as head-girl at school, lecturing a 'junior' who had put up a black.

Bianca abandoned the contest. But she relapsed into a sulky silence. This, of course, produced a sick-headache and she retired to her bed. There would be no English lesson that morning.

Katherine then had to accept the fact that life was bound to be tricky during the next few weeks. She would not find it easy to keep Bianca under control without her mother knowing. And she hated the idea of betraying Bianca even though she herself had been so let down by the girl.

The Marchesa did not wake until midday. She paid a visit first to her daughter's bedroom, then to the sitting-room where Katherine sat laboriously engaged on Italian translation.

'I am not pleased with the way Bianca looks. Was she up very late last night?' the Marchesa demanded.

Katherine could see that Bianca's mother was in one of her irritable moods. She tried to be as tactful as possible.

'No, not very late, Aunt Beatrice–' (The Marchesa had graciously asked Connie's girl to address her by that name while she was here.) 'But she has had so many of these bad headaches lately. Isn't a pity she can't find a cure?'

The Marchesa sank into a chair and gripped the sides with her nervous fingers.

She wore a black suit and a small black hat with a white plume curling to her neck. She looked handsome but haggard – at least ten years older than Mummy who was her contemporary, thought Katherine.

'We must find a new doctor who really understands *migraine*,' the Marchesa said. 'These local physicians are fools. I believe there is an American specialist visiting Milan shortly to lecture on it. We must send Bianca to him. *If we can afford it...*' she muttered more to herself than the girl.

Katherine felt embarrassed. She wished she could have told the Marchesa the truth. She would have said:

'Bianca is starving for affection and some excitement in her life. You keep her cooped up and chaperoned like a Victorian. She's quite a woman in herself – not such a baby as you imagine and she would be different if you treated her reasonably. You don't begin to be sensible and tolerant like Mummy is with me. I've always been trusted and gone around alone, and I was told about life and its facts when I was a kid. Now I can take care of myself. But Bianca can't. She's like all repressed, over-disciplined people – apt to go quite ga-ga over the wrong man. Take her out with you – dress her beautifully like you dress yourself – make her happy. Then there won't be all these migraines *– and nervous exhaustions. The whole thing is your fault because you're such a selfish woman,*

loving only yourself and Renato.'

That was what Katherine wished she could say, instead of which she stood – rather like a schoolgirl herself, she thought ruefully – hands behind her back, listening while the Marchesa talked.

She was so worried; Bianca was so abnormal. Why wasn't she a pretty, merry ordinary girl like others, and so on, until Beatrice turned her attention to 'Connie's girl'. Now *she* was most attractive with her exquisite skin, and those grey, long-lashed eyes and her fair shining hair. But *what* an ugly skirt and jumper. *Oh,* those English *'off-the-pegs'* – no cut, no style! She might send Thérèse along with that dark grey pin-striped suit she'd bought from Biki – Katherine would look a dream in it. And Beatrice had worn it once too often. Besides, she was waiting to order the Spring Models now.

'I'm off to Milan,' she added. 'Renato has already gone. We are contracting a little business, then I shall do some shopping and then come back. I leave you in charge of everything – you see how I trust you, my dear.'

Katherine coloured under the praise. The Marchesa had deigned to smile, and really she had some of her son's charm (or he had inherited hers!) Katherine reflected. She could be so very sweet. What a pity she

141

didn't love or understand her poor unwanted Bianca a bit more. How awful these mothers were who would gladly die for their sons, yet conceded hardly an inch to their daughters.

'I'm glad you have faith in me, Aunt Beatrice – I will do my best while you are away,' said Katherine and began to dread even a few days alone with Bianca in her present mood.

The Marchesa paid her more compliments; and asked after 'poor Connie' (Katherine did wish the Marchesa wouldn't always call Mummy 'poor' when she was so much happier in every way than her old schoolfriend). But the Marchesa judged people by their social status and progress alone. Constance Shaw, had, possibly, been the only 'poor' person to whom she had ever been genuinely attached.

To herself, Beatrice was thinking:

'It can't be anything to do with this girl that Renato refused to propose last night – it was my imagination – just because I'm over-anxious for him. Katherine is a sweet girl – and very self-effacing – I've nothing to worry about.'

Except, of course, her bills. But the faithful Alvise had composed a perfectly wonderful tactful letter for her to send to the creditors. It just hinted that an announcement in the future concerning the Marchese would be of singular interest to them – and would they kindly wait for their payment a few weeks longer. They would – Alvise was sure of it. They were all only too anxious to retain the good-will of such a famous Venetian family.

When Beatrice left Katherine, she was in a better mood. Katherine seemed to have that soothing effect upon people.

The grey pin-stripe suit was brought to Katherine by the French maid, who sniffed as she handed it over.

'*Mees* is lucky – it isn't every day Madame *la Marchesa* parts with her models.'

Feeling slightly embarrassed, Katherine accepted the suit, put it on, and was certainly pleased at the reflection she saw in one of the long mirrors. An expensive 'cut' paid, she sighed to herself. She looked incredibly slender and smart in this lovely tailor-made. She tucked a jade-green satin scarf which she had made herself, out of material found at *Vandelli* – into the collar, and was surprised at her own beauty.

She spent the rest of the morning wandering around the enormous house – deserted now that mother and son had gone – supervised the clearing up of the debris from the festivities of last night. Later she washed her hair, which needed doing, and sat out on her balcony to dry it in the sun there.

By lunch-time, Bianca was up and about

again, having decided that she had no more headache. (It was so boring in bed writing poetry that she might never be able to send to her Benito.) She was cross with Katherine for being so strict and unco-operative, but she could see that it would not be to her advantage to quarrel with her. So for the rest of that day she behaved with docility and a wistful sadness that was bound to touch a tender spot in Katherine's heart. They were good friends again before the day ended. And Bianca relied on her Benito's ingenuity to find a new way of seeing her. They could not exchange notes any more. Katherine knew about the gondolier.

The next day after the English lessons were over, Katherine and Bianca agreed to visit the Lido and spend the afternoon by the sea.

Incredible though it seemed in such warm sunlight and wearing only a thin coat, Katherine had to remember that it would be 25 December in a fortnight's time. *Christmas!* Somehow she could not visualize it. She was seized with homesickness. It would be the first time she had ever been away at such a time from Mummy and Daddy and the rest of the family. Bianca said that at Christmas time here, there were many religious festivals in Venice – but it was not as gay as in England. But that there would be a lot of 'fun' and a huge masked ball in the New Year.

'Let's go shopping at the Lido, and I'll spend some of my precious *lira* on Christmas presents,' said Katherine.

They caught the *Motonare* – a big double-decker streamer which departed from the Piazza St Marc – and crossed the sparkling Grand Canal and lagoon to the Lido.

Katherine enjoyed every second of that fifteen-minute trip with the sunlight in her face and the fresh breeze blowing the tendrils of hair that escaped from her head-scarf. How beautiful the fast-vanishing buildings in Venice looked from a distance! The air was exquisite – and the temperature neither too warm nor too cold today.

There were several stops – Katherine watched, with interest the crowds boarding or leaving the steamer. Black-veiled Italian women, brown-faced, swarthy men wearing berets; elderly couples with shopping-baskets full of parcels, coroneted with flowers from the market-place; amorous young couples; and an assortment of beautiful, large-eyed children – the angelic *bambini* of Italy. All muffled in shawls and coats – obviously finding it cold, although to the English girl the weather was so mild; and all giving out a strong odour of garlic.

Bianca chattered incessantly, pointing out features of interest during this trip. Katherine listened and learned. But she did not really care for the Lido. It was too *mondaine* and crowded after the old, glorious Venice on the other side. They alighted near the Casino and took a look at the fabulous Excelsior Hotel. Just at the moment it was full of film-stars; a film was being 'shot' in the district. Bianca yearned to remain in the over-heated palatial lounge with its atmosphere of women's perfumes, cigar-smoke, bright artificial lights and wonderful flowers. Katherine wanted to get out in the open air again, but to please the girl, they had tea there. Bianca was happy. She wished to be a film-star if she could not marry her Benito, she declared. Katherine tactfully avoided discussing Benito and, looking at Bianca's sallow, melancholy young face, pitied her desperately.

'Then I shall live here, and it will costa ten-thousand *lira* a day!' added Bianca.

What an ideal, thought Katherine. She would rather live on less than ten-thousand *lira* a *week* in a small *pension,* and be able to look out of a small window upon the glories of ancient Venice.

Suddenly, through the high chatter of Italian voices, came a deep English one.

'Haven't we met before?' it said.

Katherine looked round. She saw a pleasant-faced, broadly-built man in his late thirties, with a round face and clever, twinkling blue eyes. He wore an unmistakably

English lounge suit, carried soft hat and pigskin gloves and a brief-case. Yes, surely she knew him ... yet when ... where?

He supplied the name.

'Richard Kerr-West.'

'Of course,' said Katherine and stood up. Her lips curved into a smile and Richard suddenly realized how charming she was – fresh and flower-like in this hot-house full of orchid-like Continental women.

'You remember–' he went on. 'Renato and I saw you at London Airport. I had a line from him later telling me that by a coincidence you were actually travelling to his own home.'

'Yes, of course,' exclaimed Katherine. She turned to introduce Bianca. 'This is Renato's sister – the Signorina di Voccheroni.'

Bianca gave the English barrister a limp hand and luke-warm smile. He was not 'her type'; no glamour, no invitation in the formal way in which he bowed and said 'How-do-you-do...' She was not interested. Neither was Richard. He was surprised that his good-looking friend of Oxford days should have such a plain sister.

But he had a warmer regard for the older fair-haired girl beside her.

'Where is Renato? I rang the *Palazzo* and they said he was away. Bad show, as I'm only here for forty-eight hours.'

'Yes, he is in Milan on business. But do

join us – a cup of tea, perhaps?' murmured Katherine.

He refused the tea, but lit a cigarette and sat with the two girls for a few minutes.

He was representing an Italian client who resided in London but had some sort of money entanglement over here. Richard had been briefed for the case which was coming up in England, and had to meet some Italian lawyers. The client had taken rooms for his counsel here in the Excelsior.

'All too gorgeous and giddy for me,' added Richard.

'For me, too,' agreed Katherine.

'Don't you like Venice?'

'I absolutely *love* old Venice,' she answered, her eyes sparkling.

'It is my first visit here. Renato has asked me over several times but I've never managed it. Bad luck finding him away. I had no time to get in touch as I flew over with my client quite out of the blue.'

Richard stayed chatting to Katherine for a few moments, with a polite word or two thrown in for Bianca. He gathered from what Katherine said that Renato had not yet got himself tied up to any of his girl friends. He also wondered privately how Renato was getting on with *this* girl whose 'lovely legs' had inspired him to such praise at the airport. And if Renato had won his bet and had dinner with her yet. She was rather reserved, he reflected – not really Renato's type. Extraordinarily nice and knew what she was talking about; quite intellectual, in fact.

'Look here,' said Richard suddenly. 'I hope to get my business over and done with by midday tomorrow, although we aren't due to leave Venice till early the next morning. You wouldn't like to take me round Venice a bit, would you? I'm awfully ignorant about it.'

That made Katherine laugh when she remembered how ignorant she had once been.

'Bianca and I would love to show you around,' she said.

'That will be delightful,' said Richard.

But he left the two girls finally feeling that there was a good deal to be said for the truth in the old proverb, *'Two's company, three's a crowd'*.

Katherine and Bianca spent a pleasant afternoon by the sea and returned on the little steamer with quite a lot of parcels; Katherine had found Christmas things for her whole family and could send them tomorrow.

A heavenly silk, striped Italian scarf for Mummy; handkerchiefs with hand-embroidered initials for Daddy; sweets for the boys. There was such a choice in Italy. Peter and David would prefer huge slabs of chocolate to anything else. And a gay Venetian doll for little Veryan, dressed in silk and lace.

On the boat going back, Bianca moved away from her companion and stayed away such a long time that Katherine wondered where she had got to. She appeared again only when the boat moored at St Marc, with rather a flushed face. She said that she had been down below talking to an old Italian lady who was a friend of the family's.

Katherine could not spend the whole time being suspicious of Bianca's movements, so she accepted this story. But something made her look back as the crowds hurried off the steamer and she saw a thick-set man in black wearing dark glasses, the rim of his hat pulled down over his head in gangster-like fashion, hurrying off the boat. There were many men who looked like that in Italy. But this one struck Katherine as being uncomfortably familiar to her. In fact, *she could have sworn that it was Benito Usilli.*

13

Two days later Katherine wrote in her diary:

I am glad the Marchesa has come home. She came alone. She had meant to go to one or two private dress shows, but she went down with a bad cold, and when she gets them, they seem to go to her chest. So now she is in bed and Thérèse is nursing her up.

Renato has stayed on in Milan for a couple of days to attend the wedding of the Contessa Chiago's sister, Flavia, to some Count or other – I don't know the name. But it's to be a very big affair. The Marchesa seems well pleased because Renato and Violantè will be in touch all the time. I think she's still pinning everything on him marrying Violantè in the end.

It's funny but the house isn't the same without Renato. One misses him. Gloom descends upon everything when he is not here. Especially now that the Marchesa is laid up. She is in the mood to give orders one moment and cancel them the next, which raises chaos with the staff. The cook left yesterday in high dudgeon. I am sure if Renato had been here he could have smoothed things out with that devilish charm of his. She was such a marvellous cook, too.

I am not at all sure what Bianca is up to and am still ready to swear that it was Benito who followed her off the boat that day. She has a genius for spoiling things for me, too. I might quite have enjoyed my outing with Richard Kerr-West but for Bianca trailing along as the third. One wouldn't have minded if she had been pleasant, only she was so obviously bored, and annoyed because I refused to leave her behind alone. I just wouldn't, in case she got up to some mischief. But I found Richard an awfully nice man and very clever and although it seems rather vain of me to say so, I think he likes me. We got on splendidly.

I showed him a bit of the Venice I now know. Then we all went to the islands. We visited the glass factory in Murano, which I hadn't seen before. I never dreamed there could be such exquisite glass in all the world. I saw a piece of it actually being blown at the furnace; growing before my very eyes from a shapeless bubble into a lovely iridescent shape. The man who showed us round made a special little glass as a gift for me to take home. Then we went on to Burano to see the famous embroidery. Richard – he told us both to call him Dick – gave us lunch in that wonderful restaurant, 'da Romano'. We also visited Torcello and Richard seemed to know that Ernest Hemingway once stayed at a pension there, where he wrote his last book. Churchill has painted the island, too. I am not surprised, as it is unbelievably lovely – it lies like a jewel in the jade green water.

Dick was disappointed because Renato didn't come back in time to see him, but he has promised to fly over here again after Christmas. He really is a dear. He said he would get a call through to my home and tell my parents he had seen me. When he left, he said he had never enjoyed himself more and added, when Bianca was out of earshot, the he hoped the next time he would be able to take me out alone.

There was quite a significant look in his eyes as he spoke. No girl could mistake it. I felt sorry when he left. There's something awfully nice about the direct and uncomplicated attitude of a man who is a hundred per cent English, and with no difficult undercurrents. And with his fine brain and interest in everything Dick makes a splendid companion. I was bound to feel flattered by his attitude towards me. Still, when Bianca teased me last night and made one of her silly remarks like: 'Reechard lof you–' *I was cross. Bianca* will *label everything with an amorous tag. I suppose these Italians just don't understand platonic friendship. I shall, of course, be thrilled to see Dick again if he comes, but if I am to be sincere I must admit it isn't the same sort of thrill that I get over Renato. With all his failings –* I adore him. *Yes, I who thought it so stupid because everybody fell at his feet am in that humiliating position myself now. I think of him night and day. I am still quite dizzy at the memory of that moment when he took me in his*

*arms. Oh, I wish I could forget it and con-
centrate on somebody like Dick. Dick asked me
to write to him and I don't think it was only
because he wanted news of Renato. He really
seemed to like me a lot, and he is neither
married nor engaged. I don't see why we
shouldn't be good friends.*

*But the world seemed to change for me again
as soon as Renato came home. And the whole
Palazzo woke up. He is like a torch that sets
everybody alight. I can just picture the way he
scorched down the* Autostrada *to the* Pizzale
Roma, *left the car at the big garage there, and
then swept down the Canal in his beautiful
white motor-boat. I heard him come into the
house calling out:* 'Mamma mia!' *(obviously in
a good mood). We all met for lunch. Down came
the Marchesa wrapped in a violet knitted shawl
with a long fringe, having just got up for the first
time, still croaking a bit from her bronchial cold.
But she had to be down to welcome him. He only
has to go away for a few days and they all
behave as though it's a conquering hero who
returns. The entire mood of the house improves
with his presence. The servants smile and sing
more often. Bianca stops whining. He has a
mesmerism nobody can deny. God knows I felt it
when I first saw him again this time. But I tried
not to remember what I knew in my soul that I
must go on remembering till I die. I hardly dare
meet his eyes. But when he said* 'Hello Katherine' *to me, I had to answer and look at him.*

And there was something quite baffling in his smile. Perhaps one would have called it slightly ironic, or amused, and yet it seemed to appeal to me to show that I had forgiven him. So I smiled back and asked him how he had enjoyed Milan.

He said 'enormously'. Then I told him about the visit from Dick and he was very disappointed.

'Why in the name of creation did he have to come just when I was away? There's nobody I like to see better than old Dick,' he declared.

Bianca – the little horror – hung on to her brother's arm and with a wicked look at me, said, 'Reechard lofs Katherine.'

I saw Renato's smile fade. I can't imagine why. And I didn't like the way he raised his brows and said:

'Does he, indeed! H'm. It doesn't seem safe to let our young Katherine loose in Venice, Mamma, does it?' he turned to his mother.

'I really don't know,' she said.

She was obviously longing to take her son off and discuss their personal affairs with him.

Bianca can be fiendish *when she wants. She knows that my knowledge of Italian is not yet such that I can understand when she rattles it off. So I have no idea what she then said to Renato. But I heard my name, and watched his brows go up and down, and that meaning little smile curve his lips.*

I knew soon enough what she said. Shortly after lunch, Renato met me in the hall and

155

waylaid me.

'I hear you and old Dick got on like a house on fire,' he drawled.

'Yes, we got on very well,' I answered and wished my heart wouldn't beat so madly. He really has the most wonderful hands – slim, strong, brown and I had never realized before how gracefully a man could light a cigarette, put it in a long holder and place it in the corner of his mouth. Effeminate in a way, and yet he is so utterly masculine; I could feel that frightful weakness attacking my knees when his restless soul-searching eyes looked down at me.

'And I hear also that he's coming back quite soon,' continued Renato. 'He must have fallen for your charms, my dear. I congratulate you. He's been a confirmed bachelor up to now–'

Here Katherine broke off. She wrote no more in the diary. It upset her merely to remember how angry she had been when Renato had said that.

He might have just been 'pulling her leg'. She felt a fool – a prig – because she couldn't 'take it'. But somehow all her sense of humour seemed to fly when Renato made those sort of remarks.

She remembered saying that she thought that Bianca had been telling him a lot of nonsense, then she escaped from him.

But she couldn't settle down happily, even to read a newly-arrived letter from home.

She was glad that Renato had come home. Yet sorry – he was far too disturbing to her peace of mind.

What had happened in Milan? she wondered.

Much had happened that was very satisfying to Beatrice di Voccheroni if less so to her son.

A loan sufficient to relieve their temporary embarrassment had been raised. It would, of course, have to be paid back. Mother and son had to face that. And the letter dictated by the Barone had worked the oracle. The Marchesa had received assurances from all quarters that she could continue to run up bills. On the other hand, she knew that such a state of affairs could not continue indefinitely.

What pleased Beatrice most were the photographs, in the papers, of Flavia's wedding in Milan. Her son figured prominently in all of them, and mostly by the side of the extravagantly dressed Violantè. Renato had to admit that he had been extraordinarily well entertained while he was with her, and that Violantè, herself, could not have been more charming.

'Why don't you bring it off, Toto?' the Marchesa coaxed him.

He avoided her gaze. He dared not tell her that ever since he had got home he had been seething with jealousy because Dick Kerr-

West had spent so many hours with Katherine – and had appeared to like it. Moodily he said:

'After Christmas perhaps – I'll see. Give me time.'

Remembering the Barone's advice, the Marchesa did not press him further.

But the Marchesa was a scheming woman and an autocrat of the type fast dying out in Europe. She was accustomed to having her own way with her family. There was something on her mind which she had no intention of confessing to Renato. But when the time came, she believed it would be a powerful lever.

Without Renato knowing it, the Marchesa had had a long and comprehensive talk with Violantè, in Milan. The two women had been unusually frank with each other. And Violantè for all her femininity and artificial glitter was also a schemer and prepared to talk business.

She was so much in love with Renato that she admitted in her extravagant fashion she was *'ready to die with love for him'*. She was also greatly nettled by his refusal to ask for her hand in marriage. When the Marchesa delicately suggested that it was all a question of finance, Violantè listened with interest. She knew – of course – as did many others in Venice – of the decline in the di Voccheroni fortune.

Behind the Contessa lay the Chiago millions. The small loan which had been raised by Beatrice and her son was as nothing compared with what the Chiago estate – of which Violantè and her solicitors were joint trustees – could offer. Violantè suggested that a considerable sum should be placed at Renato's disposal. A little diplomacy and cunning must be employed. The Marchesa would tell Renato shortly that an 'unknown friend' had done this thing but required no repayment. When Renato was thoroughly involved, he could be told the name of the benefactor. Then, in honour bound, he would make the only amends he could; he would marry Violantè.

When Beatrice had exclaimed:

'But he might even refuse – and you cannot wish to *buy* your husband, *mia cara*–' Violantè had looked at her with big smiling eyes.

'I buy everything – why not my husband? I am not too proud. I am also, like yourself, *cara Beatrice* – a born gambler. I shall stake a lot on this – and I do not think Renato will refuse me. You will see. He will ask for my hand in marriage before the Spring.'

When Beatrice protested further, Violantè added:

'I want your son for my husband. I want it so much that I am prepared to do this thing. Do not refuse me.'

14

At first the Marchesa had refused. Pride prevented her from immediately accepting such a proposal from the woman who was so much in love with her son. Of course she knew Violantè's character. There were no great depths in her; nothing heroic or self-effacing. She was a gorgeous butterfly flitting through the fast-diminishing playground of the wealthy – one of the idle rich still able to live for pleasure alone, without giving a thought to the millions who have to work. Her personal friends were as rich as she was – American millionaires, Eastern princes, successful film-stars. She moved from one sumptuous palace or luxury villa to another. She was a well-known figure on the Riviera; she went yachting in the Mediterranean; or flew to the Bahamas, or joined the selected few who could lie in the sun on Palm Beach, Florida. There was little that Violantè had not experienced in her pleasure-loving luxurious life. The old Chiago, her husband, had in his lifetime, spoiled her disgracefully. She remained gay, inconsequent, insatiable for flattery; demanding love and attention from all men. And not averse to buying it. At times she was genuinely kind – she had no head for business and no sense of the value of money. Mainly because she had always had too much. She was accustomed to signing huge cheques – and getting what she wanted.

This, then, was Violantè Chiago. And because Renato had so long resisted her – gracefully, yes, but definitely – she wanted him more than anything or anybody on earth. If her beauty and her chic and her gaiety and charm could not work the oracle – then money must.

She continued to woo the Marchesa.

'I assure you it matters little to me if I lose the money I place at your disposal. What *does* matter is if I lose Renato – to another woman. I beg you, therefore – accept my offer. Tell him an admirer of the family who wishes to remain incognito is the donor.'

In the long-run, the Marchesa surrendered her pride. Her own thirst for money was a lash to her back, and – after all – this offer from Violantè might mean not only that she, Beatrice, and Renato could feel they had fresh forces behind them, but that Renato would finally see that he must in all honour propose to Violantè. *If* he had not done so before.

The Marchesa was not altogether a scrupulous woman, and she could shut her conscience to the irrefutable fact that what she was about to do was despicable. It was a form of blackmail. But if her conscience tweaked her at all, she shut it down by telling herself that it was for *his* good – and that he owed it to his family, who had given him everything, to marry well.

So the disgraceful pact was signed and sealed. Violantè's astonished lawyers found themselves – bound to secrecy of course – paying a sum into the di Voccheroni bank that startled even the *Signore Director,* who raised his brow, then sat down (as ordered) to write a non-committal letter to the *Signore Marchese,* telling him of the 'gift' from his unknown benefactor.

When Renato opened this letter he was in his dressing-gown, sitting as he often did, on the edge of his mother's bed, drinking coffee. He rather enjoyed talking to her like this before the day commenced. Unlike most women in the early morning, Beatrice was then usually at her best, arrayed in one of her beautiful satin bed-jackets, hair tied up in a chiffon scarf; face made up; the essence of chic. The room gleamed softly with lamplight. It was an unusually grey day for Venice. The usual carnations, deep red save for one white, from her old admirer, were on the dressing-table. The satin quilt on her bed was littered with letters and papers. Bianca had already come in to say good morning to her mother and departed again. Katherine generally appeared later on to take her orders for the day. Thérèse, well-trained, soft-footed, was quietly arranging clothes, rolling up the Marchesa's stockings that had been flung on the floor, and emptying the ash-trays. The Marchesa often stayed awake half the night, smoking and reading English or French novels when she did not take her sleeping pills.

Renato began to rip open the fatal letter, grunting:

'Another warning from the old bank, I suppose.'

The Marchesa, examining an invitation from one of her more intellectual friends, to attend an exhibition of Venetian paintings of the seventeenth century at L'Accademie, yawned delicately and glanced at her son.

'Warning – what warning, *caro*?'

Then she saw Renato's handsome face change. It was a study in astonishment. The colour flushed up under his tanned skin. He handed the letter to his mother.

'Angels and ministers of grace!' he exclaimed. 'Someone has gone out of their mind. Look at this.'

The Marchesa's heart beat fast as she took it. She knew so well what it contained. She tried to appear as astonished as Renato as she read the letter.

'But how *incredible!*' she exclaimed.

'I agree. Who can be so fond of our family that they wish to place a small fortune at our disposal and asks for neither gratitude nor return?' he said. 'It doesn't make sense.'

The Marchesa gulped.

'It seems that someone is devoted to us,' she murmured.

There followed rather a difficult half-hour for her. Renato was greatly excited and of course enthralled by this act of kindness from a mysterious friend. But he remained slightly suspicious. Who could have *done* it? That was the question. He seized his mother's telephone and rang the bank. The *Signore Director* gave him no satisfaction. He knew the name, of course, but as the benefactor desired to remain unknown, the *Signore Director* could not divulge the secret.

Renato went to the window and flung open the *jalousies* to allow the cool air of the misty pearly December morning into his mother's over-heated room. He fanned his forehead.

'Oh, Mamma *mia,* this is a *wonderful* day!' he exclaimed. But his eyes were puzzled.

The Marchesa sipped her coffee and regarded her son's back. She hoped she had done right in being a party to this transaction. She could imagine that Renato's pleasure would soon turn to horror if the name of Chiago had been broached (which of course it was not). He mentioned several of the old family friends whom he thought *might* be responsible for the largess. The

Barone was out of it, because he was one of the impoverished nobility. And one or two of their friends who might have been generous to the di Voccheronis were almost as hard hit as they were. He named one or two of the wealthier families, including his godfather who had gone to live in Brazil. He then decided that he must be the one. Yes, it was Uncle Tiepolo; only he had been so long in South America – he could not know, surely, of their embarrassment? And he had a big family of his own to provide for. However, he was the head of a prosperous firm of diamond merchants, and was reputed to have millions behind him. It must be old Tiepolo who had heard of their troubles, come to their aid, and did not wish to be thanked. It was like him. He had always been a delightfully modest person – unspoiled in spite of his success.

'Why didn't I think of Uncle Tiepolo before. Obviously he is the person, and when he comes over to Italy, I shall make him confess,' Renato exclaimed, and he refused to be diverted from the idea.

Beatrice let him think it – why not *for the present!* Now she said, tactfully:

'Do you not think it time that you asked Violantè to dine and go to the theatre with you, Toto?'

In his mood of elation, for with the arrival of this letter a terrible load of anxiety had temporarily been lifted from him, Renato pitched a crumpled envelope into the air, kissed his mother on top of the head, and executed a few neat steps around her gilded bed.

'Anything you suggest, *mamma, carissima mia*. Yes – I do owe Violantè a party. I'll ring her up and arrange it. And no more economizing. God bless Godfather Tiepolo.'

The Marchesa began to feel a little unhappier about this affair than she had anticipated. Shivering, she drew her satin wrap about her thin shoulders and begged Renato to close her windows. She could not bear the raw air. But Renato thought it a fine day. He liked Venice to look like a pearl rising out of the mist. One could have too much sun. He was going to dress and ride now, he said. First, of course, he would phone Violantè.

After he had left her, the Marchesa leaned back on her pillows and gasped. *What an ordeal!* As soon as she knew that Renato was out of the house she lifted the telephone receiver and called the Chiago establishment.

'*Buon giorno,*' came Violantè's gay chirping voice.

Quickly the Marchesa told her what had transpired. Violantè laughed until she nearly cried. The Marchesa felt almost annoyed. Violantè really was a trifle crazy – she seemed to have no idea what a serious thing she had done. However – she was full of the *joie de vivre,* because Renato had just invited her to dine with him at the Colomba tonight.

'You see – already it is working. He is happy because he has money again. We shall have good results. Do not be nervous, my friend,' she said.

'I leave it to you,' said the Marchesa rather faintly.

'Arrivederci, puo contare su di me,' said Violantè. 'I have a wonderful dress to wear. He will not resist me much longer.'

When Katherine came in to see the Marchesa, Beatrice was writing letters, but she took off her glasses and looked at the girl more kindly than usual.

'I've just had a letter from poor Connie – your mother–' she smiled. 'And I am writing this moment to tell her about you and to say I hope you are enjoying your stay with us.'

'Thank you Aunt Beatrice,' said Katherine, who always felt reduced to the level of a schoolgirl in the Marchesa's presence; besides which she could never breathe in this bedroom.

'I've also told her,' added the Marchesa, 'how much we love you, my dear, and especially my poor Bianca, who has been *so* much better since you came.'

Katherine murmured her thanks again but her lips curved a trifle mischievously. She was beginning to know Beatrice di Voccheroni. Something must have happened to put her in such a good mood or she wouldn't be saying all these gracious things. As for Bianca – Katherine wished she could tell the Marchesa how suspicious she was of the girl's behaviour.

She was soon to learn what had pleased the Marchesa. But not from Beatrice. From that inveterate gossip and mischief-maker, the French maid.

In the middle of the morning, Thérèse as usual brought coffee to *Mees* and the *Signorina*. When Bianca was not listening, she muttered in *Mees's* ear:

'Money has come to this house. There will be no more need for the *Signore* and *Signora* to worry. You will see!'

Thérèse always ended her announcements with those significant words: *'You will see.'* Disapproving though she was of servants' gossip, Katherine was human enough to feel curious.

'How has money come?' she asked.

Thérèse whispered:

'From a benefactor – I heard them discussing it. *Madame la Merchesa* is in high spirits. I do not think she will stay here for Christmas, either. I think she will shut up the *Palazzo* and go to Villefranche on the Côte D'Azur. My beloved France!'

Katherine received this news with some dismay.

After Thérèse had gone, she thought about it anxiously. She had looked forward to Christmas in Venice and to the special balls and parties which usually took place in the New Year. Bianca had promised her that there would be a *Bal Masque* – one of those sensational affairs reported in English newspapers, and which sounded so fascinating.

She had just written to Mummy and said that the whole of her life was virtually spent here 'in gorgeous Technicolor'.

Katherine decided to pass Thérèse's little bit of gossip on to Bianca who was usually left out of the family conferences.

'I hear something wonderful has happened and that a good fairy has been busy in the *Palazzo* – so don't have too many *migraines* this week, Bianca,' she smiled at the girl's dismal face.

Bianca had, in fact, heard of the mysterious 'legacy'. Renato had whispered it in her ear just before he went out riding, and told her that he would buy her a really sophisticated dress for her birthday in January.

But when she heard about the possibility of the visit to France, she went a sickly white, and turned and rushed out of the room muttering: *'No – no, is too much!'*

Katherine raised her brows. So it was like that! Bianca was still so much in love with that awful violin-teacher, she could not bear the thought of being dragged out of the country. It might not be a bad idea for her to have a complete change of scene.

But Renato put an end to any such hopes that Katherine entertained on Bianca's behalf.

They had lunched downstairs – just the three of them. The Marchesa had a 'date' at the Danielli with one of her friends. Katherine, herself, felt ill at ease in Renato's presence and tried not to catch his eye. When she did she found nothing significant in his gaze. In fact, he treated her in such an offhand way that it caused her alternate relief and despair. She was beginning to learn how awful it was to be madly in love with a man who wasn't in love with you, and whom you could hardly bear to look at. Who, if he regarded you with any kind of meaning, made your knees wobble and your throat feel dry ... and who, if he appeared casual or cold, reduced you to a state of anguish.

But it would not have been easy to guess that Katherine harboured any such feelings. She was cool and collected and for the most part rather silent during that lunch. The brother and sister chattered vivaciously together in their own language.

When coffee was served to them in the library in front of a log fire, Bianca ran upstairs to fetch a book she wanted to show her brother. Then he turned his attention to Katherine.

'Well, my dear – how goes it? As you imagine from my good spirits – fortune has smiled upon me. I've had several business worries but now the crisis is over.'

'Congratulations,' said Katherine drily.

He became suddenly strongly aware of her; of that calm personality that affected him so curiously. Did nothing ever ruffle the girl? he asked himself. Had she not even the curiosity to inquire what he meant by what he had just said. Yet he knew that she *could* be disturbed. He had once felt her trembling in his arms, under his lips. *Damn her!* He wanted to be free of her queer particular fascination. He wanted to enjoy this marvellous new relief from financial stress. He wanted to tell her all about it and yet somehow he did not. When discussing it with his mother, it seemed just a miracle that must be accepted and enjoyed. But what would Katherine think about it? He had an uncomfortable idea that she would not approve; the little prig!... She would be the kind to refuse such a gift of money from an unknown. He was willing to bet that she might even say that if a man had no money, he should try and earn it, that he should not spend somebody else's; even if it came from his own godfather! No woman – and no man for all that – had ever before worked so insidiously on Renato di Voccheroni's conscience and feelings. Katherine did not realize her power, and he could not account for it. Past discussions with her had proved that she was an idealist. He wronged her when he applied the word 'prig' to her. People with ideals were not necessarily prigs. Strangely enough those who lacked them had to be scornful of the others or admit a sense of guilt.

He began to walk up and down the library, deep in thought. Then he stopped in front of Katherine and looked down at her. It suddenly became apparent to him that she was not looking well; there were little blue circles under those beautiful clear eyes.

'Katherine,' he said abruptly, 'what is wrong?'

'What should be?' she stammered, taken aback.

'You look ill.'

'Good gracious, how ridiculous!'

'English people who come to Venice for the first time are apt to get fever,' he added. 'You must take care of yourself.'

Still more astonished, she flushed but tried to laugh it off. Why such sudden concern for her?

He asked himself the same thing, ironically. Only a few moments alone with this girl, had uncomfortable power to make him *think* rather than enjoy life just as it came. An hour ago, he had been pleased to think he was taking Violantè out to help celebrate his good fortune. Why wish now that it was Katherine who was going out with him? *Damn the girl,* he thought for the second time. She was a witch and did not know it. He did not want her spells. It was better to be gay and extract the last ounce of pleasure from life. Too much thinking could make a fellow morbid.

He said abruptly:

'We have been discussing shutting up the *Palazzo* and taking both you and Bianca to Villefranche where there is a villa we can borrow.'

'Perhaps you would rather I went back to England–' began Katherine.

'Oh, lord, no!' broke in Renato. 'Anyhow we're not going to Villefranche. It was merely under discussion. But my mother thinks she has too many commitments in Venice. She is on every kind of committee. It is rather late for us to change our Christmas plans. I think we shall have to go away after the New Year.'

Relief made Katherine's heart jolt. She said:

'I – I'm *glad.*'

'You just love Venice, don't you?'

'Yes – every stick and stone of it.'

'And you know more about it than any of

us who have lived here all our lives. You're a queer one.'

She looked at her wrist-watch nervously.

'Time Bianca and I went out.'

'Do you always do the right thing, Katherine?'

'Oh, don't be so absurd,' she was driven to a hot retort. 'I'm here in a job and Bianca's been writing all the morning – in English which she hates – and I think she needs a walk. So do I.'

He wanted to go with them. Instead of which, he had made an appointment for a hair-cut, and a shampoo, and the fitting of a new velvet dinner-jacket. He said:

'Well, you and I shall have another outing together one day – do you hear? I'll arrange it with my mother.'

Once again that anguish of consternation and delight began to disturb the girl's whole metabolism.

She started to argue – she didn't really want him to take her out. But Bianca came back, and Renato walked out of the room before Katherine finished her protest.

15

The next entry in Katherine's diary was made on Christmas night.

I am quite alone in the Palazzo *except for one or two of the servants. Even Thérèse has gone out with a new 'boy friend' who has fallen for her mature charms. I am alone and have never felt more lonely. Perhaps it is because I am so bitterly homesick. The Marchesa meant to be kind when she made me telephone to Mawgan Porth to wish them all a merry Christmas. It was a wonderful line – with just that deep hum of Continental communication behind the stillness – then came Mummy's voice – a little emotional, blessing me and telling me how they had all thought of me when they opened their stockings. They seemed thrilled with their Italian presents. Then Daddy and the boys and dear little Veryan spoke – in turn. But when David screamed: 'Hurry up and come home, Kath, we jolly well miss you–' I started to cry and I went on crying. Until, to my horror, Renato found me standing by the telephone snuffling into my handkerchief, blowing a red and unromantic nose.*

But more about that later. First I must go over the last two weeks which have been hectic, to say the least of it. There never seems any peace inside the sumptuous palace of this self-centred, madly gay family. (Madly gay with the exception of Bianca who still seems unhappy and rather hysterical and who I am quite sure is managing to get messages through to Benito. One of the servants in the house has been bribed and I don't know which. I am not likely to find out. It certainly won't be Thérèse. It might be Beppo, the pantry boy, who is a sly little devil. I caught him in the dining-room early one morning filling his pockets with fruit and nuts. I threatened to tell, and he looked at me with those big ravishing Italian eyes and begged me not to get him the sack, so of course I had to be soft-hearted and give in. But I bet he's a little liar as well as a thief. And I'll also bet that Bianca isn't above giving him a few lira *to become her messenger.)*

Anyhow, most of this last fortnight has been spent in shopping and preparing for Christmas. It turned out to be all Church and prayers today as Bianca warned me, but tonight they have all gone to another of the big palaces on the Grand Canal which belongs to Aunt Beatrice's sister-in-law. She is a dreary old bore of a Contessa and very correct and formal. But it was apparently 'a thing' that the two families always got together on Christmas night, and they've had to keep it up since the Marchese died or get into the Contessa's bad books.

Titles fly around Venice two a penny. Whenever the servants call me 'Mees', it makes me feel quite insignificant. On the other hand they are all very nice to me and I was very touched when they brought me up little bunches of flowers and boxes of crystallized fruits this morning. As for the cook – she made me a sugar 'Baby Jesus' in a manger, which is absolutely a work of art and I shall keep it until it disintegrates. Veryan will adore it.

The good fortune which fell so mysteriously on this family seems to have revived them amazingly. Renato, for reasons best known to himself, has been like a volcano in eruption and burned the candles at both ends in an incessant round of gaiety. The Palazzo seems to have been full of young Venetians or visitors from Rome and Milan; everybody dripping diamonds or shovelling out rolls of these horrid dirty notes. It just doesn't make sense when I think of the humble ten-bob or half-crown in my bag when I used to go shopping in Newquay!

When I've had time to think, and especially alone in my room at night, I've been absolutely wretched. I do love Renato so much. I try not to be thrilled when he smiles at me or starts one of his long confidential talks. But I am! I am! And no matter what happens in the future I wouldn't miss one of those precious moments.

The Marchesa has been exceptionally nice, throwing what she calls old clothes at me (to me they are new and wonderful) and sending me with Bianca and friends of theirs to concerts or on various expeditions. She even began to tell me the other day that she thought it was time I had a boy-friend and that she would ask a nice young man to dinner one night especially to amuse me.

But I don't want one. I only want Renato. Bianca was telling me the other day how different Violantè Chiago is when she is with him than when with any other man. She seems to want him just as much as I do and has far more chance of getting him. She is included in all his parties.

The strangest thing happened at the beginning of last week. I haven't got over it yet.

Renato had arranged to take the Contessa out to dine and dance. After he had gone who should turn up at the Palazzo but Dick Kerr-West most unexpectedly. He explained that there were fresh complications in his case, and he had to interview a witness here in Venice before he went off on his Christmas holiday. So there he was!

The Marchesa received him graciously, but said she was going out to a Canasta party so couldn't ask him to dinner. Whereupon Dick, with a quick look at me, suggested that I should go out and dine with him to which the Marchesa immediately agreed.

'Yes, do take Katherine out,' she said, 'she doesn't get much fun here, I fear.'

When I stammered that Bianca would be alone in the Palazzo she said that Thérèse could keep an eye on Bianca and that she was not a child who couldn't be left alone with a house full of servants.

When Dick heard that Renato was at the Lido-Venezia with the Contessa, he suggested taking me there. It was the last place I wanted to go to, but Dick said he must *see old Renato this time, and I was whisked off before I could protest. But I didn't think I was going to like seeing Renato dancing cheek to cheek with his beautiful possible-future-wife.*

I decided to make myself look my best and just show Renato that I wasn't going to turn into a a Cinderella. Not me! Nor would I let him think that I was moping around the place because of his *beautiful eyes.*

So I rushed upstairs and made up my face much more than I usually do – eyelash-black, special powder – a dab of scent – lipstick making a big red rather alluring sort of mouth. I must say I was thankful I had just washed my hair and it was shining. Then, into one of Aunt Beatrice's skin-tight black satin cocktail suits which made me look like a film-star. And a little idiotic cap made of rose-petals tilted over one eyebrow. I must admit I didn't know myself. I felt quite feverish. I remember I said to myself: I'm not going to become a good little mouse whom everybody leaves out of everything and who gets kissed only out of devilment. *I'm going to be a woman of the world – a Venetian – and turn Dick's sensible legal head, then watch Renato's surprise. Violantè's too!*

I must say when he saw me come downstairs, slinging a fur over my shoulders, Dick looked quite stupefied. He had only seen me before in a travelling coat and scarf. He said: 'Good lord – what glamour! My dear Katherine. I shall never want to leave Venice!'

That made me laugh but I felt pleased with myself as we set out for the Lido.

In that exotic atmosphere of sophisticated, beautifully-dressed women of all nationalities, dining and dancing with their smart escorts; plus the sparkling wines, rich food and languorous music, I felt like a fish out of water. But it was exciting. And when Dick and I sat down and Dick at once ordered champagne – I felt a tingle of real devilment run through me. Katherine Shaw was going to become just like those other chic, poised girls who seemed so much at ease. She would enjoy tonight to the full, *I decided. Then Renato and Violantè saw us. It was worth while, I thought, catching that first amazed glance from Renato, which altered to one of sincere admiration when he looked me up and down. Followed by an exclamation of genuine pleasure as he clasped Dick on the shoulder.*

'You, of all people. Why, you old so-and-so – what are you *doing back in Venice? Turning the head of our young Katherine, too.'*

'Not at all – she is turning mine,' said Dick.

'Well done,' I thought, and felt my face burn as Renato's brilliant eyes raked me again. He said:

'What a metamorphosis! The shy moth unfolds her wings and becomes an exquisite butterfly.'

My heart beat madly but I answered him drily:

'Oh, no, Renato, I am not the butterfly type.'

Dick was talking to Violantè. I had to admit she looked 'the tops'. In a dark-violet velvet cocktail suit, with silver-embroidered cuffs; and on the side of her red head a tiny hat with a bird of paradise sweeping across one cheek. A spray of diamonds and emeralds that must have cost a fortune glittered on a lapel of the coat.

She chattered vivaciously to Dick who couldn't understand Italian and looked awkward. But I noticed she kept a proprietary eye on Renato. The band had just struck up a South American conga. Renato suddenly pulled me into the curve of his arm.

'I'm having this one with our Katherine,' he said.

Dick politely invited Violantè to dance with him. I saw her cast a dagger-like look of annoyance at me, but she was all smiles as she drifted on to the floor with Dick.

I shall never forget that 'conga'. I couldn't dance it. Renato could, so I just moved in rhythm with his steps. He held me quite alarmingly close to him. I could have dropped down at his feet with sheer ecstasy. (Oh, Renato, Renato, what a heartbreak you can be and yet I don't think you are worth my absolute love. Why must it so often be the men who are not worth it who command that kind of love?)

I tried to appear cool and nonchalant (as I

had set myself out to be). I tried to be the sophisticated Miss Shaw. I ended as just a foolish inexperienced girl who had fallen burningly in love with Renato di Voccheroni. I don't know whether he meant to be cruel and just to test his power over me, or whether he really had some kind of feeling for me that night. Because during our dance he said all kinds of crazy things. He told me that he had never realized before what a wonderful figure I had, and that I looked heavenly in my black satin suit (I don't think he recognized it as his mother's). He said that my hair was like pale gold satin and that the rose over my ear was most provocative and that he wanted to kiss the dimple at the corner of my mouth. He told me not to go on pretending to be 'Little Miss Goody-Good' because I was just a beguiling female and knew it. He said that I knocked spots off every girl in the room – including the Contessa and that I made her look quite passé. All of which was ridiculous and I told him so. But he went on saying things and, just as the music stopped, I could have sworn he touched my hair with his lips. He whispered:

'Do you remember that time when I was so cross with you? And how furious you were when I kissed you? I apologized but I'm not sure that I meant to. I would like to repeat the kiss.'

I had had enough. I just felt in a daze and suddenly, furiously angry with him. He had no right to do this to me. I must, I thought, pull myself together and show him that I didn't care a hoot for his blandishments. I think I gave a rather theatrical laugh. I said:

'So that's the conga! Rather a silly dance and you said a nice lot of silly things to go with it. Pray excuse me, Signore Marchese, if I return to your friend the barrister who is, I think, slightly saner.'

Did that make him jealous? I did not know, but I thought he frowned. But he also laughed, and taking my elbow under one hand, guided me back to the table where a waiter was pouring out champagne for Violantè and Dick.

He wouldn't be jealous of me. Idiotic of me to suppose it. But I felt that I could have killed Violantè when she turned those huge eyes with their mascara-ed lashes on Renato and said something in Italian which was obviously very familiar. I caught the last word: Carrissimo. (Darling!) I felt drenched in sweat suddenly, and loathed both Violantè, Renato and the whole smart restaurant.

I don't how I managed to get through the rest of the evening. I just did. But it was in a bit of a daze. I ate what I could of the dinner, drank a little champagne, tried to amuse Dick, and refused to speak to Renato again. He crossed to our table once or twice to make plans for meeting his friend Dick later in the evening. And once I watched him dancing with Violantè, and saw him looking down at her in the same significant, lover-like way he had looked at me. Oh, he is

183

heartless. *Just a ghastly flirt and I must be mad to think about him the way I do. I ought to remember all the things I* dislike *in his character.*

I remember going home, as early as I could – pleading a headache. Dick got rather affectionate in the gondola but I just couldn't bear him to take my hand although I like him very much indeed, and had meant *to flirt with him. But I couldn't. With me it's just one man and one only! I wish it were otherwise.*

Why doesn't Renato end this torture and announce his engagement to the Contessa? Then I might feel better, in a queer way.

I can't say it was a very jolly night for me. Dick returned to England the next afternoon. I have seen practically nothing of Renato this week. He seemed fully occupied, and there were a lot of parties in the Palazzo *but I didn't go down to them. I'm afraid I've been indulging in a bit of self-pity and it just doesn't do. I've got to get over this wretched love affair. But I go about in a silly trance remembering the Lido-Venezia, and the orchestra-leader, Bruno Quirinetta, singing:*

Oh, dolce Italia.
dall mia terra son tornado da te
per rivedere il tuo bel ciel,
per non morir
di nostalgia!...

184

I was dancing with Renato while Quirinetta sang that sweet song in his tender voice...

Here the diary ended. Katherine could not bring herself to write any more. She felt tired and depressed. And never more inclined to pack her cases and fly back to her family. Home to quiet little Mawgan Porth, away from Venice and this fever of unrest.

Yet it had been a beautiful Christmas morning, crisp, sunny, with a clear blue sky, and the wonderful bells ringing melodiously across the shining water from all the churches. She had shared the deep religious spirit of the people and gone with Bianca to a service in St Marc's.

Afterwards they had a quiet family luncheon. Aunt Beatrice was still English enough to want to indulge in turkey, plum pudding and mince-pies on the 25th of December. But there were no crackers. It was nothing like an English Christmas. That kind of fun was to come. There was to be a big dinner-party tomorrow evening, and dancing afterwards.

The thing that upset Katherine most was the memory of her early-morning call to England to her family, and that embarrassing moment when Renato had found her alone by the telephone, crying like a homesick child.

16

Katherine had tried to hide her face from Renato but he saw the tears trickling down her cheeks. He looked shocked.

'My dear – what is it? – are you unhappy?' he asked.

She felt embarrassed beyond words – all kinds of a fool. She muttered:

'No, I've got a bad cold.'

His eyes half closed as he regarded the fair, bent head.

'Rubbish, you didn't have a cold at breakfast.'

She tried to escape but he caught her arm and pulled her towards him.

'You've just been through to Cornwall, speaking to your people, haven't you?'

'Yes.'

And she bit hard on her underlip in the effort to steady it. Now a feeling of unusual tenderness supplanted Renato's more natural wish to feed his vanity and *make* this young girl take notice of him. He raised her hand to his lips.

'Poor little Katherine. You're plain homesick and don't I know what it's like! When I first left Italy to go to school in England I felt it badly – I remember fighting someone and getting a black eye in consequence. But don't try to fight me. Let me help you to feel better. What would you like me to do? Shall I charter a plane and fly you home and surprise them all as they start to pull the crackers?'

That made her giggle. She blew her nose and snuffled into her handkerchief.

'Well, I don't like to see you miserable here in our home. I know it's not an altogether English Christmas but I can promise you a spectacular New Year.'

She avoided meeting his gaze and wished that her heart would stop pounding. She said:

'Oh, go away, and leave me alone, Renato – I know you mean to be kind but I'm perfectly all right.'

'Snubbed again!' he said, and lightly put his tongue in his cheek; but a thwarted look came to his eyes.

She frowned and then laughed again. He certainly seemed to like making her feel awkward and she was inclined to believe he enjoyed it.

'I'm sure you've got plenty to do and I know *I* have,' she muttered, 'and there's no question of "snubbing" you. You really are absurd.'

'Sorry,' he said huffily.

She tucked her handkerchief back in her

belt. She was wearing a grey jersey dress with a cowl neck. The belt was an Italian one of red leather ornated with little brass studs. Something she had found in Venice in one of those charming shops along the Mercurie. That sort of simple dress became her, Renato decided, although he had not really recovered from the pleasant shock of seeing her in her smart cocktail suit that night at the Lido-Venezia.

Katherine stared not at him, but out of the window at the bare branches of an almond tree etched in sepia against the aquamarine sky. She longed for the spring and for that bough to burst into delicate pink blossom. She loved Venice and did not really want to go away. It had only been in a foolish sentimental moment that she had felt a pang of nostalgia for home.

If only Renato would leave her *alone;* yet she supposed that he meant to be kind.

Then came the voice of the Marchesa, calling down the stairs:

'Are you there, Toto?'

'I'm beginning to hate that name,' he muttered and suddenly caught Katherine in his arms and held her for a moment against him.

'Ah, well – there's no mistletoe – but who cares? Merry Christmas, Katherine, and don't look so stern. You're so ravishing when you smile.'

She didn't know whether she wanted to laugh or cry as she felt the strength of his arms and the momentary pressure of his lips against hers. She was inarticulate. Her whole body burned with the strange, wild longing that he alone seemed able to rouse in her. Then he let her go and walked out of the room.

She waited a moment, both hands pressed against her mouth. Her eyes were very bright and this time not with tears but with fervent feeling. Then she, too, walked out of the room, fled upstairs and shut herself in her room. She didn't leave it again until she had regained her control. She could not hate Renato for kissing her. It was a man's prerogative at Christmas time, and probably the only kiss she would get, she thought wryly. But there was a cynical twist very new to Katherine Shaw's fresh young mouth when, an hour later, she saw Renato moving down the canal in his motor-boat with a couple of young Venetian friends. Bianca told her that he had gone to collect Violantè and a girl friend of hers. They were all going to the famous Harry's Bar for drinks.

She tried to discipline her heart and tell herself that she was a fool to let him hurt her. He reproached herself too for not being more content. This period of her life in Venice was a break that a thousand other girls might envy her. She had so much to be thankful for. And she could not complain of lack of generosity from the di Voccheronis. The Marchesa gave her a lovely Italian leather gilt tool desk set for a Christmas present. Blotter, inkstand and pen, all made of the same beautiful olive-green leather. From Bianca, a dozen exquisitely embroidered handkerchief. From Renato, himself, a book in a handsome red and green leather binding, gloriously illustrated: a History, in English, of the Italian Renaissance.

He had presented it to her in front of the others, and when his mother had protested that it was a 'dull choice', he had glanced sideways at Katherine and laughed:

'Oh, you don't know what a bookworm Katherine is, *Mamma mia.*'

Katherine had expressed herself enchanted with his choice – which indeed she was. There was a little card inside the book, *Best wishes for Christmas to K. from R. di. V.* Nice – but she fully intended to make him write in the book before she left Venice.

So passed Katherine's Christmas Day, which had led up to that evening alone, after the family departed for dinner with the aunt.

She saw nothing much more of Renato during the interim before the New Year, and had little time in which to think of her personal woes, or even to bother much about turning herself into Bianca's 'snoop'. Venice

190

seemed to go mad on New Year's Eve. The preparations in the Palazzo di Voccheroni were endless – as they had been for the other Ball – only this was a more general affair.

Never would Katherine forget the bewitching beauty of that clear starlit night on the last day of December. It was cool but delightful, with Venice *en fête*, brilliantly illuminated. Every bridge looked like a half-hoop of diamonds, every gondola was lit with small lamps in the prow, and festooned with flowers. All the bells were ringing, carolling gaily and – it would seem – everybody was singing; a chorus of joyful sound. The whole world streamed out into St Marc's Square to watch the dancing or take part in it. Nearly everyone wore a mask and a paper hat. Some of the men had put on painted heads of animals, or comic giants. Confetti poured down from the windows; balloons bobbed gaily upwards or came down and exploded at the touch of a cigarette, followed by screams of laughter. Pretty girls, rich and poor alike, linked hands with their escorts and filed through the narrow streets, or floated down the canals that were a shimmer of reflected colour. Venice gone mad! Then at midnight, the sound of the great clocks beating out the strokes of the dying year, and ushering in the new one. At once a roar of exultation went up from the dancing crowds.

The whole di Voccheroni family, including Katherine and several of their friends had kept together in a party so far. The Marchesa, as usual, would not allow Bianca to go off alone or take part in the public dancing, so she moved sedately at her mother's side and watched.

It was at these times that Katherine pitied the girl and felt that it was no wonder she suffered so badly from depression.

Katherine reflected that if Benito Usilli had been a nice man and not married, she herself would have been almost inclined to encourage the unfortunate girl's romance. It was a pity she had made such a bad choice.

At the moment when everybody turned to their next-door neighbour and said 'Happy New Year' – both in French and Italian – Katherine happened to be standing next to Renato. But she was not going to be kissed by him again – and she moved quickly away to receive a chaste salute on the forehead from the old Barone Alvise de Mallighi who was with the party. Amidst the excitement and laughter, Renato was quite conscious of the deliberate way she avoided him. He felt suddenly angry and even offended. To the devil with this difficult, ungrateful girl! He turned to Violantè and read the invitation in her dark eyes. She was looking most attractive in black velvet with those wonderful eyes gleaming through the slits in her mask, and her red head powdered with confetti. He caught her close and kissed lips that were only too eager to respond passionately. He whispered an Italian greeting. Now she answered seriously – without laughter – her little jewelled hands holding on to him with fierce possessiveness.

'*Io t'amo, I love you*, Renato,' she muttered the words against his lips, and it was the first time she had ever made that declaration so frankly. She added: 'Let it be a very Happy New Year *for us both.*'

He could not fail to realize what she meant and he had known for a long time that if he so wished, he could announce his engagement to Violantè tomorrow. Why hesitate any longer? True, the unknown financier had made it less essential for him to marry just in order to pay immediate bills. But the sum placed by the mysterious benefactor to the di Voccheroni account would not last long (as Renato's mother had continually pointed out). It would be madness to spend it all at the rate Renato was accustomed to spending money. He supposed that the time would come again and speedily, when they would once more be faced with a sea of debts.

Violantè was tempting – no man could be blind to her physical allure, if nothing else. Almost in that moment – his vanity piqued by Katherine's behaviour – Renato asked Violantè the fatal question. He never knew what stopped him from doing so. It was *something* – an instinct deeper and more powerful than he could fight against.

But this was no time for soul-searchings. This was New Year's Eve – and Carnival. He would not have been human if he had resisted Violantè altogether. Without committing himself, he silently returned her kiss and whirled her into the crowd of dancers. The Marchesa raised her *lorgnettes* and followed the two figures (gyrating madly like mechanical dolls), until they were lost in the laughing, jostling crowd. Then she let the *lorgnettes* fall. Her haggard face creased into a smile of satisfaction. She turned to Bianca who was looking glum and unattractive as usual. Beatrice was generally irritated by the sight of her uninspiring daughter. As she so often said to her intimates: 'I really don't know *where* Bianca gets her looks from – certainly neither from her father nor me! She must be a changeling!'

Tonight a slightly more maternal solicitude seized her. She was in a good mood because Renato had gone off with the woman to whom they were in secret so deeply committed.

'Would you like to have coffee *chez* Florians for a treat, Bianca dear?' she suggested. 'If so, you and Katherine and I will go and order it. Then you must think about bed.'

But Bianca whined that her head had

begun to ache and she wanted to go home *now.*

That put paid to Katherine's New Year's Eve. Her excitement evaporated. Most of it had gone already – for deep down inside her she had *loathed* seeing Renato disappear into the heart of the Carnival with Violantè. But she at once offered to take Bianca home. The Marchesa graciously said that she could leave Bianca there with the servants and come back if she wished. Katherine, however, decided that she had no further interest in the fête. It would have been lovely to dance over one of those brilliant bridges with *him*, but not with anybody else.

Hundreds of boys and girls danced past – arms around each others' waists – having a perfectly wonderful time in this city of enchantment that was made for lovers. Never had the old stone statues, the pillars, the domes and spires, looked more wonderful than tonight – silhouetted against a sky of glittering stars; illuminated by thousands of artificial lights, garlanded with ropes of flowers. It was an unforgettable sight. A New Year's Eve Katherine was to remember. But not only because of its gay loveliness.

There was a spectre at the feast. A spectre in the shape of Benito Usilli who had been standing not far away from the di Voccheroni party all through the evening. Wearing a mask and with a broad-brimmed hat pulled well over his eyes, he threaded his way in and out of the dancing crowds, unnoticed. *Except by Bianca who knew that he was there.*

At one interval, when everybody else was watching a shower of golden fireworks that broke suddenly high above them, he had managed to slip a twist of paper into her hand.

After reading his note, Bianca had decided to invent that useful headache, and go home. She was quite cunning enough to be sure that her mother would send Katherine with her, and not return home herself.

Now, how to get rid of Katherine? The two girls argued in the motor-boat in which they were taken back to the *Palazzo*.

'You just can't miss the Carnival. – it's quite early – only half-past twelve – you *must* go back,' Bianca declared.

'No, I've had enough, I'm tired,' was Katherine's answer.

That floored Bianca for the moment. It was difficult to go on protesting without arousing suspicion. Yet she knew perfectly well that Benito was in one of those many gondolas, with a little lamp burning in the prow, following them. She *must* manage to meet him somehow.

Katherine did not know and did not at the moment suspect. But the thrill of the gala was over for her. She could not shut out the memory of Renato with lovely sparkling

196

Violantè in his arms, waltzing madly away from the rest of the party.

She had no right to be haunted by that sight, no right to think about Renato at all. But one couldn't always control one's thoughts and feelings, she reflected unhappily. And she felt deeply unhappy as she followed Bianca into the *Palazzo*.

She tucked the girl up in bed, but positively refused to go out again herself.

So Bianca was forced to resort to desperate measures. The spirit of the Carnival had reduced her to a state of crazy longing for Benito, and defiance. She knew that he would be waiting – very well – she, too, would wait for a good hour before she made a move. First she must be satisfied that Katherine was asleep. She heard the bath running and presumed Katherine was going to bed.

But Bianca had made a mistake. Katherine had turned on the bath but turned it off again. She was, herself, in such a restless frame of mind, she could not face the thought of tossing and turning in her bed trying in vain to sleep.

She, too, made an error of judgment. She believed that Bianca's *migraine* was this time genuine. She had given Bianca cachets and the girl had taken them. So, Katherine, listening to the crackle of fireworks and the sound of music drifting over the water, was tempted out of the house again.

Wearing a coat, and with a scarf around her head, she walked down the steps of the *Palazzo*, meaning to hail a passing gondolier and watch the fun from the water – quite alone. The Marchesa had said that she could safely leave Bianca to be chaperoned by the servants, who were still in the house.

Benito Usilli, hiding a little way down the Canal, saw the slim, graceful figure of Bianca's English companion. Did she mean to go off and leave Bianca? If so it would be quite easy for him to slip into the *Palazzo* and spend a thrilling hour with the young girl who excited his jaded fancy so madly. He cautioned his gondolier to wait in the shadows.

It was then that the little drama took place. In Italy, jealous passions run hotly. And tonight there was one woman in Venice determined on a *vendetta*.

Benito's wife had found in one of his pockets a letter from Bianca – unsigned but leaving no room for doubt that the writer was having an 'affair' with her husband.

Benito's wife, too, had followed that motor-boat from the square. Maria Usilli's gondolier was a cousin of hers and only too willing to help. Maria stayed watching in the darkness among a dozen other craft in which happy lovers sat cheek to cheek, half hidden behind the little curtains as they drifted down the Canal. And she watched Benito.

When Katherine came out and stood there on the steps outside the *Palazzo*, Maria took it for granted that *this* was the girl who waited for Benito, and whom he had come out to visit. Without inquiring, flaming with jealous fury, the Italian woman ordered her cousin to bring her gondola alongside the *Palazzo* steps. Katherine was completely taken by surprise. One moment she was looking dreamily at the bobbing lights on the water; the next she was fighting for what seemed her life, with a creature who clawed at her face and hair with long finger-nails, and screamed invectives in Italian.

Benito saw it all. He recognized his wife. At once he turned and glided away in his gondola unnoticed, cursing under his breath. Bianca recognized Katherine's voice and rushed out of her room on to the balcony. She looked down and saw the two women struggling there on the steps. Katherine's scarf had been torn to shreds. In the moonlight Bianca could see that her cheeks were bleeding. Horrified, the young girl slunk back into her room and began to mutter terrified prayers. She knew perfectly well what had happened. She could understand only too well the words that were being screamed at Katherine! It was *Benito's wife! Dio mio!* thought Bianca. She had found out but thinks it is *Katherine!*

It was one of the most hideous moments in Katherine's quiet, usually well-ordered life. She had no idea what was happening beyond the fact that she had been drawn into an unseemly and degrading battle with an Italian virago. She thought the woman must be a lunatic, and screamed piercingly for help.

Desperately, she fought to save her face from the cruel fingernails. Her frenzied cries at length brought one or two of the servants out and the next moment Katherine was free from the mauling fingers. But the glittering night whirled round her. With a little choked cry, she fell down into a dishevelled heap. She had lost consciousness.

17

Extract from Katherine's diary, written in the last week of January.

It is over a month now since I felt able to write in my book again. Everything has been so grim. And I've felt so utterly disheartened.

I shall not forget New Year's Eve if I live to be 100. It really was the first day of the New Year, when that ghastly thing happened. What a beginning for anyone. And why should it have happened to me?

No one who hasn't experienced it, can believe what it's like to find yourself grappling with a kind of lunatic, trying to save your life. I really believe the poor demented woman meant to push me into the Canal and drown me! Not that I blame her when I think what lay in her mind at the time, and that she didn't know she was making such a dreadful mistake.

It was stupid of me to faint, but I think my assailant gave me a blow over the head, otherwise I wouldn't have been so weak and Victorian. However, when I came to again, Thérèse and one of the men from the kitchen, were carrying me up to my bedroom. Bianca followed, wailing like a banshee, and looking sick with fright. Then Thérèse began to bathe my face and neck, and my goodness, when I looked in the mirror, I could see what harm pointed nails can do. I had the most frightful scratches from brow to chin as well as a black eye. I looked as though I had been in a free fight all right! I would have laughed if I hadn't felt so sick and shaken. When I asked Thérèse what it was all about she gave me a queer look and said that the Signora Marchesa *would tell me, and that she was on her way up. Thérèse said that about an hour after Bianca and I had left the party in St Marc's Square, Renato and Violantè had rejoined the Marchesa and they had all decided to come home and open some champagne here. I did not know at the time, but I learned afterwards that the whole crowd came round under the arch just in time to witness the final struggle. Then the mad woman was pulled away from me.*

But I was confused and in ignorance of the real truth until the Marchesa enlightened me.

She swept into my room looking as white as a sheet under her make-up, and stood over me like a figure of wrath.

'What is this I hear, Katherine?' she demanded.

I didn't answer for a moment. I was too dazed. I suppose she must have been taken aback by my appearance, because my face was covered with wads of cotton wool and there was a bandage around my head. So she sat down and

202

relaxed a bit.

'My goodness, you look a mess!' she muttered. 'Are you sure you are all right? Shall I send for a doctor? I don't want to if I can help it. There must not be a scandal. Do you understand, Katherine? Under no circumstances must there be any scandal.'

I started to laugh and cry at the same time.

'Isn't there one already?' I asked her. I felt quite hysterical.

She admitted that it was unfortunate that her guests had seen and heard so much, but that she was going to hush it up and was not 'prosecuting' the woman, who had been taken away by her relatives.

Before going she had accused me *of trifling with her husband's affections. The* vendetta *had been boiling up ever since she had found a note I was supposed to have written. I was the culprit.*

'I am appalled!' the Marchesa breathed over me. 'I never dreamt that you could be such a little fool, Katherine.'

I lay there too utterly stupefied to answer for a moment. My head ached, my face was stinging and I felt positively nauseated – as though I had been rolled in slime or something. Then I managed to say:

'So that's it! You think that poor woman attacked me because I have been carrying on with her husband.'

'She made it quite clear,' was the answer. 'And

when Renato came along, she appealed to him. She said that she had seen her husband with you in St Marc's Square not to long ago, and that my son had also seen you.'

I felt my heart sink to the lowest depths.

'And what did he say?' I whispered the question.

'He tried to say nothing. He is so chivalrous,' said the Marchesa, narrowing her gaze. 'But he could not deny that he had seen you, or that he warned you that it was dangerous to play this sort of game in Italy.'

That was too much for me. I wasn't going to have things like that said, and I wasn't going to be a martyr for Bianca's sake a second time. So I sat up in bed (looking I don't doubt like a gargoyle) and let dear Aunt Beatrice have it straight from the shoulder. I don't remember half I said but I said it. I ended, 'You know perfectly well it was your own daughter Benito was after. You know you dismissed him because he made advances to her here. How dare you try and pin it on me? Renato may not know – but I'm going to tell him now, and everybody else, too. I don't think Mummy would be very pleased if she thought her oldest friend was mean enough to make a scapegoat of me just because she didn't want a scandal about her own daughter!'

I think it was those last words that penetrated the Marchesa's armour. She collapsed like a pricked balloon and began to weep. Of course she knew, she admitted. She knew it was Bianca.

(That terrible child!) But nobody else knew. She had kept it from Renato all this time. Of course now she would tell him the truth. He would have to be disillusioned about his innocent little sister, painful though it would be for him. But she begged me not to tell anyone else – people like the Contessa Chiago – or the Barone – or the staff here.

There followed a frightful half-hour of heated discussion, with poor me trying to defend myself, and the wretched Aunt Beatrice trying to save her 'family honour'. I was a bit sorry for her. I knew what it would mean to her to be made the laughing stock of Venice, and everybody sympathizing because she had a little cheat of a daughter barely out of school playing fast and loose with a married man. At the same time I didn't see why it should all be pinned on me. I had my own reputation to think about.

But if ever there was a determined woman it was Beatrice di Voccheroni. She discarded her wraps, sent for hot coffee and brandy for me, flattered me, cajoled, pleaded and even burst into tears, wringing her hands in the good old dramatic fashion. It was rather ghastly to see a proud woman collapse like that. She confided in me. Hinted (as if I didn't already know) about the financial spot the family was in, and how Renato's godfather had come to their aid temporarily, but how essential it was that Renato should marry the Contessa. These big important families out here were frightful snobs, she said. Violantè might cool off if she thought that Renato had a sister who had been involved with a common violin-teacher. Tongues would wag in Venice, and it might be thought that things were worse than they really were. It would mean social ruin for them all and especially for Bianca, who would never live it down. No young man of decent family out here would dream of proposing to her when she 'came out' next year. They might believe Bianca had lived with the vile fellow. People always thought the worst – they had foul, prurient minds. And so on.

The Marchesa talked endlessly in this strain. I hardly got a word in, but lay with my fingers pressed to my throbbing head, feeling that I was in some kind of nightmare. What a happy New Year! And how appalled Mummy and Daddy would have been by the whole thing. As for vendettas – they seemed to be something out of books and films; they certainly didn't happen in Cornwall.

At first I was determined not to be sacrificed. But Aunt Beatrice wore me down. After all, the only thing that really mattered to me was that I should keep my good name with my own friends and in particular with Renato. What did it matter to me if Violantè Chiago looked at me sideways and sniggered? Or any of the other di Voccheroni friends? And it did mean Bianca's whole life.

There seemed no end to the awful embarrassment of that early-morning drama. For Bianca tottered in finally, streaming with tears and fell on her knees and begged me to forgive her and help her. Then she clawed at her mother's knees and begged her not to send her to a Convent. She would kill herself if her mother did this. It was sickening and I really felt that I was going to be sick if they didn't stop. So in the end out of sheer fatigue, I told them both I'd help as far as I could, and that I wouldn't give Bianca away.

Bianca clung to my ankles and moaned. I got quite irritable and gave her a shove with my foot and told her to go to bed and try to get some sense into her silly little head.

Then I told the Marchesa a few straight truths. I felt I could afford to be daring now. I told her that she was greatly to blame for Bianca's behaviour, and the girl was a bundle of emotion and repression, because she was so neglected. That she ought to have more young people around her and a better time altogether. That it wasn't really Benito she loved and wanted – but just that she was in love with love, like so many girls of her age.

The Marchesa took it all very well, I must say. She was quite humble. She *did* blame herself, she said and would try to be less selfish in future.

'And Renato, too,' I said abruptly; 'he's not much of a brother. Why doesn't he take Bianca out a bit?'

'You're quite right, Katherine. We've both been

207

very mean to Bianca,' said the Marchesa. But added slyly: 'Renato, of course, will be married soon, and then I can devote my whole attention to poor Bianca.'

She added the promise not to shove the unfortunate girl into a Convent, or let there be any shattering repercussions from tonight's episode upon her.

'Now I must send Thérèse to bathe your poor face again. Poor brave little Katherine – I shall thank you all my life,' ended the Marchesa huskily.

I shut my eyes. I didn't want to see her. I suddenly disliked her and everybody in the Palazzo. I think she must have felt this, because she took my hand, pressed it and said:

'Please don't hate us, Katherine. I know poor Connie would never forgive me, but I'll see no harm comes to you. I won't let your reputation suffer, I swear it. I'll tell everybody that the woman was mad as a hatter and made a mistake, and that you weren't a bit to blame. I swear it. I'll see that you have a wonderful Spring here. Don't leave us. Stay and help Bianca a bit longer.'

I started to weep at that period in a thoroughly weak fashion. I was worn out and suffering from shock. But I promised the Marchesa I'd try to co-operate. I still wanted to help the wretched Bianca, and I felt that if I left she might really attempt suicide – she was so unbalanced. And having promised to support the Marchesa up to a point, I had a certain amount of power over her, and I was jolly well going to use it to make her give Bianca break.

It wasn't Bianca who needed help so much that night. It was myself. I've never felt so upset. After all, it was a nasty thing to have happened to anybody. To say nothing of my being so dreadfully in love with Renato.

Yet after they had all gone away and turned out the lights, and left me in the darkness alone with my aches and pains, and my poor scratched face, I could think of nothing but him. What he must be thinking, and what they were all saying about me downstairs. Let Renato get on with his marriage – selling himself in the money market – I couldn't care less, I told myself. Yet I would have given anything in the world to have seen him for a few moments, and make sure that he had been told it was not I who was really the cause of that sordid vendetta.

I wasn't to know for a long time what he had been told. And that was something for which I found it hard to forgive the Marchesa.

During that next week she couldn't stop showering me with gifts. Flowers, fruits, books, sweets, a new radio for my bedside – everything I wanted. The Marchesa, herself, coming in and out a dozen times a day to make sure I was all right and that my face was going to heal. Trying first this cream, then that. Then new lotions. As I got better she called in a local beauty specialist to give me a 'facial'. She made continual efforts to show her gratitude because I wasn't telling the world about Bianca. And Bianca, herself, treated me as though I was a kind of goddess, and made a pathetic struggle to stop whining and moping, and to behave reasonably.

But I didn't get the one thing that I wanted. And the Marchesa must have seen to that. For Renato didn't come near me. I hadn't the slightest idea what he thought about that ghastly fight on the steps. Neither did he even send a note of inquiry. He left Venice with strange abruptness and flew to Paris on New Year's Day, to spend a few days with his great friend, Jacques de Grenoble, Bianca told me. The announcement of his engagement hung fire, I knew. But all I wanted to know was whether he had been told the truth about me.

18

Then, suddenly it was Spring.

Mysteriously, as though a magic hand had been laid overnight on tree, bush and plant – the tight green buds opened and the first delicate exquisite colours of the year transformed Venice into a fairyland.

Never would Katherine forget her emotions when she opened her shutters that warm, misty morning and saw the loveliness of the scene before her. A scene that might have been painted by the greatest water-colour artist in the world. Golden light piercing the translucent pearl of the awakening day and dipping into lavender water. The sudden poignant beauty of peach and pear blossom; of slender almond; cream-petal and delicate pink; delicate green leaves. Where yesterday it seemed there had been sober plants in the great stone urns, or tubs behind the wrought-iron balconies and gates; now one could see breath-taking splashes of vivid colour from a thousand opening flowers.

Spring in Venice! The mists vanishing, giving place to the luminous blue of a cloudless sky. Spire, dome and tracery of carved stone-work upon roof and cupola looking gilt-edged against that blue, blue background while the sun rose higher every hour.

Golden sunlight; golden bells; rippling water changing from amethyst to amber and then to emerald and aquamarine as though all the jewels in Italy had drowned themselves in the mirror-like canals of the most beautiful city in the world.

Katherine was in a grave mood when she got up that Spring morning. It had not, after all, been much fun living here these last few weeks. In fact, January and February had dragged miserably for her, for she had been a prisoner in her bedroom for the first fortnight after the 'incident'. Encouraged by the Marchesa, she stayed quietly upstairs while the nasty scratches on her face healed. Katherine had felt the confinement and lack of exercise, and taken some little time, too, to recover from the shock of that brutal attack by Benito's jealous wife.

She had also felt compelled to write home without any of the careless happiness that used to shine through all her letters before that sinister end to the New Year's Eve carnival. She could not possibly explain what had actually happened and did not wish to worry her parents. But it had been difficult to send the weekly budgets to Mawgan Porth and make them appear gay or contented. She knew perfectly well that even if her father was deceived, her mother would guess something was wrong, and Mrs Shaw did. She wrote and asked 'if Kath was quite sure she was well, as her last letter had seemed strained'. But Katherine had at once written back to relieve her mother's anxiety. She might tell her all about it one day when she got home – but not now.

Katherine's chief pleasure during those days of virtual imprisonment lay in watching Venice from her balcony. She spent hours out there in the sun; and in teaching Bianca, which had at last become a real job. Bianca seemed pathetically sorry for her past misdeeds and so terrified of being sent away from home into the dreaded Convent, she could not do enough to please Katherine. She studied, read, conversed with real energy, and was beginning to speak much better English.

The Marchesa, herself, informed Katherine that she had written to Benito Usilli and warned him that she would place the whole matter in the hands of the police and accuse his wife of assault, if he made one more attempt to see the Signorina Bianca. Since when had come a full apology; a crawling, whining letter in return, begging her to pardon him and overlook 'his demented wife'.

The matter therefore seemed closed.

The Marchesa was, in her turn, making the effort to be more thoughtful for her young daughter and had held several lunches in the *Palazzo* for young people of Bianca's age. It was also broached that once Katherine was fully recovered they might all go to Rome for a few days and see a theatre, visit the Opera House and buy new and more attractive clothes for Bianca.

Katherine, in deference to the Marchesa's wishes, appeared before none of the staff, save Thérèse who brought up her meals and was inclined to mutter such things as *'I know ... tien! tien! I know what it did happen!...'* But Katherine refused to be drawn into gossip or make explanation of her torn face – as Thérèse so avidly desired.

The one burning question in Katherine's mind, however, remained unanswered. How much Renato knew of the truth. Renato had as good as vanished from her life since the night of that attack.

When Katherine plucked up the courage to ask for news of him, Beatrice di Voccheroni vouchsafed only to say, 'Oh, my son is abroad.' And Bianca seemed to know little more about her brother.

It was maddening to Katherine not to be told exactly where Renato had gone and why he had left home so suddenly and completely. She was not sure that she trusted the Marchesa; and that Renato *had* been told the truth about Bianca and Benito. She made several efforts to question the Marchesa and each time was given a vague non-committal answer accompanied by a blank kind of smile. Resentment was born in Katherine and fostered by the continued mystery made of this. Yet the cruel fact stood out that she had absolutely no right to be so interested in Renato or his reactions towards herself. So she was forced to brood in ignorance of facts and chafe against her present position. Of course she did not intend to put up with it for much longer, she told herself.

Then, on this glorious morning of Spring, she decided to rebel. Bianca had gone out with her mother. Katherine took a long look at her face in the mirror. There were practically no more marks left of those cruel, long finger-nails. Only the faintest pink line here and there. She used some of the lovely cream the Marchesa had given her, powdered her nose, and wearing a light grey flannel suit and white blouse, went downstairs. Her first venture below for many weeks.

She must go and have her hair cut, she thought. It had grown so long and thick – it needed attention. She had tied it back with a black bow belonging to Bianca and looked very little older than the younger girl this morning. She had lost her appetite lately and grown much thinner.

She had barely reached the big hall down-stairs when the doorbell rang. No servant appeared – they were probably drinking coffee and gossiping and did not hear. Katherine, herself, opened the door.

Richard Kerr-West stood there. A gondola was moored at the entrance steps behind him. He took off his hat and greeted Katherine with enthusiasm.

'Why, Katherine, how lovely! This is what I hoped for, but I couldn't get an answer to my telephone-call from the Danielli just now, so I half feared you were all away. May I come in?'

Her face flushed and her eyes brightened as he walked out of the warm sunshine into the shadows of the big cool *Palazzo* and took her hand. It was good, after weeks of mental and physical discomfort, to see Dick's cheerful, nice-looking face and feel that she was in the presence again of somebody who really wanted to see her. She said:

'Oh, Dick – it's grand to see *you*. What a surprise!'

She put, perhaps, more warmth into those words than she intended. To her constern-ation he mistook her meaning. She might have realized that he had fallen in love with her when he was last in Venice. Without further ado he laid down his hat and gloves, seized her and gave her a hug that might have been brotherly but for the kiss that followed and that was full on the lips – and passionate.

She was so startled that she said nothing for an instant. Dismayed, her clear grey eyes blinked short-sightedly up at him under the long lashes that he always found so disarmingly attractive. He put out a hand and touched the burnt-gold hair and the bow.

'Darling child, you look about sixteen,' he murmured, 'and I would be accused of baby-snatching if my friends at the Bar could see me now.'

'Oh, Dick!' she whispered helplessly.

He gave a quick look round the hall. The *Palazzo* seemed deserted. Somewhere from the back came the sound of an Italian tenor voice singing gaily. But the rest of the family were conspicuous by their absence.

He made another attempt to kiss Katherine. She eluded him.

'No – you mustn't.'

'Why not? I love you,' he said recklessly, 'I've fallen head over heels in love with you, Katherine. I think you must have known that when I was last here.'

Her face flamed and now the marks of finger-nails showed very decidedly under the cream and powder, but Dick did not notice. He went on:

'I came back to Venice, not to see a client this time, but to see *you*. I adore you, Katherine. The nicest thing in the world for me would be for you to tell me you like me a bit, too. I dare say old Renato will be pretty amazed. It was he who first noticed you at London Airport that day, you know. The cad!' Dick laughed in his happy fashion. He was a cheerful optimistic man. He had no great depths or violent passions. He was warm-hearted and had an easy-going disposition. He rattled on for a few moments about his feelings for Katherine – still holding her in his arms – now and then squeezing her shoulders gently with his hands and bending to kiss her hair since she would not lift her lips.

'Hope this isn't too much of a shock, darling. I've thought such a dickens of a lot about you. I wanted to send you a Christmas present but didn't get any further than a foolish card. You got that, didn't you?'

'Yes, yes, I did,' she stammered. Her heart was pounding, but not with love for Dick and she knew it. It certainly *had* been a bit of a shock to come downstairs and find *this* crisis awaiting her. And although she could not deny that it was very pleasant to know that a man like Dick loved her and so openly showed it – it put her in a frightful dilemma, for she knew that she just could not give him the answer he wanted.

At length she pushed him away from her, gently but firmly. With a look of deep

218

embarrassment, she said:

'Dick dear, let's go and talk. Don't rush me, please.'

He drew a sigh and straightened, fingering his tie. He, too, was flushed and a little breathless. But he laughed.

'I'm all kinds of a fool and I ought to know better. Mr Richard Kerr-West, the ruthless and forbidding counsel who floors his victims under cross-examination with a single deadly word – goes to pieces because Katherine Shaw has eyelashes two inches long and the most beautiful legs in the world.'

His humour relieved the situation and Katherine found herself laughing with him as he took her arm and walked with her into the library. The *jalousies* were shut and the room still smelt of stale cigar-smoke, although it had been cleaned. Katherine wrinkled her nose and, at her bidding, Dick flung open the *jalousies*. The sunshine poured in like molten gold. Dick took a deep breath of the sparkling air.

'Spring in Venice. It's wonderful! I've landed on the right morning. I only decided late last night to fly over. Just finished a case and had too much time to think about you. So I told myself the best thing was for me to come and see you and get it over.'

He turned back to her with a boyish grin which she found friendly and appealing.

And she wished in that moment that she could have loved him. Her parents would have liked him so much. And he was a barrister with a fine job, money, and much to offer. Many people would say that she would be mad to turn him down. And yet ... the memory of Renato and her love for him was so firmly embedded in her mind and heart that it was not to be erased. Katherine was coming face to face with her real self these days and it was quite certain that she was not a girl who could love easily, nor forget.

Dick moved towards her and would have pulled her back into his arms but she stopped him.

'No, Dick. Please let us sit down and talk.'

The look of disappointment in his eyes upset her but she held firm. She took his arm and led him to the sofa by the big stone fire-place. She found it difficult to say anything under these circumstances but knew that it must be done. She wasn't going to play fast and loose with a man like Dick or make use of him in any way. And it wouldn't have been difficult to have what some girls might call 'a good time' at his expense. Easy though it would have been to indulge in a nice emotional affair and keep him hanging on and see which way the wind blew in the future. Katherine was far too honest for that.

'Look, Dick,' she said. 'This is all a bit un-expected and I admit I feel rather awkward. But I've got to be truthful.'

'And what do you do when you are being truthful?' He tried to carry on with the humour, but his heart sank as he caught her meaning. He had not really known until he saw her again and kissed that fresh lovely young mouth of hers, how deeply he had fallen in love with Katherine Shaw.

She went on:

'I like you terribly, Dick. We had great fun together last time you were here but I did not think you were – so serious.'

He picked up one of her hands and examined it. A capable, nice little hand, he thought; no scarlet varnish on the nails ... just a pale-pink polish. And a skin with a slightly boyish tan. He liked those hands.

'Well, I'm afraid I'm dead serious,' he admitted. 'I hoped to be able to tell the di Voccheronis that I was taking you away from your job. In other words, I want to marry you, Katherine.'

'Oh dear!' sighed Katherine.

Disappointed though he was, Dick burst out laughing, and pulled one of her hands up to his lips.

'You say that just as though you'd lost a bag of sweets or missed a train! Don't I mean any more to you than that?'

'You mean a lot as a friend and I can't tell

you how much I need your friendship at this moment,' she said the last words significantly. 'But – I – just – couldn't marry you.'

'Why, my dear? Am I so boring and repulsive?'

'Oh Dick, don't be so ridiculous. You're the nicest man I've ever met.'

'Except–?'

'What do you mean by "except"?' she whispered.

'My dear, I'm not a barrister for nothing. I've rushed in this morning where angels fear to tread but I'm not quite as half-witted as I may seem. I deal with a lot of women in my career and I often know it when they say what they don't mean. What *you* mean is that I'm the nicest man in the world except the one you are in love with.'

That floored her. She cupped a burning young face between her hands and bent her head.

'Oh, lord!' she said.

A brotherly tenderness replaced some of the natural desire Dick had to make love to her, because he was, after all, genuinely in love for the first time in his life. There had been others – one girl in particular, but she had been a very sophisticated poised young woman who played the devil with him for a few months and then married a title. Katherine was not only young and fresh, but charmingly sincere and he felt a new emotion – the wish to be very gentle and to help her. If she wanted his friendship she should have it, and he told her so.

'Don't worry about what I have just said to you. Forget it. You *are* in love with somebody else – aren't you?'

She nodded speechlessly. Dick pulled his pipe from his pocket and stuck it between his teeth. He did not bother to light it but he enjoyed chewing the stem. Putting out a hand he tweaked the silky bow on the gold of Katherine's vital hair.

'Don't be embarrassed by me. I'll say "hey presto" and turn myself into a good uncle or something. I'd like you to confide in me. Of course it's Renato – isn't it?'

That was altogether too perceptive and Katherine shrank from the truth even as she heard it. The fresh colour ebbed from her face when she raised it to Dick and she looked suddenly pale and tired. He also noticed suddenly how thin she had grown since Christmas.

He frowned.

'What's going on, Katherine? I sense an atmosphere. Where is everybody, by the way?'

'The Marchesa and Bianca are out shopping and then having coffee at Florians.'

'Have you been ill?' he asked abruptly. 'You don't look too good.'

She hesitated, wondering whether to tell

him the truth, and then decided that she couldn't for it was Bianca's story, and she had promised the Marchesa not to tell a living soul. So she stammered:

'N-not very well – t-touch of fever. N-nothing to worry about.'

'But you've lost weight.'

She tried to giggle.

'Just as well out here where one eats nothing but spaghetti and ravioli – all the fattening foods, fried in oil!'

He glanced at the slim lovely lines of the figure beside him and raised an eyebrow.

'I don't think you need worry. However, are you going to tell me about Renato?'

'I don't want to very much,' she said in a small voice.

'Forgive me for being persistent or even impertinent – and it is so to pry into your private affairs but I feel I want to know, because I love you so much. I'd like you to tell me if there's a chance for me, Katherine.'

She looked up at him and gulped, her eyes suddenly brimming with tears. When he saw them he at once put down his pipe, and gripped her hands.

'Oh, good lord, I didn't mean to make you cry, Katherine. I'm dreadfully sorry, darling. No, I mustn't call you "darling", must I?'

The tears were spilling now and rolling down her cheeks. She shook her head dumbly, sniffed, then laughed.

'How stupid of me. Lend me a hanky.'

He handed her a beautiful silk, handkerchief.

'It's a shame to use it,' she said with another laugh and dried her eyes.

'Look here,' said Dick abruptly, 'something's happened. What the devil is it? What goes on in the Palazzo Voccheroni?'

'I really can't tell you,' she whispered, and blew her nose forlornly.

'Is it to do with Renato?'

'No. Not really.'

'Then have I made a mistake? *Aren't* you in love with him?'

'I suppose I am—' the admission was dragged from her and she added quickly. 'But I oughtn't to be. I can't say he ever encouraged it, and please don't ever tell anybody, *please*, Dick.'

'I'm not likely to, Katherine. I shall always respect your confidence. After all I care very much what happens to you.'

'It's so terribly nice of you,' she said in a choked voice, 'and I wish—'

He held up a hand.

'Now don't start wishing that you could have loved me or anything of that sort. You don't, and that's that. But if you need a friend – well – you've got one in me for life.'

'Thanks awfully,' she whispered.

He pursed his lips and put his pipe between his teeth again.

'I might have known that you'd fall for Renato – they all do – they all did at Oxford. None of the chaps got a look in when Renato was around. Of course he's a delightful fellow and I'm devoted to him but women seem to find him irresistible. It must be that slinky touch of the 'Iti'. I don't possess it obviously.'

'Oh, Dick, you are funny!' she laughed, grateful for his sense of humour. It relieved the tension. Then he said on a graver note:

'When's Renato due back from Morocco?'

She stared at him. She felt suddenly enlightened. So *that* was where he had gone. Nobody had seen fit to tell *her*.

'I had a letter from him,' added. Dick. 'He said it was a very sudden decision. He just packed a suit-case and flew down to the South of France and joined a friend of his, Grenoble, I think is the name, who was about to take his yacht to Casablanca. Renato decided that he needed a change, and that it would be a good chance to get away.'

Now she understood. Renato had been cruising in Jacques Grenoble's yacht – lying in the sun in Casablanca. But why – why had he so suddenly rushed away from home?

She sat silent, perplexed, listening to Dick.

19

The one person in the world whom Renato di Voccheroni did not want to see at the moment was Violantè Chiago.

But the very moment he stepped out of his Alfa-Romeo which he had driven at a furious pace from Milan – and walked from the garage in the Piazzale Roma into the sunshine – he ran into her. For she, too, had just been driven by her chauffeur from Milan and the two cars had swept along the Autostrada almost within sight of each other.

Renato muttered something under his breath but forced a smile as he faced the beautiful, elegant young woman. He was I no mood for dalliance. Especially not with her. He had no interest in the supreme beauty of that golden noontide, either, although as a rule he loved the first rapture of the Venetian Spring. And it seemed now that he had never been away; forgotten the very pleasant lazy life on board Grenoble's luxury yacht; the hot sunshine and Oriental splendour of the villa in Morocco. Looking down into Violantè's huge brown eyes – heavily made up as usual with mauve-

shadowed lids and glistening black lashes –
he cast his mind back to that dreadful New
Year's Eve when he had seen her. To the
moment when he, laughing and gay in the
motor-launch, with Violantè hanging on to
his arm, had heard those terrible screams
and seen the two women struggling on the
steps outside his home. He had felt an
unforgettable horror when he had recognized one of them as Katherine Shaw – and
realized that it was she who cried so shrilly
for help.

The hour that followed was also imprinted
on his memory. Katherine being carried upstairs unconscious (he had barely glimpsed
that blood-stained young face). Then his
mother, taking him into a room alone to
explain that this was a *'vendetta'*. And of
course he realized that Katherine must have
continued to meet that fellow he had seen
with her in St Marc's Square; she had been
foolish enough to encourage him; a married
man and the wife had taken her revenge.

At first – well aware of the love for Katherine that had become so strongly rooted in
his heart – he had wanted to rush to her –
make sure she was all right. Then he had
passed from anxiety to disgust. Incredible
though it seemed, Katherine was – well –
just like *that*, he had told himself. Behind
their backs, despite his warning, she had
carried on an intrigue. Renato had no

further use for her. He had felt a white-hot rage because she had spoiled an ideal; his ideal of Katherine Shaw.

Then followed the episode with Violantè; embarrassing, one of the most awkward of his life.

She had seen him abandon his party and rush out of the *Palazzo*, and followed. She had not, of course, realized why he was in such a 'state' and she had questioned him:

'What a scandal for your poor mother – what has the silly English girl been doing?'

He had not replied. He had felt too bitter, too upset by the whole sordid incident. He had not even bothered to protest when Violantè insisted on joining him in the motor-boat. He wanted to get away from the *Palazzo;* right away. Then came the inevitable moment when they were alone on the dark dimpled water under that glorious starlit sky, with music drifting across the lagoon, that Violantè showed her feelings for him, recklessly. With her arms around his neck and her red lips lifted for his kisses. He had not wanted to kiss her, but in a moment of frustration she sobbed on his shoulder and begged for his love. Then he had gently but firmly said:

'I thank you, *mia cara* – you are wonderful – I admire you enormously. But quite honestly I do not want to marry *any*body.'

There had followed more tears; her pride

lay in tatters – and he, like a weak fool, had caressed her, grateful for her generous passion, yet despised himself for his sensual weakness; for going so far as to return even one of her kisses. To end the trying scene, and the very trying evening – he had said:

'I must go away, Violantè. I have been asked to join Jacques Grenoble who is sailing to Casablanca tomorrow. I had refused. But now I shall go – I need to get right away from Venice – from everybody I know – to think things over.'

She had accepted that; temporarily mollified by his kisses and his flattery. She let him go and said no more. She had even begged his forgiveness and understanding of her breakdown. She knew that he loved her, she said; but it was just that he hated the idea of giving up his freedom. But she *knew* that by the time he returned – all would be well – he would feel he could and would ask her to marry him.

There had been no sleep for Renato that difficult emotional dawn. He had felt he would never sleep again under the same roof as Katherine Shaw – loving her, hating her, *horrified* not only by what she had done but by what had happened to her.

At breakfast time he had presented himself to his mother fully dressed, suit-case in hand, and told her he was leaving Venice at once. He would stay abroad until

February. Nothing Beatrice could say altered that decision.

Unfortunately for Renato, the long, peaceful days on board Jacques's yacht had not altered the deep love he felt for Katherine. He had calmed down; become more philosophical, even cynical about her 'affair', and told himself he was all kinds of a fool to care. But he remained in love with her – rather than Violantè Chiago.

He had returned to Venice this morning half hoping not to find Katherine at the *Palazzo;* confident that his mother would have dismissed her because of her folly on New Year's Eve.

Now he found himself forced into a position with Violantè again and all he could do was to take off his hat and lamely say: 'How are you?'

'How handsome and well he looks,' she thought, her blood stirring as it always did at the sight of Renato. Darkly bronzed by the Moroccan sun – he looked if anything more Italian than English today. She had staked everything on the belief that his feelings for her would grow fonder during his absence – and that he would return to Venice to ask her to marry him. She had *paid for it* – a high enough price, too – the Contessa reflected rather pettishly.

But Renato evaded an immediate 'show-down' with the woman whom he knew to be so violently enamoured of him; lamely announced that he had to 'rush to a business appointment' – and left her.

Violantè looked after the white, gleaming di Voccheroni motorboat as it glided over the sunlit shining waters of the Canal. An ugly twist to the red lips spoiled her beauty. Tears of frustration magnified her eyes. All her passionate Italian blood stirred and boiled into feminine fury. She was not going to be 'put off' by Renato much longer. She was *not* ... no, even if she had to tell him how deeply (if unknowingly) he was in her debt.

Renato meanwhile entered the *Palazzo* in a state of mental disturbance – even though he felt so physically fit after his two months' cruise. He began to think that very soon he would be compelled out of sheer longing for peace and quiet – to marry Violantè and settle down. It would settle his mother's troubles too. These women were 'getting at him' he thought morosely. Why *not* marry Violantè? Why worry about a silly little English girl who had a penchant for low-born Italian musicians?

With such thoughts in his head, he walked into the library and was amazed to find his old friend Dick sitting there with Katherine. Delighted though he was to see Dick, whom he greeted warmly, he eyed the girl critically. So she was still here! Strange that

232

Mamma had not sent her packing. He had half wanted to find her gone – out of his life. Yet he knew beyond all doubt he was glad to see her again, and that his heart played tricks with him the moment he met the level candid gaze of the bright eyes she turned upon him. He also noted her extreme slenderness. She had a new air of fragility.

'Well, well!' he drawled, taking the gold cigarette-case she knew so well from his pocket and handing it first to her, then to Dick. '*You* look as though you have been through it. Oh, well, I'm not surprised!'

Katherine stood up. Her fingers twitched nervously over Dick's handkerchief which she was still clutching. Her cheeks flamed. And at once she *knew*. He had not been told the truth. By the very way he spoke and looked at her; that cold, unfriendly *scornful* way. She swallowed once or twice, murmured, 'Yes – I've – been – ill–' and then turned to Dick.

'I – I must fly. See you later.'

She dashed out of the room as though it upset her to stay there another moment, went straight upstairs and locked herself in her bedroom. She sat down and hid her face in her hands trying not to cry. Her heart thumped and every nerve in her young body cried out against the injustice of it all.

It seemed only a few moments later that a knock came on her door.

'Who is it?' she asked huskily.

'Me – Renato,' came that deep, lazy voice that had such infinite power to charm – and to hurt her.

She answered:

'I – I'm busy at the moment. What do you want?'

'To talk to you,' came from Renato authoritatively.

She looked at the closed door in an agony of nerves again. *Why* wouldn't he leave her alone? What could he possibly want to say to her?

'Quite honestly, Katherine,' came his voice again, 'I expected to find you had gone back to England. But since you are still here – I feel I'd like to ask you a few questions.'

Her whole body began to tremble.

'Why – what about?'

'You know,' came from Renato significantly.

Her chin went up. The fighting blood in Katherine suddenly replaced nerves and emotion.

'Are you by any chance referring to that squalid fight you witnessed on New Year's Eve?' she demanded.

'Yes, I am,' said Renato bluntly.

Then Katherine pursed her lips, marched to the door and opened it. She faced Renato, her cheeks poppy-red, her eyes blazing.

'You have no right whatsoever to cross-question me whatever you may think about that night,' she said, 'but one thing is obvious to me. You haven't been told the real facts – have you?'

He stared at her, frowning. If he had expected to find a humble, shame-faced Katherine, he was surprisingly wrong. With a characteristic gesture he smoothed back his hair and fingered his tie, as though it was his turn to be nervous.

'What facts do you refer to?' he asked.

'Well, since you're so anxious to know, we'll go downstairs to the library again and I'll tell you,' she said.

And as she ran down those wide beautiful stairs, with Renato following, she felt that she was in the grip of all the emotions any woman could be capable of feeling. Love, passion, hate, *all* of them rolled into one.

20

Once down in the library, facing Renato again, Katherine experienced a revulsion of feeling. She was almost frightened now of telling him the truth. After all, nobody liked giving anybody else away. Katherine was still young enough to remember vividly those schooldays in which one learned not to 'sneak'. It was against every instinct in her to betray that silly little Bianca to the brother whom she so adored. On the other hand it was high time Renato learned what had happened. Why should she go on being a martyr? It was obvious that the Marchesa had not kept her word. Renato knew nothing. So it was left to Katherine to pass on the unpleasant truth.

She found herself trembling and felt quite cold although the warm spring sunshine flooded the beautiful library, illuminating the magnificent gilt and leather of the books that lined the walls, glittering on the golden ormolu candelabra that stood on each end of the high carved marble mantelpiece. Oh, the beautiful, beautiful sunshine of this Venetian Spring for which she had waited so long! Oh, the romantic loveliness of the almond blossom adorning the brown branches of the little trees out there. Why did all this unpleasantness have to be? Was it a jealous fate anxious to draw a gloomy veil over her rhapsody.

Renato lit a cigarette and put it in a long holder which he placed in the corner of his mouth. He felt a certain amount of embarrassment because he could see that Katherine was disturbed. She looked scared.

He was confused.

'Now look here, Katherine, Dick said a lot of queer things about you to me once you had gone,' he began. 'I don't begin to understand them and I don't know whether I have got to congratulate you on your engagement to him or not but if I have – *alora*–' he ended with the Italian word and a significant shrug of the shoulders.

'I'm not engaged to Dick nor likely to be,' came from Katherine in a low voice.

'In that case I'd like you to tell me more about New Year's Eve.'

'Are you sure you want to know?'

She shot the question at him, her teeth clenched. Her colour kept fading and then rushing back in a crimson flame. What havoc this man could play with her! How dared he stand there so cool and debonair, so *critical*, smoking his cigarette in that lazy way and taking upon himself the right to pry into her private life. Suddenly, her spirit reviving, she flashed at him!

'Why should New Year's Eve concern *you,* anyhow? Once before you tried to interfere with the life I lead outside this house and I told you it was none of your business.'

'Ah, but you were mistaken,' he drawled, 'I didn't mean so much what you did *outside* the *Palazzo,* as the repercussions your actions might have upon my family and our good name. I went away immediately after witnessing that repulsive scene between you and the wife of this fellow with whom you are supposed to be involved – I just couldn't *take* it. It was too much for me and–'

'Too much for *you,*' broke in Katherine breathing hard, 'and what about *me?* Don't you think it was too much for *me?* You've been gone a couple of months! You didn't wait to see what happened to my poor old face,' she broke off with a hysterical laugh.

He frowned and averted his gaze. He felt suddenly that he did not want to search that indignant young face for scars. He was still blinded by his own conception of what had taken place on the night of the Bal Masque. He said:

'I'm sure it couldn't have been at all pleasant for you, but you asked for it.'

'Are you so sure, Renato? What makes *you* so sure? Tell me, I'm interested.'

He frowned harder.

'My dear Katherine – perhaps you'll

remember that night in St Marc's Square when I warned you about the hot blood of our Italian men. After all you are a young girl living under my mother's roof and I am head of the house. I owe you some protection. If your father knew about this, he would blame me for letting such a thing happen to you.'

Katherine had to bite her lips hard to keep down her rising hysteria.

'Oh, you don't know how silly you are – how absurd, with your stupid conceit and dignity – all this business about the fine name of the di Voccheronis – of Italian pride–'

She broke off choking. Renato stared at her, shocked to the bone. His face went scarlet.

He removed the cigarette from his lips and laid it down on an ash-tray.

'You are being insulting, Katherine.'

She faced him, no long afraid or embarrassed. She was not to be intimidated. In this moment the extraordinary love that he had awakened in her hung in the balance on a fine thread. In another moment she knew she was going to hate him. The time for dissembling had passed. She was going to be frank with him now. In that moment of extreme tension, she remembered something that her father had said – not so very long ago. She had always been a spirited girl, gentle of heart but never the timid, easily influenced type, easily diverted from her principles. She had once had an argument with her mother. One of those quite ordinary domestic disputes which can take place between mother and daughter in any household, no matter how much they love each other. Katherine had thought herself in the right at the time. But she had repressed what she had wanted to say in rising temper to her mother and instead of being honest and blunt had gone around the house for two days in sullen silence – weeping at intervals. Then she was hauled into Daddy's study for 'a talk'. Wise, kindly Daddy had asked her what it was all about. When he had heard, he had made that unforgettable speech to her:

'You have been wrong to keep silence. Always say what is in your mind, even to your mother – politely and firmly. When there is a dispute between two people, it can be fatal if one or the other represses the truth. The truth may be unpleasant. It may cause momentary pain, but anything is better than distortion of fact, or allowing things to be misconstrued. Many lifelong injuries and broken friendships result from people being too scared to say what they *really* feel. Go to your mother and tell her what is in your heart, however much you dread it. Then you will see how much better everything will become at once. What a relief there will be.'

And he had been right.

Mummy *hadn't* exactly liked what Katherine said but she had thanked her for being frank, and they had kissed and made friends again. After that, it was all over and forgotten. No more misunderstanding. The young girl had learned her lesson; learned that it was the half-truths, the lies, or alternatively the dangerous silences that can breed the greatest trouble. So now, with that memory to spur her on, she decided to come into the open with Renato, even though he might withdraw his friendship from her for ever.

'Look,' she said, more calmly than she had spoken until now, 'I have no wish to insult you, Renato. But I do think you are wrong to be so inflated with self-conceit that you imagine the di Voccheronis can never be wrong. I shall tell you exactly what happened that New Year's Eve. I did not want to – because it means giving away someone *you* love. Your mother knows, of course, and I asked *her* to tell *you*. But as she hasn't done so, here goes. I shall begin from that night in St Marc's Square. It isn't *I* who went to meet the Italian musician. Nor I who have been having a love affair. It is–'

She broke off, flushing to the roots of her hair. Even now she shrank from saying it. But Renato caught her up.

'Well – well who was it if it wasn't you?'

241

'Bianca,' she said in a low voice, then turned, walked to the window and stared blindly out at the gleaming waters of the Canal.

She heard Renato's shocked voice:

'Bianca! Are you mad? She's only a kid–'

Katherine did not even turn round.

'That's where you and your mother have made a mistake. She's *not* so much of a kid. And she is much more Italian than English. You ought to know that. She's horribly emotional and mature. I tell you, your mother knows all about it. The stupid affair began when she was having violin lessons from Signor Usilli.'

A moment's silence. A gondola passed by the *Palazzo*. Through the open window came the swish of the oar, the gay tenor of the gondolier's voice singing an aria from *Norma*. It smote Katherine's heart. It seemed to bring to her mind so acutely the peculiar charm of Venice. And for her it was all over. She would *have* to leave the *Palazzo* now, she thought abjectly. Spring had come to Venice. But for her, it would end almost as soon as it had begun.

Then she heard Renato say in a queer voice:

'Dio mio, I'd never thought of that. Never, *never.'*

Katherine turned to him. Her grey eyes were swimming with tears.

242

'I am awfully sorry. I was afraid you would be upset. I hate to be the one to tell you.'

'Upset,' he repeated, and he looked at her now as though she were a stranger whom he had never seen before – and felt indeed as though he were seeing her for the first time. 'Oh, my God,' he repeated the words in English. 'Upset is hardly the word. I am staggered, and so deeply ashamed of all that I have said – thought – about *you.*'

She made haste to apologize for Bianca.

'She is of course in some ways only a foolish child and she didn't realize what she was doing. You needn't take it too seriously. There's been no harm done except for the scandal that night. But everybody thought it was me, so it doesn't matter. It hasn't besmirched the fine old family name – has it?'

This time, if she was sneering at him, he did not notice it, nor would have minded if he thought so. He saw her only in the light of a heroine – a perfectly wonderful person who had taken the blame for something she had not done. Mingled with his remorse for misjudging her was a happiness that surged up and increased with every passing second. For once more, she was his ideal – his untarnished, adorable Katherine whom he had thought from the beginning such a very special person.

He took a step towards her.

'You've taken all the wind out of my sails,'

he said, 'and I haven't the least idea what to say to you. I can only offer you my profoundest apology.'

'Oh, that's all right,' she muttered with a slightly boyish embarrassment.

'But it *isn't* all right and never can be. It's simply ghastly to think that you were so involved. I suppose that creature who attacked you made a frightful mistake and pinned it on *you*.'

Katherine nodded: 'Yes.'

Renato sat down. He put his head between his hands and closed his eyes.

'How simply terrible! The more I think of it the more it horrifies me. But it just never entered my head that it could be anything to do with my sister. Yet you say my mother knew?'

'Yes.'

'Why wasn't I told?'

'In the first instance, after she dismissed Usilli, it was because poor little Bianca didn't want you to know. She was so ashamed and your mother promised that if she behaved herself it should be kept from you.'

'I see.'

Silence again, only broken by the distant chiming of the inevitable bells from one of the great churches across the water.

Katherine looked at Renato's bent head and felt a mad desire to run across the room, put her arms around him and comfort him.

She had a pretty shrewd idea that he was suffering not so much from distress because his young sister had acted so foolishly, as from injured pride. It must be very humiliating for him to realize that he had made such a grave mistake. Awkwardly she said:

'I should forget about it if I were you, now that you know. Honestly, I hated telling you but—'

Now he raised his head, looking at her with the deepest gloom in his handsome eyes, and interrupted:

'I ought to have been told long ago – and when my mother comes home I shall ask her why it was kept from me!'

'Perhaps she didn't have time to tell you before you left,' said Katherine and coughed.

Renato stood up.

'Oh, don't go on apologizing for my family. You know perfectly well that she had time to tell me. She had other motives. My mother has a motive for all her actions. But to let you take the blame – to allow all our friends to think it was you – good heavens, it is iniquitous! I can't think what possessed her.'

'I told her that I didn't particularly mind what your friends imagined,' said Katherine. 'It couldn't mean as much to me as to Bianca, who *lives* in Venice. It wouldn't be very good for a young girl to start life with a tarnished reputation.'

'That's very generous of you, Katherine, but you're only a young girl yourself. Good heavens, and I have been talking about what your father would have said–' Renato laughed harshly. 'I would like to know what he would say about *this*. I shall not be satisfied until everyone in Venice is informed of facts.'

'No, no!' exclaimed Katherine vehemently. 'Under no circumstances can you rake up that old story and drag Bianca into it. Let it alone. Once I've gone home nobody will remember me. But Bianca has to live here.'

He stared at her for a moment incredulously.

'I can't think of anybody else on earth who would be so enormously kind or considerate. Katherine, you–'

'Oh, please don't start praising me. I couldn't stand it,' she broke in.

He took a step nearer to her and caught one of her hands.

'Whatever I do about Bianca, I mean to make you understand what *I* feel about you. All those weeks that I was away in Casablanca I misjudged you. I felt disgusted – yes, I admit it now – disgusted by the memory of your poor little scratched face. The scratches that Bianca should have had, the young *idiot!*'

Katherine tried to pull her hand away, all her body on fire at the physical contact with him, and at the new light of admiration in his eyes.

'Oh, don't – I don't want to be thanked!' she exclaimed. 'I only wanted *you* to know. I promised your mother to keep silence in public, on those terms.'

He retained his grip of her fingers and deliberately pulled her nearer him.

'Why did you so much want *me* to know?' he asked in a queer voice.

She stammered, her body beginning to tremble again.

'Oh – because you are one of the family – because you were my friend – because I knew you were so contemptuous of me – and – and–' she broke off. She grew speechless. For this time whatever her principles, her philosophy, she could not tell Renato the burning truth; admit that it was because she *loved* him that she could not bear his scorn.

But now it was as though the devil entered Renato. And he was not going to let her go until he heard her say what *he already knew.* For with all his experience of women, *he did know.* It was written there on Katherine's young fine honest face and in those tell-tale eyes. It was revealed by the quivering of her fingers and the agitated rise and fall of the slight, pointed breasts. She loved him. Well – he loved her, too. He was virtually at her feet in a white-hot fervour of admiration for all that she had done – of gratitude because she had sacrificed herself in order to defend his sister.

Forgotten, the languorous eyes and lips of Violantè Chiago. Forgotten the family crisis and financial needs, and the marriage that he ought to make. He was being true to himself for the first time in his life when his arms went around Katherine and held her fast. She tried to get away, but he would not allow it. His lips covered her hot face with fervent kisses and finally came to rest on that fresh young mouth which he had kissed once before, but never as now, with the deep passionate kisses a man can give only to the woman he truly loves.

Katherine struggled no longer. She was lost. She gave him back kiss for kiss – helpless and enthralled, loving him with all her young brave heart.

And it was at that moment that the Marchesa, followed by her daughter, returned from Florian's and, laughing and talking, walked into the library.

21

Extract from Katherine's diary written on the first night of Spring:

I can hardly write these words because my fingers are shaking and can hardly hold the pen. They seem to have been shaking all day, certainly since the scene with Renato this morning. Oh, Renato, Renato, *I love you. I love you so much that I want to die. Of course that's absurd and exaggerated. One doesn't want to die in these circumstances. One wants to live and be happy. But I don't see any chance of happiness and I see every prospect of going on living, and being terribly miserable.*

People say that hearts don't break. I can just imagine when I tell Mummy about this, she'll assure me that I'll get over it and find someone else. That's because I'm supposed to be so young and to have my life before me and so on. But she'll be wrong, and people are *wrong who say that you can always find another man in this world.*

I mean every word of it when I write that I shall love Renato until I die and that there will never be another man in my life. *If I can't marry Renato – and of course I can't – I shan't marry anyone else. I shall remain an old maid. There are lots of old maids in this world who have only one love, like Daddy's sister, Aunt Susan, whose fiancé was killed in the First World War. She never got over his loss and stayed alone until she died the other day at the age of seventy. Daddy always said she took it badly and I've heard him tell Mummy that it was silly of her to let it wreck her life. But I understand poor Aunt Susan now and I don't think she was silly. Because that's how I feel. Renato is not my fiancé, but he is the only man I can ever love. I could never let anyone else hold me and kiss me as he did this morning. I've loved him really since that day we flew together to Milan. Of course I've had moments of almost disliking him and disapproving of his mode of life. I've found him conceited and I've thought him horrid to go around flirting and breaking hearts. I've hated his attitude towards money, and his laziness. Yet I love him.*

My knees absolutely shake when I remember the way he kissed me and how close we were. Oh, I adore you, Renato. *I want back those moments when those wonderful hands of yours caressed me and you drew the very soul out of my body with your long, long kisses. I'm not Katherine any more. I'm a woman madly, hopelessly in love. And it's all for nothing. I've got to go away and never see you again. That's why I feel tonight, at least, that I want to die.*

It was awful when the Marchesa and Bianca

came in and found us standing there in each other's arms. I tried to break away but Renato insisted on keeping one arm around me. His mother looked absolutely staggered and white as death. Bianca, the little beast, began to giggle. The Marchesa sent her out of the room and then spoke her mind. I really did not hear half she said, but most of it was telling Renato that he was an unscrupulous fool. Unscrupulous because he didn't seem to mind what girl he made love to so long as it fed his vanity, and a fool because he behaved like that with a girl under his own roof. As for me, she told me I was sly and deserved all I got although she supposed I might be excused for having my head turned as Renato was so fascinating and I was still so young.

Then Renato, still keeping his arm around me, said the most astonishing thing. He said:

'Well this time you've got it all wrong, Mamma mia, *because I'm not playing the fool with Katherine. I happen to be in love with her.'*

Of course, I never expected him to say any such thing and I was ready to sink through the floor with sheer joy. He was in love with me? *Could that possibly be true? Or was he just being perverse and trying to upset his mother? But he qualified the statement. He went on to say that he loved me as he had never loved any other girl or ever would, and that I was worth more than all the beauties from Italy and America put together, and that he would never*

251

forgive her, the Marchesa, for not having told him about Bianca, and for allowing him to go away believing I had been responsible for the scandal on New Year's Eve.

The Marchesa listened to all this in silence. Looking pale and a little frightened, she sat down and began to remove her hat and gloves. The strong sunlight showed up all the lines under the powder and paint, and made her look old and hard, and yet in a way I pitied her because of the fear in her eyes. They must once have been beautiful eyes, like Renato's. Yes, I could see how handsome the young Beatrice must have been, and understood why the old Barone had adored her. She was so elegant, so poised, so admirable in her way. But oh, what a lot she had missed in life! She had had a hus-band and children and position and in a feverish kind of way enjoyed her life of gambling and parties and social success. But she had never really loved anybody but herself.

The Marchesa listened now to what her son had to say and regarded him with a kind of horror. Her skin looked damp as though she were perspiring. She raised a clenched fist and beat it slowly against her lips. In a muffled voice she spoke to him.

'You are mad. You don't know what you are saying.'

'I know very well,' was Renato's reply. He spoke in a short, dry voice and his long fine fingers stroked my shoulder. 'I love Katherine.

252

How many more times do you wish me to repeat that? I love her.'

I felt as though my heart would burst with emotion. As though all the humiliation and physical distress of the past eight weeks meant nothing any more. It was bliss enough just to hear him say those words so firmly. He really astonished me. I had not thought it possible that the Signore Marchese di Voccheroni would deign to love me, the daughter of an impoverished country doctor – and be quite as definite about it. Or express it like this to the autocratic mother who had made it quite plain that she wished him to marry the Contessa – or the American girl, Hilary.

I felt enormously proud. I instinctively leaned closer to his side. I had a feeling this magic moment might not last and that I had better make the most of it. I loved the very odour of Turkish cigarette-smoke and the particular brilliantine he used, which clung to him. Quite stupidly I shut my eyes and sniffed it and wished madly that Aunt Beatrice would go away and let me hurl myself into his arms again and be kissed and kissed until I was breathless. What a little fool I was. Or am. I still feel the same now, this moment, as I write. What is that silly song?... 'Mad about the boy. I know it's foolish but I'm mad about the boy...'

Well, I was. I am. Oh, Renato, why should you possess the power to turn me into this strange crazy person? I used to be the old sober-sides of my family. *Practical, sensible Kath, they called me.* Look at me now!

Well, to continue – Renato went on (he was crazy, too, of course) to say that he wanted to marry me. That practically made my heart stop beating. My brain hadn't travelled as far as that. But it seemed to have an electrifying effect on the Marchesa. I knew she would be upset but that blunt statement from Renato did more than upset her. She sprang to her feet and her eyes looked like two coals burning in her haggard face. She spoke to him in Italian. Through her teeth. It was awful – rather like an animal snarling. Streams of Italian. Naturally I couldn't understand. I turned and searched Renato's face for some explanation. He made none but seemed to look all wooden all of a sudden – no – worse – as though turned to stone. And a kind of greyness tinged his marvellously brown face. I've never seen two people alter so in a moment. They both became different – seemed sort of paralysed, staring at each other. Until that shrill of Italian from the Marchesa ceased.

I grew quite scared. Especially when Renato's arm fell away from me. It seemed to leave me denuded and vulnerable. I was shivering like anything. I spoke to him.

'Renato,' I said, 'what has she just been saying? Or oughtn't I to ask? Perhaps it doesn't concern me.'

He did not answer. He did not even look at me, although a moment before his hand had been warm and tender upon me. I began to wonder if that old cat the Marchesa had said something unfair and beastly about me. I started a protest and she shut me up.

'Be quiet, please Katherine. This does NOT concern you.'

I began to mumble like a schoolgirl:

'Well, it won't be fair if you—'

Then Renato interrupted. He turned and suddenly caught both my hands, doubled them, kissed them, hotly, and rather despairingly I thought, and said in a low, thick voice:

'You'd better leave us, sweet. My mother is right. This does NOT concern you. Nothing has been said about you nor ever can be again, unless it is good. You are the finest person I've ever known. I repeat that I love you and want to marry you. But my mother has done something – something—' his voice cracked and he dropped my hands and turned and dropped on to the sofa. He actually hid his face on the curve of his arm. 'Oh, Mamma, how could you put me in such an impossible position? How could you?'

I stared at him and at the Marchesa. She walked up to the sofa and laid one of her long bejewelled hands on Renato's shoulder. She looked positively sickly. I hadn't the slightest idea what this was all about or what she had said to make him go to pieces like that. It was all Greek to me. But I knew that she had obviously some power over him and was using it. He made no more delirious declarations of love for me or *offers of marriage. He seemed just sunk – abject – awful. It made me feel sick. My whole body felt cold. I really had a ghastly sensation that I was the innocent witness of some awfulness that Aunt Beatrice had done, and that Renato deplored but couldn't alter. Anyhow, it was nothing to do with me. They said so. I had as good as received my* congé *from Renato. The Marchesa behaved as though I didn't exist. I walked out of the room and Renato made no effort to stop me. But I heard him speak as I closed the door. He said:*

'I'll never forgive you for this as long as I live, Mother.'

I couldn't help hearing her answer. She made it in English this time, and although I was still mystified – it gave me some bearing on the matter. It concerned the Contessa. For her name came into it.

'I had *to tell you, Toto. Now you see, don't you, that you can't just marry any girl you happen to fall for. You've* got *marry Violantè.'*

I waited to hear no more. It was too unnerving. Of course I don't know why *he had* got *to marry Violantè. I could make a dozen wild conjectures – and did – and they might all be wrong. But I did know that fate was inexorably closing the door on the maddest, most stupendous happiness I have ever known. I rushed up to my room and sat there on my bed, trembling, wishing I had never, never come to Venice. Wondering how I could gather myself together,*

256

buy a ticket and get back to England to my own people today. *I must go. I couldn't stay under the di Voccheroni roof with* him *and watch him being married off to Violantè against his will. It was* too *horrible.*

Bianca tried to come into my room. She called out: 'Kathee … Kathee…' That was the name she had been using, affectionately, since my 'accident'. I was not fond of her in the true sense of the word – nobody really could be; poor Bianca, because she was so furtive; there was nothing sweet or wholesome about her. Yet I was always sorry for the girl and had been from the beginning. I called back that I had a bad headache and would she please leave me alone. But of course she knew. *She had seen me locked in her brother's arms and I wondered if she was laughing at me. It was all so degrading.*

I decided that I could not stay up in my room. I must get out – right away from the Palazzo *– in case* he *tried to find me. It was all very mysterious – this battle of words between him and his mother, but one thing was plain to me. He would never repeat those words which had been so intoxicating for me to hear: 'I* love her and I want to marry her'. *I could not trust myself to think of Renato and marriage. Of what it would have meant to me to be his wife.*

I had a sudden nostalgia for Cornwall. I had a vision of Mawgan Porth – the cluster of white houses with their red roofs and flower-filled gardens on the cliffs. The narrow path winding down to the rocks. Here – the exotic beauty of Venice hurt me – even caused a revulsion in me. I pressed my fingers against my hot eyelids – and thought what it would have been like on the Cornish coast at home this morning. Sunny – perhaps – but a much paler sun than this one – a much paler sky. The sea would be blue, green and limpid, the strong curving breakers rolling in a long line over brown sands and jagged rocks that glistened blue with mussels, and with slippery brown seaweed and millions of pink shells. There would be seagulls volplaning overhead or swooping down into the water after food, uttering their strange harsh cries. There would be old Jake, the fisherman, going down to his lobster pots, and the usual morning activity in the small post-office at the top of the cliff. That wonderful little shop with a grand display of all the traditional postcards, shrimping nets, buckets and spades, groceries, papers and sweets of course – things of absorbing interest to my two little brothers and baby sister. They used to be exciting to me, too, when I was small.

I wanted to go back to Cornwall, to sanity and to the peace of my old life. I wanted to make myself believe that I did not really love R di Voccheroni but was only infatuated. That even if I could *marry him* I wouldn't *because it would never do*. Katherine Shaw would not make a suitable Marchesa to step into Aunt Beatrice's shoes!

I put on a short coat, tied a chiffon scarf over

my hair, opened my door quietly and slipped downstairs. I hoped nobody would see me. Renato and his mother were still talking in the library because I could hear their voices. His angry and bitter – hers equally angry, punctuated by sobs. Some awful degrading argument was still going on.

I hailed a passing gondola and told the gondolier to take me to St Marc's Square. I had so looked forward to going out today and although half-dazed with misery I could not even then be blind to the brilliant beauty around me. In the strong sunlight the tall narrow old houses on either side the Canal looked every shade of blue and pink and saffron yellow; the bridges were fantastically beautiful; the stone-work as delicate as dark grey lace. Everywhere there were tall Easter lilies in pots, and as we pulled up beside St Marc's Square, I thought I had never seen the great Doge's Palace, or the sculptures, look more splendid. Florian's Café was crowded as usual – everybody seemed to be sitting out of doors in the sunshine this morning drinking coffee, watching the pigeons flutter among the marble columns, or wing upwards towards golden cupolas on the cathedral, shining against the deep blue sky.

I knew it all now by heart. It was not strange to me to toss the correct amount of lira *to the gondolier and say 'Grazie', and see the inevitable admiration in his dark Southern eyes as he touched his forehead and answered: 'Grazie,*

Signorina. Buon giorno.'

Now for the first time since I had rushed out of the library, the tears came to my eyes. Somehow I groped my way to a solitary table, sat down and stared miserably before me. Gone was the nostalgia for Cornwall. Gone the desire to weep on Mummy's shoulder, or listen to Daddy's advice. I was in love with Renato and with Venice. I wanted him – *wanted him back as I had him for those few ecstatic moments in my arms.*

A smiling cameriere – *they are always so gay in Venice – came up with his little pad and said:*

'Cosa desidera, signorina?'– *'What would Mees like?'*

I ordered black coffee. I needed something hot and strong. As I stared before me I remembered that first day that Renato had taken me around Venice and the feeling of comradeship and intimacy that had grown between us. I would have to say good-bye to all that, to leave Venice and him, and I would never come back. How was it possible to be so young and to have one's life before one and yet feel as I did this morning that my life was done.

A man's voice interrupted my thoughts. I looked up. It was an American voice and belonged to a typical American wearing rimless glasses, wide-brimmed hat and gabardine suit; the inevitable camera slung over his shoulder and guide book in his hand. He grinned and lifted his hat.

'What did you say?' I asked stupidly. I felt stupid.

'I asked if I might sit down and take coffee with you.'

I swallowed hard and replied rather rudely, I'm afraid:

'No.'

He was a nice boy and went pink but continued to grin. 'Okay, okay,' he said, 'forget it. I just thought you looked kinda lonely. I reckon I am, too that's all there is to it. So long, sister.'

Wretched though I was. I had to smile because there was something so frank and pleasant about him, and he made me feel as though I had slapped a nice friendly child in the face. I felt my cheeks grow crimson.

'I didn't mean to be – to be – to be – oh, it's just I wanted to be alone,' I stuttered.

He eyed me solemnly, without the grin this time, and shoved his hat on to the back of his head.

'English, aren't you?'

'Yes,' I said.

The lonely young American seized his opportunity to talk – and how he talked! Standing there firmly, he launched into a detailed description of his birthplace, Colorado; his parents, his job (with tractors); this trip to Europe; what he thought of Venice; what he thought of England. What he thought of the English climate! He ended:

261

'Gee! I've seen everything there is to see and yet I realize I ain't seen nothing yet. Too much of a good thing in too short a time. I've fed the pigeons in Trafalgar Square and now I'm going to feed the goddam pigeons in St Marc's Square but you kinda get to the point where you'd like a nice girl to talk to!'

I looked up at him with a certain amount of sympathy but smiled and shook my head.

'Sorry,' I said. 'I'm not the girl for you to choose.'

I saw his gaze travel over me.

'You're mighty pretty,' he began. But that was enough and too much for me. My fingers went to my lips and pressed them. I began to tremble. For I'd seen a tall figure in grey flannels coming through the crowded square. Renato. He stood still and seemed shading his eyes with his hand, and looking round. Looking for somebody – it might even be me – or was it Violantè Chiago? I asked myself with uncontrollable bitterness. And now I was rude to the American again.

'Go away' I said, in a smothered voice. 'Oh, please go away and leave me alone.'

22

When Renato caught sight of Katherine's slight girlish figure sitting there in the crowded square talking to a stranger – obviously an American – he was filled with a bitterness which robbed him of the last shred of his boyish *joie de vivre*. He stood there staring at her, wondering what mad impulse had led him to rush here in search of her. What was the use? She was not for him. The lanky youth with the rimless glasses, grinning down at her, stood a better chance of marrying her – if he so wanted – than the Marchese di Voccheroni. His own mother had ruined his chances – and his happiness. The thing that she had done stood between him and Katherine like an impenetrable barrier.

When he had first heard what his mother had to tell him, first realized how deeply he and the whole family were in debt to Violantè Chiago, he had almost hated the Marchesa. That was a terrible thing – to be near to hating one's own mother. With all the passionate Italian blood swelling up in him, he had stormed at her. How dared she do such a thing behind his back? How could she have lowered her pride and implicated *him* in such a degrading manner? It was infamous – unpardonable. He never wanted to see her again. He would leave the *Palazzo,* and Venice, for good and all.

And then the Marchesa had burst into tears. He had witnessed the unhappy spectacle of a once-arrogant ambitious woman undergoing a kind of horrible disintegration. She had actually gone on her knees to him, tears streaming down her haggard face.

'I did it for you, Toto – my darling boy – I did it for *you.*'

He kept repeating:

'But how *could* you ask, let alone accept, a loan of money from a woman like Violantè?'

The Marchesa had moaned a garbled explanation, trying to condone her action. They were so hard up. The future looked black. Bianca had to 'come out' next year. They were all in debt. And it was really *his* fault because he would not make up his mind to marry a rich wife.

'So,' Renato had said through his teeth, 'you sell your own son.'

At that Beatrice di Voccheroni had given a hollow laugh and risen to her feet, trying to regain some of her lost dignity.

'Don't be too dramatic, Toto. If you marry for money you won't be the first man to do it, and Violantè understands the situation. She is crazy about you.'

'That–' Renato had said with a dark bitter look at her, 'is the most unscrupulous remark I have ever heard. I always guessed women were more treacherous and dishonourable than men. You have proved it.'

So they had continued to rail at each other. Finally, the Marchesa broke down again and in floods of tears implored Renato to forgive her and right the matter by marrying Violantè.

'Don't you see?' she had asked in a strangled voice, *'you must now.'*

Sick to the soul, he answered:

'That's the terrible part of it. You have forced me into a loveless marriage. I don't see I can do anything else *but* propose to Violantè. At least it would help discharge our debt.'

But the moment he had seen the relief spring into his mother's eyes, he had felt near to hating her again.

'It's nothing to *you,* I suppose, that you have ruined my life and that I've got to break the heart of the nicest, sweetest girl in the world,' he had added.

The Marchesa, her spirits revived, sneered at this.

'*Basta!* Sickly sentiment. And anyhow Katherine can't mean so much to you – she's a nice girl but very ordinary, and before she came you found Violantè most attractive.'

Then he had tried to impress his mother

with the fact that Katherine was far from ordinary and worth twenty *Violantès*, and that he had never wished for more than an amusing friendship with the Contessa. But he had soon stopped. What was the use? Suddenly feeling that he could no longer breathe the same atmosphere as his mother, he had marched out of the room. He drove his motor-boat to St Marc's Square.

At least he must see Katherine; explain what had just taken place.

Now – seeing her with the American tourist he asked himself if it was worth while making the explanation. Why not just fade out of her life? Yet – surely he owed it to her to tell her why he could not stand by that grave declaration of love for her which he had made in her presence to his mother.

But he dreaded further contact with Katherine. He knew as he saw her again – the fair neat head, the serious grey eyes – all the firmness and integrity and candour that was Katherine, and made her so adorable – how much she meant to him.

He had a swift flash of remorseless insight into his own life. He had reproached his mother, but he, himself, deserved rebuke. For now he knew he had merely wasted his life and youth in the futile pursuit of pleasure – and mad extravagance. If he had been a little less mad and self-centred, this sort of thing might never have happened.

His mother was not the only one who had gambled with the family fortune. Tens of thousands of *lira* had slipped through *his* fingers, too – like fine sand. And on that shifting sand he had built the structure of his life. Now it had collapsed ignominiously. And he had lost Katherine. That was what mattered. *He had lost Katherine.*

He saw her get up and knew that she had sighted him. He also saw the American boy salute her, like a soldier, and move off. Katherine took off her glasses as Renato walked up to her table. She looked flushed and embarrassed.

'Oh, hello,' she said lamely, and sat down again.

He did not answer but took the seat beside her, and hailed a passing waiter who recognized him. There were few inhabitants of Venice, including the regular staff at Florian's Café, who did not recognize the young man. Beaming, the waiter hurried to fetch coffee and a brandy as ordered by the Signore Marchese di Voccheroni.

Katherine, her throat dry, her pulses racing, said timidly:

'Well, I can't quite understand what all this is about but I suppose you've come to tell me.'

Renato put on a pair of dark glasses and she replaced hers. The sun was very strong this morning. Now they looked at each other through a grey-tinted world. So, Renato mused, it would be forever more for him. A grey, colourless world. There was nothing left for him but to treat this young girl with the honesty she deserved.

'I want you to listen to me carefully, Katherine,' he said. 'You are right. I have come to tell you what has happened. And you aren't going to like it. I, personally, loathe the very thought of what I've got to tell you.'

She shivered as though a cool wind had struck her. An orchestra started to play a gay tune from an American musical. But she hardly heard it. She felt unhappy and apprehensive and she could see from the way that Renato spoke that she need not expect good news. Her heart began to sink even before his next words. And once he had said them it was as though he had reached out an icy hand and frozen her very heart.

'I did hope to ask you to marry me at once. That is what I want and what I meant. I believed that you would marry me. I love you. Of that there isn't any doubt at all. But something that my mother has done makes it quite impossible now for me to do as I wish.'

She swallowed hard and her lips formed the word: 'Why?'

He told her, sparing neither his mother nor himself.

'I am as base as mother. She did the actual deed and made that revolting bargain with Violantè. But she did it for me as much as for herself. The di Voccheronis are broke. I am as responsible for that as anybody – plus, of course, the new frightful taxes and the repercussion of two wars. In my grandfather's day the di Voccheronis were one of the wealthiest families in Italy. Mother and I have both squandered away what was left. We have behaved singularly badly both to Bianca and to ourselves. I don't mind it particularly – that is, from the financial angle – but I do object to being forced into a marriage I have no wish to make. As you know, I have tried to avoid it for a long time. Once you came into my life I knew *why* I was avoiding it. In the old days, perhaps, I might have made up my mind to marry either Violantè or a girl like Hilary Drumann, in the long run. But you brought new meaning into my life and set a new standard. You made me realize that a man needs more than beauty or fascination or amusement from a woman. You are, in fact *true* woman. You can be gay or serious, woman or child. You have all the virtues, and just a little of the devil. You are a darling, Katherine, and I love you – truly I do.'

She had sat stupefied during this long speech – and conscious almost of horror at what he told her. But those last few simple

269

words came near to breaking down her self-control. She could have burst into tears then and there. To prevent herself from doing so she dug her nails into the palms of her hand. She felt hot and cold in turn.

'Oh, Renato,' she said under her breath. *'Renato!'*

The waiter set down the coffee and cognac. Renato paid for them. 'Sure you won't have a drink?' he asked her.

'I want nothing, thanks,' she whispered miserably.

Renato drank his brandy at a gulp. He needed it to steady his jumping nerves. Then he said:

'Well, now you know everything. A very pretty story, is it not? I've had enough for one day. First to learn about Bianca and how deeply I have wronged *you,* my little love; then to be told that my mother has *bought* me a rich wife!'

Katherine winced. Oh, if only this were not happening she thought with passion. If only she were not sitting here, having to listen to such terrible things! Everything was spoilt! How ironic to think that she had dreamed of and waited for this golden Spring in Venice, and now it was all hideous and she wished she could put back the clock and that it was Winter again. She would never be able to look at pictures of St Marc's Square in the future – the pure sculptured beauty of wonderful buildings and colonnades, the flash of the pigeon's wings against that bright blue sky, without remembering this morning. This deadly conversation – this good-bye to Renato. For, of course, it was good-bye.

'Say something, Katherine,' she heard Renato's low urgent voice.

She took off her glasses and turned to him. It cut him to the quick to see that those fine grey eyes no longer looked so young or so eager as when she had first come to Venice. They were the eyes of a woman – full of pain, swimming in tears.

'Put your glasses on again, for God's sake, I can't bear it,' he muttered. 'The worst thing of all to me is that I've *hurt you.*'

'I can take it,' she said with an attempt at slang and flippancy.

'It's more than I can do,' he said through his teeth.

She chewed at her lips and blinked back her tears.

'I shall always be proud to know that you wanted to marry me, Renato.'

He put out a hand and gripped hers, crushing it so that her fingers hurt.

'When I hear you say that it puts the devil in me. It makes me feel that I cannot and will not marry Violantè Chiago. Oh, *why, why* wasn't it my godfather who put that money in my bank?'

Her fingers clung desperately to his. She

loved him so very much. Nothing that he had told her about his mother, or himself, and their mutual orgies of spending, could make her feel anything but an intense love and almost maternal compassion for him. He looked so unhappy – the once gay irresponsible Renato. He seemed somehow younger today, in his humiliation and grief. That was evocation enough for her tenderness.

Suddenly she said, awkwardly:

'Have you spent everything that the Contessa lent you?'

'Good heavens, no! Luckily the beastly bargain hasn't been in operation very long.'

'But you mean you can't pay her back what you *have* spent.'

'Not without considerable embarrassment; I suppose you'd almost call it ruin.'

'What would "ruin" mean? You don't mind me asking, do you, Renato?'

He pressed her hand and gave the ghost of a smile.

'Darling, you have every right to ask. After all, it concerns you – doesn't it?'

'I suppose so,' she said in a small voice.

'It's all very complicated,' he muttered, 'even if I could pay Violantè back, *lira for lira* – I suppose I'd still feel I owe it to her to marry her.'

'*Do you?*'

He took off his sun-glasses and stared at

272

Katherine, a deep scowl contracting his brow. What did she mean? What was she thinking? He said:

'Supposing the shoe were on the other foot. Supposing you felt you ought to marry some rich man to bolster up your family fortunes and educate one of your brothers? And supposing the man concerned had lent your father money – oh, I needn't go into details – just switch the whole sordid tale into reverse and look at it from your angle – how would you feel about it?'

Katherine, who was not given to hot impulse, considered this question in grave silence before she answered. It presented quite a problem certainly. But the answer was not long delayed. It seemed to clarify in her mind quite quickly.

'I would never under any circumstances marry a man I didn't love, Renato,' she said. 'I don't think such a marriage can be acceptable in the eyes of God. Oh, don't think me too terribly religious or a prig or anything, but I have got definite ideas about right and wrong. And I think it is bound to be wrong for two people who do not love each other to get married. The one who *is* in love, is certain to become frustrated and unhappy, and the other one will be equally so. As for marrying to help one's family – that's an old-fashioned idea – one reads of it in books – there were lots of martyred Victorian heroines forced into rich marriages by unscrupulous parents or who went willingly into them as a sort of martyrdom. But I think it was crazy. I'd rather see my brothers and little sister go to a cheap school and my parents have to struggle than marry a wealthy man I couldn't love. Two wrongs can't make a right. My marriage would only be a failure and start another sequence of mistakes. It *couldn't* be right.'

Renato went on staring at her. He lit a cigarette and smoked it quickly, nervously for a few seconds, then drank his coffee. What she had just said started a new train of thought in his own mind. Finally he said:

'So you don't think I'd be doing the *heroic* thing to marry Violantè?'

'No, not at all,' said Katherine, 'and *please*,' she added, 'don't think I'm arguing like this because *I*, personally, don't want you to marry her.'

'My darling, you're incapable of dishonest argument.'

'Thanks,' she said and continued, 'Well, I don't think it would be heroic for the reasons I've just stated. You might be quite attracted by Violantè now, but you'd grow to hate her because of the price you had to pay, then you'd make *her* unhappy in turn. She's a very possessive, demanding sort of woman – isn't she? You'd never be able to live up to her – be the husband she would expect, and in the end you'd split up. Besides – you've got to live with *yourself*. How could you possibly do so, knowing that you'd been a party to such a bargain? Surely it wouldn't be enough for you just to feel you'd given her your name – or paid for a big splash when Bianca came out – or found yourself able to keep up the *Palazzo* for your mother?'

Renato shook his head slowly as though confused.

'Dear life!' he ejaculated, 'What a clear vision you've got – what a philosophy! You make me feel a fool – a blind fool – and a creature unworthy of any woman's love. Heaven knows why you care a rap about me – I don't.'

She looked up into the brown handsome face which was so haggard and depressed this morning. Her whole being seemed to ache with the vast pain of loving him.

'But I do love you – I do – no matter what you've done or what you will do in the future, I shall always love you,' she whispered.

He pressed her fingers hard and then dropped them.

'So,' he said under his breath, 'you still think I ought not to do as my mother wishes?'

'Oh, it isn't that, Renato. But you should do as *you – the real you –* feels to be the right thing. Right for the deepest possible reasons – not just money or power, or because it's the easiest way out!'

Passion and despair and bitterness mingled in the man. He suddenly beat one clenched fist against the other.

'It's damned easy for you to preach. You're not in my position.'

Her face burned scarlet.

'I didn't mean to preach. You asked me what I thought and I told you.'

'Perhaps you think I shall enjoy taking the easiest way out and marrying Violantè and her millions?'

'But it *wouldn't* be the easiest way,' she protested. 'Not in the long run. It would lead to the most hideous difficulties and complications in the future. Apart from growing to hate her, you would grow to hate *yourself.* That would be the worst thing of all.'

He lit another cigarette, his hand shaking.

'What shall I do?' he said under his breath. 'What the hell shall I do? *What do you want me to do, Katherine?*'

She averted her face a moment, her heart thudding painfully.

'It's becoming too difficult – I can't answer that question.'

'Why not?'

'Because I'm too deeply concerned. I love you, Renato. If I could marry you, I would – so I don't want to see Violantè Chiago get you – do I? I'm being honest now all right.'

He leaned across the table and gripped her hand again, his tanned face reddening.

'*Dio mio* you are, my darling – honest as daylight. And it makes me feel inches higher to hear you say you love me like that. But why should it prevent you from telling me what I ought to do'

Katherine snatched her hand away – her pulses on fire. She stood up. Without looking at him, she answered:

'Because it looks as though I'm just – trying any old way to get you for myself.'

Now he, too, rose. Taking her arm he walked with her through the sunshine towards the emerald green waters of the Grand Canal where the motor-boat awaited him.

'I can't talk to you any more in this damned crowd. Come, we'll find a quiet spot and you shall tell me what's in your mind. No – don't try to get away. I insist. I have a right to know.'

Katherine did not speak again until they were right away from the square and the crowds and Renato took the boat under one of the many little ornate humpbacked bridges in a back water – a narrow canal that shone like glistening oil. The houses rose tall, narrow, shuttered and secret on either side. They were in shadow here. Cool, remote, altogether alone. And here, Renato switched off the engine and the boat drifted a little, quietly. He, smoking, heard now what was in his Katherine's mind.

She astonished herself by her own frankness. But it all came out – like a torrent – something that had been locked up inside herself and must be released even if it meant that she never saw him again. After a fashion she was being hard and cruel; she knew it, but for that he must blame the frankness of her nature, her very simplicity which had a diamond-hard quality. She said:

'No man worth the name could ever marry for money, no matter what was at stake – his family, his fortune, all the treasures in Venice. No reason can make it right or proper for *you* to marry the Contessa when you love *me*. Even if I didn't come into it, it would still be wrong, *knowing* you don't love her. It would end in bitter misery for you both. And for me, if you wish me to include myself.'

'I do,' he said.

She sat pale and tense, her hands clasping and unclasping, her short-sighted eyes peering up at him under the thick lashes in that serious, intelligent way he had grown so to love.

She continued:

'Well – if you were anything of a man you'd decide to work – yes, *work*, Renato. Have you never considered that? Are those attractive hands of yours too soft and idle to do a job? Why should you waste your good brain – all your fine education? You and your mother belong to the old régime of the so-called "idle rich" which led Europe into most of the disasters that wrecked it in 1914 and again in 1939. You think you and your sort are privileged beings who can spend money you've never earned, or been left by other people. Why should you avoid working? I – oh, *how can I talk to you like that?*' she added in a low voice, her cheeks crimsoning.

'Go on,' he said, his arms folded. He was without any colour now. 'I can't begin to think how you can love this soft, lazy, despicable degenerate you describe. But go on. I can take it.'

She felt suddenly unnerved.

'I'd rather not–' she muttered.

'Oh, but you've got to. You can't start something like this and half-finish it. You've only half killed the brute, my dear. Let him have the *coup de grâce*. It's unkind to leave a fellow bewildered and writhing in agony. Annihilate him – *do* – and quickly.'

'You're being sarcastic–' she began, choking, her courage failing her.

'Go on!' Renato interrupted, and shouted as though in a passion. 'I tell you *I can take it.* What I feel doesn't matter. But I want to know what YOU are thinking.'

She somehow managed to end what she

had commenced in the extremity of her own pain and loss.

'Well then – if I were in your shoes, Renato, I'd pay back every single *lira* I owed the Contessa, even if it meant selling the *Palazzo* – which is, of course, worth a tremendous lot – full of its terrifically rare antiques and treasures. And I'd get my mother to sell her fabulous jewels and furs and I'd teach Bianca that life isn't so easy – not just a question of enjoying herself and making a good marriage. I'd make her develop *her* talents – and get a job – work just like millions of other girls. *We,* the Shaws, are jolly poor. Our home and the sort of life we lead would appal your mother. But at least we can stand proudly on our own feet and know we don't owe a bill in the world. Oh, Renato, you may hate me after this, and I expect you will because I've been so cheeky – saying such awful things to you. Yet I tell you I love you. Yes, yes, *yes,* I do, and it's because I love you so much that I want to see you do something *big;* not just marry a wealthy woman and *be paid for,* for the rest of your and your family's lives!'

She was breathless, eyes swimming in tears when she had finished. Renato stared at her. She stared back. He seemed dumbfounded by this extraordinary outburst. But every word of it had sunk into his most profound consciousness. She had an incredible

280

effect on him. The quiet girl from Cornwall had torn his soul out of its very roots and shown it to him. In the daylight it looked ugly, he thought with a shudder; bleeding, confronting him with a terrible clarity – a hideous picture of himself. This creature was a Renato he despised and never wished to see again. A spirit he wished to destroy. But out of the ashes a phœnix could rise, a creature more worthy of Katherine's respect; *of his own respect*. That was what she was trying to tell him. That he must be able to live with himself and not feel ashamed.

He put the back of his hand against his wet forehead. He was breathing fast and his teeth clenched as though his agony in this moment was physical as well as mental. From some dim consciousness there was dragged forth a biblical quotation – a memory from his earliest Sunday school lesson. He repeated the words under his breath:

'"*What doth it profit a man if he gain the whole world and lose his own soul?*"... That's what you mean, isn't it, Katherine?'

She heard and nodded, but she had reached the limit of her own powers of perception, of endurance. She flung herself into his arms, no longer strong and heroic, attempting to turn him from the Renato-that-was into the Renato who might-have-been. She was all woman in this second, completely in love, devastated by the fear of losing her lover for ever. Face wet with tears, she clung to him and he held her with a passion to equal hers, smoothing back the fair, thick hair, kissing every inch of the small fine-boned face.

'My darling, my *darling* – I love you beyond all words,' he said. 'I don't resent one single word you've said. It is all too shatteringly true. Only I've never wanted to face up to the truth before. As God is my Judge, Katherine, I haven't particularly liked myself lately. I've been ashamed and wretched and I haven't known what to do. You have shown me the way and, no matter what faces me, I'm going to do as you want me to and be what you want me to be. But not alone. If I chuck everything – everything I've ever held dear in Venice or out of it – if I stop this playboy act, and take on a job of work, you must come with me. Will you share the work and the poverty? You're very strong, Katherine. Are you strong enough for that?'

She looked up at him, speechless with her love and joy. Then with her hot wet cheek pressed to his she whispered:

'You must know I'll come. I'd follow you in rags to the ends of the earth if I had to, darling Renato. And if I had anything valuable – I'd sell it and–'

'No thanks–' he interrupted, and held up a hand – eyes grim, warning her. 'Once is enough. I'll never again be beholden to another woman for a single farthing – never until I die – so help me God!'

'Oh, Renato–' Katherine sighed the name and looked up at him half fearfully. She could not begin to visualize what this conversation meant – what her outspoken condemnation of him was responsible for. She only knew that events had taken a sharp turn – and for the better so far as they two were concerned. It looked like financial ruin for the di Voccheronis. For her, poverty meant nothing so long as she could be with *him*. But what would it mean to Aunt Beatrice – to Bianca?

Renato began to talk rapidly, his arms still holding her in a jealous kind of way as though afraid to let her go. He must go to Violantè and explain the situation at once, he said. She, Katherine had made him see that it would not be an honourable act to marry her but an act of madness, of egotism, leading to worse wrongs. Violantè must be thanked – for she had done this crazy thing out of her love for him; he knew that. But he would repay her with money – not as she had hoped – with himself as a husband. His mother, too, must be forced to capitulate and agree to sacrifice her own desires. As for Bianca – it might be the making of the sly little devil if she had a job to do, instead of too much time in which to mooch around, bemoaning her headaches. And he, he would go immediately to Milan. He had strings there he could pull; an old friend who was the owner of one of the biggest car factories in Europe. He might start off by getting a job in that concern – and become the London representative. He would benefit by the fact that he spoke and wrote fluently in both Italian and English. She, Katherine, must marry him as soon as he was established. He might, with luck, be able to save enough out of the wreckage – (after selling up the di Voccheroni possessions) to allow his mother a small income, pay for Bianca's training, and then start a small home with Katherine.

'We will have to push off in a tiny apartment in Milan – then perhaps a small flat in London–' he went on feverishly. 'But I'll work like hell, darling. I'll get on – I'll give you everything one day and–'

But now she stopped him, her hand over his mouth.

'Renato – wait – oh, darling – you're making me dizzy. It all sounds too gorgeous – and so *unexpected*. I thought you'd come to say good-bye to me!'

'I did. But now we've had this talk, wild horses won't drag me away from you – except for a few necessary weeks.'

'Wait,' she repeated, her eyes like stars, her heart hammering wildly. 'Oh, Renato, what

284

will your *mother* say?'

He put his tongue in his cheek.

'Mamma deserves her disappointment. She has got me into this. Now she'll have to help get me out.'

Suddenly Katherine whispered:

'Somehow it's Violantè I pity most. She must have loved you a lot.'

'She'll have to learn the same lesson – that money can buy everything but love and self-respect. As for me – I've damn well done nothing to deserve you, Katherine.'

'You haven't got me yet,' she said mischievously.

'Katherine, *Katherine!* But you will marry me. Say you will. Kiss me, my darling Katherine.' He breathed the name again and again against her lips.

The saffron-hued houses with their dusky green shutters and the water lapping against the slippery stone steps; the chipped statues, the carved urns, the blue chink of sky overhead; the brown eager face of Renato, himself, faded from her sight. She had closed her eyes. His warm, fervent kisses were upon her lips and those sealed lids, upon her throat and fair, tumbled hair. And she returned his kisses. Until she knew that whatever he was – or might be – whatever the future held – whatever trials or setbacks awaited them she must be with him – she must go on loving him – until she died.

23

An hour later, as the Marchesa and her
daughter were finishing lunch *à deux* in the
big ornate dining-room, Katherine returned
home alone.

Beatrice di Voccheroni put down the peach
she had been peeling and walked into the
cool hall to greet the girl. The elder woman
was dressed as though ready to go out, and
wearing a small plumed hat. She looked very
chic but pale and her eyes were red-rimmed.
She gave Katherine a suspicious look.

'Where have you been? You didn't say you
would be out for lunch.'

Katherine had entered the house full of
courage and dizzy with happiness. But now
some of her tremendously high spirits left
her. She answered nervously:

'I didn't know I would be.'

'Where have you been?'

'Oh – to – to Florians.'

'All morning?'

'N-not exactly–' Katherine began to
stammer under the cold scrutiny levelled on
her by the Marchesa.

'Have you seen Renato?'

Katherine's courage almost completely

deserted her now as the older, more experienced woman of the world shot this question at her. But she decided to answer truthfully.

'Yes, I have, Aunt Beatrice.'

'Where?'

'At Florians.'

'For lunch?'

'No.'

'Where is he now?'

Katherine answered:

'He has just gone to the Chiago residence.'

That was enough for the Marchesa. She relaxed. An expression of relief crossed her haggard face. She turned and walked back into the dining-room. Bianca peered through the doorway and her dark discontented eyes regarded Katherine inquisitively. She called out:

'Where have you been, Kathee? Come and have a snack.' She used the last word proudly, to show off her slang. Katherine called back:

'I – don't want anything, thanks. I've got to write an important letter home. See you later.'

And she fled upstairs, anxious to avoid further cross-questioning. She wanted no lunch. The fever of excitement was still tingling through all her veins; the mad happiness of knowing that Renato was not lost to her; that he loved her enough to abandon his project of marrying Violantè for money –

and that she, Katherine, was to be his wife and share his new poverty.

For him, it would mean hard work, hitherto avoided; an uphill climb; a relinquishment of all the luxuries he loved. But for her, it would be nothing new to have to 'save'. But she would be rich – rich in his love and her own heart's glorious contentment.

He had asked her to say nothing to his mother. He himself wished to break the painful news to her, after his interview with the Contessa! The unhappy interview he must now be having at this very moment.

Katherine fully anticipated the storm that would break over her head as soon as Aunt Beatrice was told. She would start packing now. On Renato's advice it was best for her to leave Venice and go home – until he had prepared the way for their marriage.

'Then I shall come over and see your parents and fetch you, my love,' he had said before he left her.

Fetch her; like a prince in a fairy-tale, carrying off his princess, Katherine thought dizzily. She walked out on to her balcony and stood a moment, drenched in amber sunlight; all the vivid colours of this sweet Venetian, Spring afternoon dazzling her sight. She whispered:

'Venice – dear, wonderful Venice, I love you! I shall long to come back. Not as

288

myself, Katherine Shaw – but as *his* wife!'

She turned back into the room, trying to recover some modicum of sanity which seemed difficult, for so many feverish emotions turned the practical, cool young Katherine into the craziest of girls. She opened the big carved oak cupboard and began to take down her dresses and fold them ready for packing.

It must have been about an hour later when the door of her room was burst open, unceremoniously, and Thérèse rushed in, her face yellow, her eyes rolling with fright.

'Mees – *mees* – come *queeckly.*'

Katherine dropped a coat-hanger and spun round to face the Frenchwoman.

'What on earth is it, Thérèse? What has happened?'

'The *Signora Marchesa...*' panted Thérèse, a hand held dramatically to her heart. 'She was just for go out. She had a *rendezvous – vous savez* – and a telephone call – it come from the Contessa Chiago. I do not understand but the Marchesa, she scream something, then drop the telephone and rush upstairs. Her face it look terrible. I see it *Mees* – I am afraid.'

Katherine's heart jerked.

'Where is she now?'

'Lock in her bedroom. I am afraid. I hear her sob and scream. I am afraid she might *keel* herself. She has sleeping pills in there –

many of them. Something *terrible* has happen. *Mees,* oh, where, *where* is the *Signore Marchese?* Come and help me break down the Marchesa's door – *queeck.*'

24

From Katherine's diary:

I don't think I have ever known a more difficult time although I must say it has had its compensations. For despite all the difficulties nothing has been able to alter the fact that Renato and I love each other. There had been no turning back from that *since he took me in his arms that day of Spring – asked me to marry him.*

I've been through some perfectly ghastly moments. One complication after another has cropped up and I've certainly learned the truth of the old saying that the course of true love never ran smooth.

First, the sensational illness of poor Aunt Beatrice. I say 'poor' because I pity her *even more than Violantè, who is merely disappointed in love. But Violantè shouldn't have tried to get Renato in that underhand way. It was all so* shameless. *I do hate rich people who try and get what they want quite unscrupulously, using money as a lever. It must be very nice to have a lot of money, but one shouldn't use it as a weapon to beat those who haven't got it.*

No – Violantè seems to me just a horribly vain

spoiled woman – rather feline and savage now – because she has not got her man. But more about her later. I want to write first about Aunt Beatrice.

She is no longer young or fit and she is Renato's mother, and in her queer misguided fashion she did it all because she thought it best for him, as well as for herself. Mummy says she used to be so generous at school but that she had the makings even then of an autocrat. Nothing must ever stand in her way. And I think she only made Mummy her best friend because Mummy is gentle and self-effacing. I can quite see that she would have admired Beatrice and been a little over-awed by her magnificence, because even at school the young Beatrice was given masses more pocket-money than anybody else. Her parents used to fetch her away in a large car, and Mummy once stayed with her and returned to my grandmother quite shattered by the luxury – the way Beatrice was coddled. She grew up into the haughty dictatorial girl who married the Marchese di Voccheroni, and he, according to Renato, was a bit crazy – suffered from what the French called the foli de grandeur. He encouraged his wife to throw lira around and behave as though they were royalty. She had her gambling weaknesses too, and once her finances took a downward dive, no doubt she gambled even more heavily in the effort to retrieve her personal losses. She just couldn't imagine an existence without luxury and servants. Women *who had to economize – and quite enjoyed life (like 'poor Connie' as she calls Mummy) – were in her opinion out of their minds. Her attitude was not really a pose – she had lived and breathed in a hothouse of unlimited money for so long that she was hardly aware of the cold winds of poverty that blew outside. They had never touched her. And it was of no interest to her that that particular wind blew upon the vast majority, and that she belonged to the fortunate few. Unfortunate I think, because her long selfish life in which she regarded herself as a special person brought her none of the warmth and sweetness of true human love. Even her daughter was a bore to her. The only real love she felt was for Renato. Now, in her estimation, he had failed her utterly, and chosen poor little me instead of a wealthy woman.*

I can see that it was no small shock when Violantè telephoned (which Renato told me afterwards was the case) in a screaming passion and informed her of Renato's decision, and she realized her mercenary schemes had failed.

In a flash she must have visualized the end of her wonderful 'special life'; of being the dictatress of the Palazzo; of being able to go down to the Côte D'Azur, and into the Casino in the hope of running a bank at chemin de fer, and winning another monk coat, or diamond clip. The end of the crazy spending and entertaining, and being able to snap her fingers at those who had neither money nor position.

293

The grim revelation was too much for her. She could not face it. So she rushed up to her bedroom to pull out those sleeping pills on the pretext that she needed them to 'soothe her'. But Thérèse, who knew her mistress, was afraid she might take one too many.

What a scene followed. Thérèse and I rushed up to the Marchesa's door, but couldn't open it. Our knocking and calling received no answer. We only heard a low moaning. The Marchesa might or might not have taken her sleeping pills, but we simply must *get to her. We knew that. Bianca, who was never either a brave or practical person, had started to fling herself around the house and yell – 'Mamma, Mamma mia!'* A lot of help *she was.*

I must get hold of Renato, I told myself, so I put a call through to the Chiago residence. To my intense relief a maid told me that the Signore Marchese had just left. But added that the Contessa had left with him. I could think of northing worse than Violantè arriving in the midst of this fracas. And I had an instant of ghastly fear that she had got round Renato somehow or other and was coming with him in a proprietary fashion.

I was to feel remorseful for that instant of doubt when he explained all to me. He had had a frightful scene with Violantè who had passed from slanging him and calling him every name under the sun, to wild appeal. Sort of winding herself around his knees, telling him that she couldn't live without him. *Apparently she excused herself for what had seemed a horrid attempt to 'buy him', but saying that she did it out of her great love. I can see that put Renato in an awful position. After all, he had spent some of her money. But when he told that he was going to pay her back every lira, she tried to soften his heart by pointing out that she didn't need the money but that it would be such a dreadful humiliation for her if he wouldn't marry her.*

Now Renato may be spoiled, used to women tumbling over themselves to get him and so on – but he has the sweetest possible side to his nature. He can be quite soft-hearted and hates to hurt anybody. He didn't want to hurt Violantè. He said he just stood there, and sweated while he listened to her and wished the earth would swallow him up. She must have looked awful as he described her, her mascara was all running and that big red mouth smudged with lipstick, while she clawed at his ankles and wept. However, he managed to calm her down and made her understand finally and absolutely that he did not intend to marry her, by breaking to her that he was going to marry me. That, so it seemed, finished her. She rose to her feet, asked him to wait a moment and solemnly left the room. When she returned she had made up her face again and looked all beautiful and sort of dim-eyed with crying, and had got herself into deepest black, as though she was in mourning.

These Italians do like a drama! Renato (when we were all peaceful and things had simmered down) made me laugh at his description.

'I think she thought she was playing La Tosca,' he said. 'She had a black veil wound round her head, and it only needed a couple of candles to complete the effect. Just imagine what my life would have been with Violantè as a wife! I would have found myself forced to play a different sensational role with Violantè as my leading lady every day.'

Anyhow, she then put on a sweet, sad sort of act with him. It was obvious, she said, she had lost him, so she must try to accustom herself to it, but she would not accept any repayment at the cost of her dear friend Beatrice's comforts, or his belongings, and so on. As for his decision to marry me, she thought he must be out of his mind, but she would only believe it when we were actually married. (I think she thought that he was just using my name in order to slide out of his commitments with her!)

Violantè is a very stubborn character. She was not going to release her stranglehold on Renato easily. She would return with him to the Palazzo Voccheroni to talk over money matters, she said. Poor Renato! He said he did everything to try and dissuade her from it but she wouldn't listen. And after the scene they had just been through, he could not be thoroughly rude and refuse to take her. So that was why she was with him when he came back.

By that time Renato's valet, Luigi, had succeeded in forcing the lock of the Marchesa's bedroom and Thérèse and I got in there.

Our fears about the sleeping pills were not justified. But there was every need to call a doctor at once. Unknown either to herself or anybody, Aunt Beatrice had a 'heart'. The violence of her feeling had affected it and brought on a slight attack. We only just reached her in time. She lay on her bed, lips blue in an absolutely grey face, and her teeth chattering with agony. Thérèse rushed for brandy – Luigi to the telephone. Really, when I look back on it, it was short of a ghastly nightmare. I've never seen anybody have a heart attack before and I did not know what to do. (A nice admission for a doctor's daughter!) However, the brandy revived her a little and it wasn't long before her medical adviser reached the Palazzo. By a stroke of luck he had just gone back to his own house to fetch some instrument he wanted, when Luigi's call came through.

That long black day ended with the strangest possible gathering downstairs in the library. It consisted of Renato and myself (sitting side by side on the sofa), Violantè lying back in an armchair, exhibiting her exquisite legs, for she was wearing a very short skirt, smoking one cigarette after another in a long amber holder, and with a black chiffon scarf wound theatrically around her red head. She did not speak much but looked mournfully through her *fantastic lashes at Renato. Bianca, her face puffy with crying, wore a somewhat sly smile of pleasure on her lips, no doubt because her mother was too ill to order her about, and it looked as though she might have a few days without discipline. The old Barone, Alvise di Mallighi, was there, too. The old boy had pathetically called at the Palazzo, as usual, with his beautiful red carnations for his old amorata, and been told that she was seriously ill, following a heart attack. Nothing would induce him to leave again, then. Day and night nurses had been installed, the telephone cut off, and the Marchese would be unable to see anybody or do anything for some considerable time. He was appalled by this disaster.*

Certainly it was a pretty kettle of fish for me. I couldn't even rush back to England as I had meant to do, because it didn't seem fair now for me to leave Bianca while her mother was so ill.

Aunt Beatrice rallied sufficiently to ask to have a word with her children. It appears that she had for a few moments thought that she was about to die. She had told them that she was dying, and quite humbly asked them to forgive her if she had failed them as a mother. She, who used to be so worldly and scornful of weakness, became within a few moments a tearful, feeble old lady. Renato said it was the most ghastly change and it upset him terribly to see her. Poor boy, he naturally began to blame himself for everything, yet his mother was really more to blame than anyone. But she had whispered to him that she hoped he would be happy with me (if, indeed, he meant to marry me), and that she would like me to stay and look after Bianca, because she trusted me. That was quite something *from Aunt Beatrice who had so recently accused me of being a snake in the grass trying to seal her son.*

So, here we were – and Violantè, simulating enormous concern for her beloved Marchesa (and for the whole family), refused to go home.

We all dined together – a most unhappy, constrained meal. Nobody ate much. Afterwards – several times – Renato hinted that it would be best for Violantè to go, but she literally stuck. *I don't think I have ever disliked anybody more than I didViolantè that evening, when I was just longing to be left alone with my darling. It was almost as though she* sensed *what I wanted, and out of sheer malice remained*

On one occasion Renato flicked an eyelash at me, intimating that he wanted to speak to me, and we left the room together for a moment. He drew me into a little room that was hardly ever used, on the other side of the hall, and gripped both my hands, looking down at me in a frustrated sort of way.

'Dio Mio! What a day!' he exclaimed. 'I'm half-dead and you must be, too, my poor little Katherine. Do you think my mother is going to die? Have I killed her?'

'No, of course not,' I said. 'I had a word with

the doctor. You know he speaks excellent English, and he assured me that all danger is past and that she must just be careful in the future.'

A look of despair crossed Renato's handsome features.

'Careful, living where and how and on what?'

'Oh, darling,' I said. 'Don't try and work that all out now. It's too much. Things will resolve themselves – they always do.'

For a moment he held me close and put his cheek against mine.

'You're the one sane thing left in my crazy world,' he said.

It took some courage for me to say what I did then, but I said it!

'You know, don't you, Renato, if you feel you want to cancel us – and marry Violantè after all, you–'

He did not let me get any further. He covered my lips with his in a long deep kiss which left no doubt in my mind how much he loved me.

'My beloved Katherine,' he said, 'there can be no question of "cancelling us" as you call it. You've shown me quite definitely how wrong it would be for me to marry for money, and I'm sticking to that, no matter how awkward things become. Of course we didn't anticipate poor Mamma having a heart attack. But it's just one of those things that happen to complicate an already delicate situation.'

I couldn't help breathing a sigh of relief. I

300

hugged him close.

'Oh, Renato, if I were only able to help.'

'You do help by just being you. Even Mamma wants you to stay because she trusts you. We all do. Don't leave us, darling.'

I told him that nothing on earth would induce me to, if I could be of help.

Then I asked him what he thought Violantè had at the back of her mind.

He frowned and twisted his lips.

'I don't know – but it can't be anything helpful. She's driving me mad hanging about like this, doing her Tosca act.'

'Why don't you tell her right out that you must take her home because there's so much to do.'

'You don't know Violantè,' he said grimly. 'She would just say that that is why she is staying – in order that she can help me do it.'

I couldn't resist being a bit sarcastic then.

'Maybe she's going to offer to pay all the doctor's bills,' I said.

Renato turned red and muttered under his breathy.

'Any more offers of financial backing from Violantè and I'll pick her up bodily, put her in the launch and send her home.'

However, Violantè did not offer to do anything so tactless as to pay bills, and of course I was only joking when I suggested it. But she stayed, under the pretext that she adored Beatrice and must be near in case Beatrice wanted to see her, *and she might be of use to us. And kept making significant remarks about wanting Renato's help and advice about her estates, and 'hoping if he had a moment to spare tomorrow he would take her along to see her bank manager'.*

'It's so hard being a poor little woman without a husband to advise when financial problems arise,' she said, when we were all sitting in the library. (I knew enough Italian now to follow Violantè's speeches when she didn't accelerate them beyond my powers of translation.)

The old Barone said little but sat drinking old brandy and smoking one of Renato's cigars, his mournful, noble face looking as pale and fine-cut as a cameo. Every now and again he raised his glass, inhaled the bouquet and drank a toast to the health of his beloved Beatrice.

I felt sorrier for him than I had ever done. The dear lonely old man whose love for his Beatrice had never wavered with the misfortunes of years. He, more than any of us – suffered with and for the woman upstairs. He paid little attention to anything that Violantè said. He did not like her. But once or twice he stroked Bianca's hand and called her his 'poverina'.

Meanwhile there had been no mention of my relationship with Renato. Violantè was behaving as though Renato had never told her about me, and I suppose he did not think this was either the time or place to announce an engagement. Which it wasn't!

The first person to break up the party was

Bianca who said she felt a migraine *coming on and wanted to go to bed. I went upstairs with her, but Renato followed and called out 'Don't be long – and don't for goodness' sake leave me alone with Violantè.' So I only stayed a moment with Bianca. But she quite touched me by flinging her arms around my neck and saying:*

'I really love you, Kathee, and I am sorry if I have been very naughty. It is true that you are going to marry my dear brother?'

I felt the blood creep up under my skin.

'Would you mind?' I asked the girl.

Somehow I was comforted and pleased when she answered:

'I think very glad. I would love you for my sister, Kathee, cara mia. *And you will make a wonderful wife for our darling Renato.'*

'Oh, I hope so – I hope so,' I answered fervently and kissed the girl's sallow cheek.

But I was worried as I went downstairs. I could not yet see daylight. Nothing could be plain sailing for Renato and me. And this feeling was intensified when I saw a white-veiled nun who had come to nurse the patient, emerge with a tray from the Marchesa's bedroom. It reminded me of present circumstances in this house.

Renato had been so right when he had expressed anxiety about how *his mother would live in the future – and where – and* on what!

25

The Barone had gone. Satisfied at last that his beloved was not about to breathe her last, he took his departure from the shadowed Palazzo Voccheroni and went sadly back to his hotel in a gondola – conducted by one of the oldest gondoliers in Venice; a white–haired Venetian who used to bring the *Signore Barone* here in happier days.

But Violantè stayed on.

Katherine got up once or twice and made an effort to go to bed – exhausted by the entire proceedings of the long day. Each time the look in Renato's eyes implored her to remain, so she sat down again.

When the hour of midnight was tolled sonorously from the Campanile – the Contessa grew restive. She was thoroughly annoyed by now and reluctant to continue playing a waiting game. She stumped the end of the cigarette she had just smoked, into an ash-tray and frowned at Katherine. Rising to her feet, she brushed some ash from her lap.

'I am going!' she announced.

There was no mistaking the expression of relief that crossed Renato's face. He jumped to his feet and eagerly suggested sending her back to her villa in his motor-boat with the chauffeur.

Violantè bit her lips. She had seemed calm and good-tempered, but inwardly she was a raging tornado of frustrated passions and had been so all the evening. And she had been observing, closely, the girl whom Renato declared he wanted to marry. Like one fascinated she had watched Katherine. Why, *why* – she asked herself a dozen times or more, had this quiet English girl won Renato di Voccheroni when all the most attractive, spectacular women on the Continent – or from the United States – had failed? *What* was the secret of her attraction? Violantè could not understand it. In her opinion Katherine had a good figure, beautiful legs and a fresh unblemished skin. But that was all. Her eyes were weak. She had to use glasses for close work. Her hair was thick and fair but there was nothing chic about the way she did it. She looked rather school-girlish, in fact. She possessed *none* of the seduction that Violantè believed necessary for the ensnarement of men. And last, but not least, she was penniless. Side by side with *her*, surely Katherine was what one would term 'a poor catch'.

The knowledge that her ruse to get Renato had failed so dismally was a blow from which Violantè found it hard to recover. A blow to her prestige and her genuine desire for Renato. But love for her was not a question of self-sacrifice or service. It was a raging tempest – a burning thirst to be assuaged. With Renato's mother behind her, she had staked everything on getting him in the end.

She had tried this evening to appear sympathetic and helpful, and prove to Renato how necessary she was to him. She had now to confess herself beaten. So she was determined not to go out of his life for ever without making Katherine 'squirm' a bit.

She did not take the coat Renato had fetched from the hall and handed to her. She said to Katherine:

'You understand my language now, do you not?'

'Yes, Contessa,' answered Katherine. She felt uneasy. She did not like the ugly look in those huge, feverish, dark eyes. Violantè continued:

'Then I will say to you what is on my mind.'

Here, Renato, also a trifle suspicious, put in:

'Don't you think it is a little late for discussion?'

'Late?' She swung round on him like a tigress, her face flushing scarlet. 'No – unless it is too late to save you from yourself.

Yes, it may be too late for that, Renato.'

He stiffened. Katherine felt desperately inclined to escape from what looked like being a most unattractive scene. She felt so sorry for Renato. What an impossible position his mother had put him into with this woman. And how cruel and un-scrupulous the Contessa could be! As cruel as a foolish thoughtless child who had been denied a toy she particularly wanted and was trying to vent her spite on the one that refused it to her.

'I beg you not to make another scene, Violantè,' said Renato quietly. 'It is very late and we are all tired. Besides – Mamma is very ill. We are all upset and it would be more tactful for you to–'

'To go meekly home and hand everything I have staked on getting to Katherine!' Violantè broke in shrilly. 'Oh yes. I am sure you would like that. You would like me to smile at Miss Shaw and congratulate her.'

'Violantè – please–' Renato began.

She stamped her foot.

'I will not be silenced; nor sent home just when you think you have finished with me. As for your mother's illness – what has caused it but the way in which *you* have behaved? Your terrible selfishness.'

'*My* selfishness?' Renato repeated, and laughed sarcastically. 'Really, Violantè!'

'I repeat – *your* selfishness. Poor Beatrice

relied on you. You, alone, could have saved her lovely home and put things right for Bianca. You and I – together. And you have walked out on us all.'

Katherine blushed for the other woman. She could not conceive of any human being behaving with such lack of delicacy or pride. Unrequited passion seemed to have brought out the very worst in Violantè. Renato saw the hot red sweep Katherine's face. He guessed how she was feeling about this. And he had never loved her more. She contrasted so favourably with the stupid, jealous, ranting creature beside her. In his eyes, Violantè had nothing left of beauty or attraction. She was ugly – repellant – in her uncontrolled fury.

'I beg you to put an end to this and leave us,' he said more coldly than he had ever spoken to her. 'Katherine and I are going to be married and that ends it all.'

Violantè gave a strangled laugh. She turned upon Katherine.

'Oh, yes, I know! A nice thing! To marry *her*– What can *she* give you? I have every-thing – she has *nothing*.'

Renato went to Katherine's side and put an arm around her, drawing her close. He could feel her shaking. He said:

'I am sorry to be rude – but you have asked for it, Violantè. The fact is that I find Katherine has *everything* and you – *nothing!*'

Katherine wriggled uncomfortably.

'Don't – don't go on – let's break it up,' she muttered.

'I have nothing?' screamed Violantè. 'And what about my money? Money you have already spent! I have everything, I tell you. And we could have been happy together if that miserable girl had not come here and taken you from me.'

Katherine looked at her speechlessly, she felt quite incapable of replying to such an unjustifiable accusation. Violantè continued to yell:

'She pretends to be so quiet and good, but she comes between us like a thief who stoops to steal another woman's lover.'

'*Really – honestly–*' began Katherine, and felt the sweat break out on her forehead.

'Don't speak to her, darling, let *me* answer,' said Renato through his teeth and added: 'You know perfectly well, Violantè, that I never belonged to you, so Katherine cannot have stolen me. This is all a lot of dramatic nonsense.'

Shaking from head to foot Violantè pointed a finger that glittered with diamonds at the unhappy Katherine.

'What sort of a wife will she make for the Marchese di Voccheroni? A little governess – totally unfitted to be your wife or to act as hostess for your friends. If she had really loved you she would have refused you. She would have known that it was only a passing fancy on your part. Instead she is relentless – going to ruin your life.'

Katherine felt sick to the soul. Those were ugly words and even if there was no truth in them, they stung. They seemed to rouse Renato to such a pitch that he almost lost his own control.

'Be quiet, Violantè!' he shouted back at her.

'It's true – it's true.'

'It is not true. It is a deplorable lie. Every word. Katherine did not come between us and I am not merely infatuated. I love her with all my heart and I know of nobody more capable of making a wonderful wife for me. The only doubt is what sort of a husband *I* shall make for *her.* She has all the graces. I have none.'

Violantè gave a hysterical laugh.

'And you have no money either, *mio caro,* beyond what I have lent you–'

Renato's face crimsoned then went deadly white.

'You shall be paid back *lira* for *lira,*' he said in a low, furious voice. 'It is only to be deplored that my misguided mother ever struck such an infamous bargain with you. But I thought we had settled all this in your house earlier on and that you realized how I felt about it. I do not understand what you hope to gain by this beastly sort of battle of words. I thank you for your original generosity and for your deep interest in – shall we say – my family. But it must end there. My bank manager will communicate with yours tomorrow. I am putting the *Palazzo* up for immediate sale, and with it, all our valuable collection of tapestries, pictures, and other things. My mother will have to dispose of her jewels. We should then be more than able to pay you back what has been spent out of your loan. After that – what happens to us is our affair. It is obvious that there can be no friendship in the future between us. I am sorry, Violantè,' he added on a more gentle note. 'The di Voccheronis and Chiagos have known each other a long time. It is most unfortunate that it has to end this way. Believe me, I am very unhappy about it. Katherine and I would have preferred to keep you as a friend rather than have you as an enemy.'

It was that last remark that broke the Contessa. Afterwards when Katherine thought over it, she felt really sorry for the silly, infatuated woman. She seemed to be able to hold her own and battle and sneer, until Renato bracketed their names so quietly and definitely. *'Katherine and I'* – he had said. For Katherine it was an enormous thrill to hear those words spoken. For the woman who had lost, it was the final nail in her coffin. She broke down. With her face in her hands, she stumbled to the sofa and began to cry, dreadfully.

Renato and Katherine looked at each other. Katherine, so typically English and controlled, found Violantè's complete loss of dignity deplorable. It embarrassed her. Renato, more used to emotional storms in his father's country, was not so much scornful of it as worried, because he did not know what to say or do in the circumstances to help her. She had an unfortunate way of making him feel entirely responsible for her misery.

At length he put his hands on Katherine's shoulders, kissed her on the forehead and whispered:

'You'd better go, darling, I'll deal with *her*.'

Without the smallest pang of jealousy or apprehension, Katherine turned and left the room.

What had *she* to fear now? Nothing. *'Katherine and I,'* he had said. Dear, wonderful words to hold to her heart and remember. Somehow they seemed to bind her to him irrevocably.

Let him try and comfort the miserable Violantè if he could. But for a moment she had writhed under Violantè's remarks about her being 'unfitted to take her place as the Marchesa di Voccheroni'.

Long after she was in bed, Katherine lay

awake in the darkness brooding over that – trying to visualize herself as the future Marchesa. In a way, it frightened her. Those horrid words screamed at her by the Contessa had an insidious effect.

'Delayed action,' Katherine told herself, 'I am beginning to get cold feet!'

She tried to imagine what her family would think about it all. Mummy would probably be thrilled that her daughter was going to marry the son of her oldest friend, and – like all mothers – be pleased that she had chosen such a distinguished man; as well as one whom she loved. Neither of them would care whether Renato had money or not as long as he could give her a reasonable life. There hadn't been much time to talk things over since this had all transpired, but Renato had made it plain to Katherine that they would never be really *poor*. That was, not according to the Shaws' standards. Even a small private income, as well as what a man earned, meant a lot in Katherine's world of economy. It was only in the eyes of the di Voccheronis, one was 'penniless' unless one had huge capital.

But to own a title – to have to mix with Renato's rich titled friends – how *would* it work? Katherine found herself wondering and worrying until the early hours of the morning. Once – with her sense of humour asserting itself – she drew a mental picture of herself facing her small brothers, David and Peter, and hearing them 'rag her'. Their Kathy – a Marchesa!

She also had to remember she would say good-bye to that English name of which she had been so proud. Half English though he was by blood, and educated at an English public school and varsity, Renato remained an Italian by birth. She would, therefore, become the wife of an Italian. She could retain her British nationality – that was permissible nowadays – but she would still become a woman with an Italian title.

How would she fit in? How would she like it? She felt herself shivering a little with nerves; she pulled the bed-clothes up to her chin and lay wide-eyed, her mind going round in circles. She tried to concentrate on the memory of her love for Renato and his for her. She could not but feel enormous pride because he had put her in front of everybody else in his life. What was he saying to that wretched girl downstairs. It was to be hoped that she had gone home by now, and that they would never see her again.

Katherine at length fancied she heard voices and some sort of commotion in the corridor outside her room. She switched on the lights and found that it was four o'clock. Putting on her dressing-gown and slippers, she opened her door and looked out. Renato stood there, whispering to the nun who was on night duty with his mother. When he saw the girl in the rose-pink candlewick dressing-gown, her fair hair tied back with a ribbon, looking so enchantingly young and sweet, his lips curved into a pleased smile. He said good night to the nun who gave a quick, curious look at Katherine and disappeared into the Marchesa's bedroom. Renato came to Katherine's side.

'You ought to be asleep, sweet,' he said, and gently took her hands and kissed them.

Her heart began to pump.

'I haven't been able to – I keep thinking – and I thought I heard something going on out here.'

'Sorry, darling, I'm afraid we woke you – so thoughtless to chat right outside your door.'

'How is your mother?'

'Better, and sleeping quite soundly. The sister thinks that it will only be a few days before she is almost herself again. It will be a question after that of keeping her quiet. She won't be able to lead her old, full life dashing about the Continent.'

'Oh, Renato–' began Katherine and stopped.

He read what was in her mind. He smiled down into the grey eyes that were so sweet and drowsy with fatigue. His own face was haggard and he stifled a yawn even as he spoke to her.

'Not now, my darling – don't start worrying about the future any more tonight – or rather this morning. I'm so damned tired, I wouldn't mind if there was a bomb under my bed, I'd still go and lie on it.'

Katherine smothered a laugh.

'Darling, there is a bomb – under all of us.'

'Then let it explode – so long as we go up together.'

'Has – *the bombshell* gone?'

'Yes. She went an hour ago. I can't tell you what it was like trying to calm her down. But I managed it. Violantè is a very excitable person and she hated defeat. A bad loser, my dear, that's it! I think she thought that I did not mean it when I first told her about *us,* so she came along and tried to get at me again. You see, you can't make a woman like Violantè Chiago understand that money is not the most important thing in the world.'

Instinctively, and rather sadly, Katherine's gaze wandered to the Marchesa's door. Once again, Renato read her thoughts and shook his head.

'No, don't worry about Mamma. I know her. She has her faults, haven't we all? And this time she nearly lost me for good and all. But I shan't bear her a grudge. And you'll see – she has great courage, and she's practical – like all English women. Once she understands there is absolutely nothing more she can do about it – she'll accept our marriage and our altered circumstances and make a go of it – I am quite sure she will.'

Katherine's eyes silently questioned him and once more he seemed aware of what was passing through her mind.

'Yes, I know it's a poor show that she's going to be an invalid and have to lead a quiet life just when money is short,' he went on. 'But it may turn out a mixed blessing. If she can't go out and spend money – she'll have to sit quietly at home and read, won't she?'

'Well, that's one way of looking at things,' murmured Katherine.

She felt that this was neither the time nor the place to voice all the anxieties that had been besetting her. Another time, she would have to talk things over with him and satisfy herself, that she was, after all, the right person to step into the shoes his mother had worn with such imperiousness for so long. Katherine sighed and stared down the wide majestic staircase at one of the Gobelin tapestries adorning the wall, and at a vast glittering chandelier swinging from the painted ceiling. She looked at the flowers; at a very fine sculpture on an onyx and marble pedestal close by her. She thought of all the magnificence in this Venetian palace, now so familiar to her. Renato's home. *The Palazzo Voccheroni.* Wasn't it rather terrible to think that it would pass into a stranger's hands.

Wasn't it Renato's rightful inheritance?

And yet ... she could remember once at home when her father was discussing traditions and legacies, he had remarked that no man should have a *right* to inherit anything just because he was fortunate enough to be born of wealthy, landed parents. The only right a man had, he had said, was to live the life God had given him and make the best of it through his own hard labours.

It was the first time in Katherine's life that she had been faced with a problem of such a kind. And in this hour she could not altogether agree with her father. She wanted passionately to be able to give Renato back his inheritance. She had a sudden mad wish to be as rich as Violantè.

But this time Renato did not suspect what she was thinking. He only knew that he loved her beyond anything and that he was desperately tired. He took her in his arms and laid his cheek against hers, closing his eyes, inhaling the fresh, faint fragrance of her crisp hair.

'My darling, *darling* Katherine,' he whispered.

All troubles fell away from her like a cloak. She reached up and put her arms around his neck and hugged him passionately.

'I do love you so much, Renato.'

'I don't know why,' he whispered, 'but it is enough for me that you do. Good night, my sweet, try and get some sleep. Tomorrow we'll make further plans.'

'Tomorrow, I've got to think of going home,' she reminded him.

His arms tightened their hold of her.

'No – you promised you wouldn't go until Mamma is on her feet again. *Please*, Katherine!'

She answered breathlessly, 'Oh, very well!' Her pulses were on fire as she felt his lips stray from her cheek to her throat. She knew she must stay if he wanted it. A new passion mounted in the man and his fatigue was replaced by an ardent desire. An impatience to bind this girl to him completely and absolutely ... as though he could not feel secure again until she was his wife.

'Katherine, Katherine, don't let's wait. Let's go to Rome and get married at once – as soon as I can get a licence and fix thing with the British Consul,' he said urgently.

26

If ever Katherine was tempted to do something crazy – it was then.

Her brain spun at the thought of rushing to Rome and being married by special licence to her wonderful Renato. He saw her hesitancy and felt her quivering cheek against his. Tenderly he kissed her warm white neck. His fingers shook a little as he untied her hair ribbon, let loose the thick, sweet-smelling hair and buried his face in it.

'You don't how beguiling you are, my Katherine. Marry me tomorrow – the next day – *any* day this week you like, but don't ask me to go through one of these long drawn-out engagements,' he said huskily.

She tried to keep her head. Her hands gripped his shoulders and pushed him a little away from her.

'Oh, Renato, Renato, *you* are the one who is beguiling – you're so crazy – and I do want to marry you so much!'

His brilliant eyes laughed down into hers and he pressed a kiss into each of her soft palms.

'Then let's do it – I'll get in touch with the Consul tomorrow.'

Her gaze wandered to the Marchesa's door. She thought of the woman lying behind it, with her tired heart and broken dreams and the tremendous sacrifices that lay ahead of her. Young though she was, Katherine had a strange capacity for understanding and sympathizing with the sorrows of others. And because poor unhappy Aunt Beatrice was to become her 'mother-in-law' she felt a new affection for her.

'Renato darling, we can't do it to *her*–' Katherine nodded at the door. 'You know what she'd feel about it. She wouldn't think it was you, anyhow – she'd say it was *me* and she'd never forgive me for what she would think, my rushing you into marriage.'

Impatiently Renato moved his head from side to side.

'Must one always be sensible and do the right thing? Why can't you be crazy like myself and turn into an egotist for once. Would it be against all your principles, my good little Katherine, to "rush me into marriage"? I'm the one that's doing the rushing anyhow, and you know it. What does it matter what *anybody* else thinks?'

She bit her lip and caught her breath on a laugh.

'How impossible you are.'

'I know. I always was, and I guess I always will be,' he grinned suddenly like a boy. 'So if you don't want to take me on – say so now, and I'll swim the canal to the Chiago residence.'

'Renato!' she protested.

'Is the dear little girl shocked because I tease her?'

She went pink and hot.

'Sometimes you make me feel I'm a prig and a fool and that I'm quite unsuited to be your wife. But I'll talk to you about that tomorrow.'

His answer was to pull her back into his embrace and kiss her with such fierceness, that her lips stung and her senses reeled again. Now, with a hint of tears in her eyes, she appealed to him.

'I love you so much – don't make it more difficult for me.'

'But I'm not – I'm only trying to get you to marry me at once.'

'But darling, I feel it would be wrong. Your mother would simply hate it and we must give her time to get used to the idea.'

'After what she did behind my back, she doesn't deserve consideration from either of us.'

'Then what about *my* mother? She has always looked forward to my wedding – she has said so heaps of times. She would be bitterly disappointed if I just wired to say that I was already married.'

Renato rolled his eyes heavenwards.

'*Dio mio!* Are all women the same? Even

my beloved Katherine? Must it be a white bride – veil, orange blossom– "The Voice That Breathed O'er Eden" and the villagers throwing flowers at our feet, saying: "'Aint the bride beautiful and 'aint *he* a smasher?"'

Katherine leaned her forehead against his shoulder and giggled.

'You're abominably conceited.'

'And you're horribly practical. Whenever I want to do something quite delightfully mad, you switch on the red light and say stop and make me put on all my brakes.'

'No, darling – you shall always do exactly as you like and I shall have no control over you at all in the future. I haven't much control over myself this instant if you only knew. I'm hanging on to a mere thread of sanity tonight.'

'This morning,' he corrected, and touched her lips with his again. But this time she drew away and opened her bedroom door.

'I refuse to say another word to you – or kiss you. Let's both get some sleep, darling, and please let's try not to hurt anybody else. I do want our life to start by being right.'

'It shall be as you wish. Good night, angel,' he said.

'Good night. Good *morning*,' she whispered, and the door closed behind her. Renato, with a sigh, walked along the corridor and into his own room. For a moment he stepped out on to his balcony and looked at the rosy light of dawn that was just breaking in the East, touching the dome of the Basilica with fingers of fire. The water below was a dark, cool green. The air blew chill, and a faint mist hung over St Marc's Square. He stretched his arms above his head. How tired he was! And how deeply, beautifully in love with his Katherine. She was exactly what he needed in his life; what he had always needed. With her beside him, he could do any job – and like it – he who had once thought it would be terrible to have to work.

She was right, of course. It wouldn't be fair to the parents on either side if they raced into a marriage, that one was too ill, and the other too far away, to attend.

What a frightful day it had been! What an *appalling* scene with Violantè! Even at the bitter end, she had made another effort to get him.

'You'll never be happy with that English girl,' had been her parting words.

But, strangely enough, he had no doubts at all about his happiness. He knew he could never be happy with anybody *but* Katherine. There were certain aspects of the future that were, naturally, not attractive. But he could face up to them. He would not, for instance, enjoy selling his old home and all the beautiful things that his father had passed on to him. It would be a wrench to leave the

Palazzo Voccheroni for good. It would give him a pang to sell his motor-boat, and his Alfa-Romeo. A new experience for Renato di Voccheroni to find himself in a Milanese factory (if he had the luck to be taken on there); to come down to a small run-about, a modest apartment. A very new experience to have to count the *lira* before he spent them. But Katherine would be with him. Katherine, with her youth and beauty and strange wisdom; her generous heart, her genius for loving and for inspiring love.

He turned from the window and the pearly morning and threw himself down on his bed. Fully dressed like that, he fell into a sleep of exhaustion.

Katherine was up long before Renato awakened. When Luigi, as usual, took in the coffee-tray and *croissants,* he cast a pitying look at his master's weary, young face and that long, tired body stretched out on the bed in the crumpled suit, and left him again. The *Signore Marchese* needed rest. Yesterday had been terrible. The whole staff had whispered during breakfast that it was not only that the *Signora Marchesa* had had a heart attack but that some dire misfortune had overtaken the house. There were no gay voices raised in song in the *Palazzo* to greet this new golden day of Spring. Thérèse went about with red-rimmed eyes and a sniff. She, who did quite a bit of eavesdropping, was more aware than the rest of the servants that the main trouble came from lack of money, and she saw herself out of a job. The Marchesa would no longer be able to afford a personal maid.

Katherine, although heavy-eyed and still tired, got up at her usual hour. There would be plenty to do this morning. She resisted all Thérèse's attempts to gossip, or extract information from her.

Possibly the one truly contented person in the *Palazzo* that morning was Bianca. Things were going her way at last. She had received by first post a letter from a girl of her own age who had been at school with her in Paris – the one good friend she had made – she had invited Bianca to Lausanne where she was going with her mother to spend a fortnight's holiday, following an operation for appendicitis.

Bianca showed this letter to Katherine. Her sallow face was quite pretty because she looked eager and happy.

'You will *make* Mamma let me go, won't you, Kathee? I've never been to Switzerland, and my friend, Claudine, is a year older than I am and has many admirers. I think she would be pleased to pass one on to me and we should have great fun together. She says that her mother thinks it would be good for her to have my company. There is lots we can do in Lausanne, and it is a very fine climate for my *migraine*,' she added slyly.

Katherine was at once sympathetic. It would be the very thing – to get Bianca out of this harassed household at the moment. So with Bianca hovering in the background, agitated and nervous, Katherine duly approached the Marchesa.

The nun who was on day duty said that her patient had breakfasted, and was quite anxious to see *Mees*.

Katherine's heart jolted a little as she tip-toed into the Marchesa's room. In the old days she had always felt some trepidation before an interview with Aunt Beatrice; who even when she was her most charming, scared Katherine. This morning she found no reason to be in the least scared. But only to feel pity. As Renato had said, his mother had aged overnight. Katherine was shocked to see the Marchesa without any make-up – without any of that usual chic or coquetry of the elderly woman who seeks with the aid of cosmetics and smart clothes, to retain a semblance of her youth.

Beatrice di Voccheroni, this morning, sat propped by many big pillows, looking strangely small and wizened. She seemed to have shrunk. The lace-edged pink satin bed-jacket looked incongruous against her pale, unpainted face. Her hair was limp, her whole appearance limp, too – like a doll that had lost its stuffing. Only the handsome eyes seemed alive and they even smiled at Katherine as the girl approached her bed.

'Come on – I'm not going to eat you,' she said.

It was at least the voice of the old Marchesa – dictatorial, expecting to be obeyed.

Katherine sat down beside her.

'I do so hope you're feeling better–' she began.

But somehow the apology stuck in her throat and she became obsessed with a feeling of guilt as if she, as well as Renato, had struck this pampered, exacting woman a blow from which she would never recover. How ill she looked! Yet the nun had said her heart was very much stronger and there was no longer cause for alarm if she took things quietly.

But somehow it was a pathetic change coming in here and finding this orderly 'sick room'. Everything put away – not an article of clothing in sight. No flowers had come up as yet. It seemed to have lost all its glamour. What a contrast to the old days, with Aunt Beatrice screaming down the telephone as she ate her breakfast, screaming orders at Thérèse, at *her;* the bed littered with papers and letters; the room full of flowers, perfumes, lights.

Oh dear, thought Katherine, in another moment I shall burst into tears.

The Marchesa had nothing unkind to say

to Katherine. She had come face to face with her own soul since yesterday and found it wanting. After the first storm of rage and disappointment that had so nearly wrecked her, she had undergone a strange spiritual transformation. Maybe it was because she had been afraid that she was going to die. Those few moments of dreadful pain and frantic effort to breathe had left their mark, not only physically but mentally. She had imagined it to be the end. Seen herself suddenly, as a selfish, irreligious woman about to be hurled into Eternity with few good deeds and a great many unattractive ones to her debit.

She had known an instant of terrible fear as well as terrible pain. Deep remorse – the natural sequence – had followed the fear. Once she knew that her heart attack was not fatal and she was to live, fear departed and remorse remained. She regretted not only the bargain she had struck with Violantè, but the fact that she had for so many years encouraged her own son to live the life of an idle spendthrift. She was ashamed because she had neglected Bianca. There was no end to the things that she regretted. She had awakened early this morning and lain here with the tears rolling down her cheeks. This was her punishment. She must not blame Renato for his refusal to make a loveless and mercenary marriage. If it had turned out a failure she would only have added another regrettable misdeed to her record. She must be glad that Renato had chosen a nice girl who would make a better wife than *she*, Beatrice, had ever been a mother. And if bankruptcy and social ruin stared them in the face – that must be accepted as part of her penance.

Such was the mental state of the Beatrice who received Katherine this morning. But the transformation was by no means complete. There lurked in her yet a dozen or more human sensations of regret – not for what she had done – but for what she was losing. She hardly dared dwell on the future. It was such a ghastly thought – giving up *everything* that in her estimation used to make life seem worth living. Her long, thin fingers twitched on the monogrammed sheet. She looked at Katherine. The girl looked back, pale, tired but composed, as usual. Beatrice envied Katherine her serenity. Poor Connie had been just the same – no matter what the trouble at school – Connie had never turned a hair. How nice it must be to be born placid! Again there was the trace of the old, nervous, excitable Beatrice as she said:

'Don't sit there staring – tell me what's been going on.'

Katherine flushed.

'I – I didn't mean to stare, Aunt Beatrice.'

'I suppose I don't look my best,' said the Marchesa with a dry laugh. 'That good creature who is nursing me looked so horrified when I asked her for my make-up box that I told her that I wouldn't bother. What's the use of making-up, anyhow? I'm finished. I shall never again care what I look like.'

'Oh, Aunt Beatrice, why should you feel like that? You mustn't!'

'Could you tell me what there is to look forward to?'

Katherine felt a hot prickly sensation down her back; acute embarrassment.

'But – why – not? There will be lots to look forward to.'

'My dear, the di Voccheronis are ruined and you know it.'

'I don't know much about the money affairs,' stammered Katherine, 'although Renato says that a great deal will have to be sold up.'

'Everything will have to be sold. Violantè must be paid back, at once, and in full.'

Katherine nodded miserably. Beatrice shut her eyes.

'What a fool I was ever to suppose that it would turn out for the best!'

'But in another way perhaps it *will* all turn out for the best,' Katherine ventured to remark.

'For you, no doubt, my dear child. You've got the man you wanted – a man whom a great many women have wanted – and you've never had money so you won't miss it.'

Katherine pulled nervously at her collar.

'Oh, Aunt Beatrice,' she broke out, 'I wish I knew what to say. It's all so tricky! You see, I love Renato terribly and I know that he loves me and that we're going to be very happy, but I do realize how disappointed you must be, and how hard it will be for both you and Renato not to be rich any more. But I'm sure he'll make a success of whatever job he takes over. He's a wonderful person – oh, please forgive me for all this if you think any of it is my fault,' she added, and her lips quivered and the tears rushed into her eyes, try as much as she could to stop them.

It was the sight of those tears and the brave simplicity of her speech that touched the depths of the older woman's heart. The desire to be bitter – faded. She felt a sudden genuine tenderness for this girl; a new understanding of why her 'Toto' loved Katherine, and not Violantè Chiago.

She put out a hand. Katherine gripped it with her warm strong fingers. In a shaken voice, Beatrice whispered:

'My dear, my dear, you don't have to be sorry about anything. I know how wonderful my son is and how can I blame you for loving him? You just don't quite realize how different the sort of lives we have led, are from yours and your mother's. There must be a great deal you don't understand, just as I have never understood how people who lack money can be content. But we'll just have to learn to try and see each other's point of view. One thing I'll tell you – I agree with Renato, that you're a darling. I shall enjoy having you as a daughter-in-law very much – only just give me time to get used to the general change in our conditions.'

Katherine, quick to respond, was on her knees now beside the bed. She leaned her cheek against one of the Marchesa's hands and kissed it.

'Oh, Aunt Beatrice, I love Renato so much – and I want to love you, too.'

The Marchesa stroked the fair, bent head.

'All right – all right, my dear – we'll get on very well. I'll try and grit my teeth and watch the old home being sold up. No doubt, as Renato has already told you there will be enough left for me to live on, in a modest and retired fashion. I can see myself becoming one of those impecunious old women who creep into the Casino and stake a few francs on the roulette table and then creep out again to buy themselves a glass of milk and a bun.'

'Oh, Aunt Beatrice, you'll never be like that!' Katherine said with a mixture of a laugh and a sob.

She was beginning to feel self-confident and happy again. Gloriously happy because Renato's mother did not hate her. She added: 'I must go downstairs and fetch the most beautiful red carnations which have just arrived from the Barone. He left them early this morning with a note for you.'

Fresh remorse plucked at Beatrice's heart-strings.

'How can I be so wicked as to complain about my life when I have the love of a man like Alvise di Mallighi,' she whispered. 'Every day for twenty-five years he has sent those carnations and always the one white flower for *me*. So patient – so faithful! I don't deserve it, Katherine. It should be a black flower not a white one, shouldn't it?'

Katherine shook her head, near to tears again. And then with a pang remembered the real reason why she had come to see Aunt Beatrice. She spoke to her about Bianca and the invitation to Lausanne. The Marchesa gave permission without argument.

'Poor Bianca – she's had the thin end of the wedge lately – let her go and enjoy herself. I know Claudine Mirreville's people – they're very nice – I don't think Bianca can come to much harm.'

Katherine walked out of the room and straight into Bianca who was anxiously hovering outside. The girl was ecstatic in her delight when she heard that her mother had given permission for her to accept Claudine's invitation.

'Oh, how wonderful, Kathee – I know I'm going to be happy and I shall owe it to you!' she said, flinging her arms around Katherine. A voice said:

'We all of us in this house owe a lot to Katherine.'

The two girls swung round. Renato stood there – still in his dressing-gown.

'It's time I was up and about. I've got to learn to get up early and go to my office, haven't I, Katherine?' he turned to her with a grin.

'But, of course, darling,' she laughed.

But he saw the tears on her lashes and came quickly to her side.

'What's upset you? Have you seen Mamma?'

'Yes – but if I'm upset it's not her fault. She's been perfectly sweet to me. It's just as you said – she's going to make the very best of things. I've never admired her more.'

'I'll look in and kiss her good morning,' said Renato clearing his throat.

Katherine smiled as he walked into his mother's bedroom. She was glad, because she knew that that kiss from Renato would be more than a reconciliation – it would be the tonic that Beatrice di Voccheroni needed to help her get well again.

Thérèse met her as she was going down-

335

stairs and said that the Englishman, Mr Kerr-West, had telephoned.

'Oh, lord,' thought Katherine, 'poor old Dick, we'd all forgotten *him*.'

When she answered that call – try as she would to remember to let him down lightly – she could not keep the exultation out of her voice.

'It's all going to be all right, Dick. Renato has asked me to marry him.'

An instant's silence and then Dick made his big gesture.

'I congratulate you with all my heart, Katherine darling. And I congratulate Renato. He is the devil of a lucky fellow. How has it come about?'

Katherine said breathlessly:

'It's all rather involved – but do come round and let's tell you. I know Renato will want to see you.'

'And ask me to be best man?' came from Dick with a touch of dryness.

'Oh, Dick,' began Katherine remorsefully – but he broke in.

'No, you needn't say it. I don't want sympathy. I'll get over it. I'll come round and tell that old son of a gun that he's got to settle down and make you happy, or I'll soon be on his trail.'

'Then we'll all meet at Harry's Barn later in the morning,' said Katherine and put up the receiver, her heart singing.

27

From Katherine's Diary, June 11th:

Tomorrow is my wedding-day. I am so excited that I hardly know how to write. I've already made two ink-blots because my fingers shake and my fountain-pen wobbles! I really must calm down and pull myself together, otherwise a fine bride I shall make tomorrow. I, who am supposed to be so placid.

I look around me and say to myself: 'This is the last time Katherine Shaw will ever write in her book. Tomorrow she will become Katherine di Voccheroni.' The Marchesa di Voccheroni to give me my full title. But it's such a mouthful. It sounds so odd for little Kathy – she can't take it in yet or credit the fact that it is really going to be her name!

I look around this little bedroom that I've occupied as plain Katherine Shaw for so many years. I see a brand new cabin-trunk on the floor, lid open, inner straps still undone, a gleam of pink satin shining through a layer of tissue. That would be my bestest satin night-gown with the lovely lace. Mummy made it. She has been an angel and made me several heavenly bits of lingerie. She always was good at that delicate sort of work. My pink velvet dressing-gown is a work of art, lined with silk-chiffon. My undies are too fragile and gossamer for me, really, but Mummy says she knows Renato by now and that he is the sort of artistic man to appreciate a wife with a glamorous trousseau and that I must start off by pleasing him. Bless her – she's never done anything but try to please dear old Daddy, but not by wearing glamorous undies. He'd be better pleased if she saved the money!

He adores her really and she, him – but it isn't the way Renato and I adore each other. We are just not in this world. We live up among the stars. Very nice too. We mean to try and stay up there even if we have to descend occasionally to mundane levels and study that grim question of economy which will loom pretty largely in our lives for a bit.

I want to write in my diary today. I haven't opened it for nearly four months. Yet I'm fascinated by the things in my room. The sun – not as hot and glittering as that lovely sun in Venice, but mild English sunlight – is trickling through my casements. I hear the hum of bees in the honeysuckle; the deeper hum of the sea down below the mighty cliffs. The occasional whine of a seagull, circling round the flagstaff at the bottom of our garden. The boys and Veryan are eating a picnic tea out there, having just come in from bathing. I can just see their faces – brown, sandy, sticky, grinning at each other. Veryan's hair is wet, hanging in straight strands. I can *hear their laughter. They're so full of beans as usual and looking forward to tomorrow. Veryan is going to be a bridesmaid – she looks too adorable in the little rose-pink organdie dress mummy has made her and her tiny cap of silk rose-petals. She's going to suffer for my sake, bless her, and go to bed tonight with that straight hair in curlers. She may be only ten but she wants HER share of glamour, she says. David is so shy he refuses to take part in the wedding, but Peter has consented to be an usher and is terribly proud of it.*

I'm to be married in the lovely old church at St Columb. It's where Mummy and Daddy were married too – and where we children were all christened, so it's a nice thought.

The old homestead will be packed to overflowing before this afternoon is over. Aunt Vera – Mummy's only sister is coming to stay the night – all the way from Bath where she has lived ever since she was widowed. And Daddy's brother, my Uncle Everard, a retired Naval Captain, and Aunt Katherine who is my god-mother and who I was named after, are coming from Plymouth. The boys are sleeping out, in a tent in the garden tonight and thrilled at the idea. I bet they'll never sleep a wink all night. Mum is sure they'll get rheumatism, but Daddy says it can't hurt them with a groundsheet. They're Boy Scouts, anyhow. And Veryan will be in a camp-bed in the parent's room. I offered to have her with me but Mummy says the bride has a right to be quiet and alone on her wedding eve and I must say I shall appreciate it. All this excitement makes one so tired.

My attention strays again. I look at my wedding-dress on its hanger outside the wardrobe. I can't stop looking at it. It's really beautiful and I really did look nice when Miss Christy tried it on me in Newquay for the last time yesterday. I didn't want satin – everyone has that. So we found a lovely fine grosgrain – white with a tinge of pink – cut lowish in front and tight across the breast and with long tight sleeves. The Marchesa sent over her very own veil from Venice, by a friend who was coming to England. I've never seen a more exquisite piece of lace – it falls right to my feet. With it I'm to wear a quite simple coronet of orange-blossoms. And round my neck, Renato's main present to me. A triple-row of glorious real pearls with diamond clasp. They belonged to his grandmother and he refused to let his mother sell them with all the other jewels that have 'gone with the wind'.

'My wife must have some decent jewellery,' he said, and out of the Marchesa's wonderful collection (it raised an enormous sum at Rome), they kept back my pearls, an emerald and diamond ring – it was my engagement ring – and a pair of emerald and diamond clips and ear-rings to match. They cost a fortune but the Marchesa and Renato insisted on me having them, so I'm terrifically lucky. She kept little for herself. Just one or two pieces. But more about

my future mother-in-law in a moment.

I am looking at my wedding-dress. At my new silver shoes. My going-away ensemble, a beautifully cut dress, navy blue thick, silky material and short coat to match, with white collar and cuffs; my new white doeskin gloves and bag and tiny white hat made of silk flowers. The Marchesa has also passed on one of her many fur coats to me. She sold a superb wild mink in Milan. It raised millions of lira; kept an ermine coat for herself and gave me a short summer-ermine jacket which she said was the least sophisticated and suited me the best.

I look longest at the suit-case – also open, packed ready for my honeymoon, and think about it. We are spending part of it in Cornwall which Renato doesn't know but wants to explore – South Cornwall, beginning with Mullion – then we go right up to far-away Scotland, to stay at the Royal Hotel in Scalloway which is an ideal spot for lovers. We both were absolutely in agreement that we wanted to find a place out of the world we knew and that knew us – away from England and the excitement of the Continent – and up to those misty, lonely, romantic isles in the far North. Two weeks up there – then back to Mawgan to pick up my things and the presents Mummy is storing for us, then to our home ... *in Milan. There to begin our new life. A small but pleasant apartment in a quiet avenue of trees in the great, noisy, fascinating city where the Cathedral towers over all – a*

*gigantic triumph of architectural magnificence –
and the industrial heart of Italy throbs in so
many large factories. In one of these factories,
owned by one of Renato's great friends, he will
start to do his first job. And it won't be easy for
him. There is never an easy road to victory for
the working man.*

*One thing we will have is an elegant home
because Renato kept some of the things he
particularly loved out of his home. An assortment of glorious antiques and ornaments. My
curtains, too, will be sumptuous – cut down from
the lovely Florentine brocades which used to
hang in the Palazzo's large salon.*

*But I don't seem to be beginning this diary
where I should. So much as happened during
these few months.*

*Aunt Beatrice got better quickly – I call her
'Mamma mia' now, at her request (but I shall
never use her 'Toto' for my husband because I
don't think it suits him, although, of course, like
all mothers, she remembers him as her small
boy).*

*Well, she recovered and except for one or two
lapses into melancholia – generally bemoaning
her lot – she has behaved like a brick. Mummy's
quite right when she says the worst has got to
happen in order to bring the best out in some
people. And just as too much money spoilt
Mamma, the lack of it seems to have turned her
into a much nicer person.*

Venice, of course, once the news became

general, buzzed with gossip for days. The phone never stopped ringing and people never stopped coming round to sympathize, because the Palazzo *was up for sale. Mamma was quite ruthless and broke off relationship with everybody except her greatest friends who came to see her out of* real *friendship and not mere curiosity. It is amazing how many of the so-called 'cream of society' dropped out altogether once they knew they would never be entertained in the old manner again.*

Bianca went off to Lausanne and sent us rapturous letters and postcards. She even found a nice young doctor from one of the big clinics there who became interested in her, and took her out. So she *benefited by the family upheaval. When she came home, she was crazy about her doctor, and Benito Usilli was a thing of the past. Mamma was sensible and encouraged her correspondence with the young Swiss. As she remarked to Renato and to me: 'It might be just Bianca's cup of tea to do good works as the wife of one of "those dull Swiss!"' The old, cynical, worldly Beatrice was far from dead! But she was so much warmer and more friendly in her general attitude, and showed a sense of humour even when the sale took place. A masterpiece went for a song and one painting – Beatrice herself had done it as a girl – fetched a far higher price! It made her laugh. The* Palazzo *was, in the end, purchased by no less a person that Mr Drumann – Hilary's father.*

Renato had written a short note to Hilary telling her of his forthcoming marriage to me, and of the financial collapse. She wrote the sweetest letter – she really is a nice girl – wished us both luck and said she had asked Pop to buy the Palazzo at any price. If she couldn't marry a di Voccheroni she was at least going to live part of the year in their glorious home, she said. Old man Drumman gave a wonking price for it and bought in a lot of the treasures too. He called it 'an insurance for Hilary'.

We all felt quite glad that such a nice creature as Hilary would be the future chaletaine. Thought Mamma winced at the idea of what she called 'a tin-can millionaire' in her aristocratic home where some of the most cultured people in Europe had gathered.

Well, anyhow, enough money was raised on the sale of the Palazzo and its contents to more than pay back what was owed to the Chiago estate. Let us draw a veil over Violantè! She disappeared after that appalling night of Mamma's heart attack, and soon afterwards we saw in the papers that she had married again – an Italian, younger than Renato, and heir to another old title. Renato said he had a lot of property in the south, but was 'a poor type'.

Violantè and the di Voccheronis never met again, but I can imagine what she felt when she saw the announcement of our engagement which Renato put into all the Continental and English papers.

Now follows the saddest part of my story – the final packing up and exit from the Palazzo. *We'll have to draw a veil over that, too, because I'm afraid poor Mamma broke down and cried and Bianca cried in sympathy and Renato looked grim and was obviously very moved. The whole staff wept, too, although the Drumanns had wired that they wished to keep on Mamma's wonderful cook, and Luigi. But Thérèse – who had recently indulged in enough general gossip to last a lifetime – returned home to her native France. After that – the motor-boat went. Then the Alfa-Romeo. Then, for the time being, good-bye to Venice. Beautiful, enchanted city of waterways, of golden light, of heartache and happiness. Dear Venice where I learned to love, to suffer, and to be made whole again. One day Renato and I are going back after we are married, but not just yet while the memory of the selling up and departure is still a fresh wound. But one day, darling Renato said to me in one of his best and most humorous moods, 'One day we'll take our children there and you shall have your little guide-book that you love, and tell them all the things. And of course we'll be quite humble and hire a third-rate gondola. And they'll suck cheap sweets, and you'll be wearing last year's model bought from a rich friend, and I'll be pretty shabby, but we'll stop in front of the* Palazzo *and say: "This is where your dear father once lived, and fell in love with your dear mother." And it will still be called the* Palazzo

Voccheroni, *so we'll all get a kick out of* that. *Then we'll go and eat – not at the Danielli – oh no! much too expensive – but in one of those little modest cafés; but we'll think how rich we are, because we're so monstrously happy.'*

Oh, I loved *that! Not only did I love to think of our children (what could be more wonderful for me than to have a family of Renato's?), but because he really* means *it when he says we shall be so happy.*

He got his job – in the car factory in Milan. His friend, the Signore Director, *turned up trumps and said he would be delighted to welcome such a distinguished young man into the firm. But that he'd got to start at the very bottom. True, he can work up to becoming General Manager, which carries a very big salary, but he won't be at all important for a long time. He'll even wear overalls and go into the works where he'll learn all about that particular make of car, and then, afterwards start on the administrative side. There is nothing the General Manager hasn't got to know. But Renato doesn't seem at all depressed by the idea. He has always adored cars, and is going to like 'tinkering', he says, instead of handing the engine over to a chauffeur.*

We had a perfectly wonderful few days in Rome – we all went to a very small, quiet hotel where I helped to 'settle Mamma and Bianca in' and where she intends to live while she looks for a small apartment. They are going to stay in

Rome. Nobody was miserable. It was a warm, comfortable little place, and the di Voccheronis have many good friends in Rome, although at times Mamma missed the Palazzo – *and Thérèse to wait hand and foot on her. But she got used to it and she won't be so poor – because there is still the trust money – the capital they* couldn't *spend. As for Bianca – she started at once to train for a secretarial job, and seems enchanted by the idea and not nearly so prone to her* migraine. *All that girl needed (as I always thought) was something interesting to do, and a bit of a thrill out of life; more independence.*

I thought the most touching thing of all was the way in which the old Barone Alvise di Mallighi followed his adored one. Yes, he actually moved from the hotel in Venice where he had lived for twenty years, *to Rome, to the same hotel as Mamma and Bianca. And believe it or not as you like, soon after his arrival he proposed all over again, red carnations – one white one – and all. Mamma told us about it. He said she might just as well let him look after her for the rest of her life. He had small means, and he would like to share them with her.*

Of course, Mamma refused him. But the last letter I had from Bianca said that she wouldn't be at all surprised if Mamma did become the Baronesse di Mallighi, in the long run.

Mamma and Uncle Alvise are inseparable these days and it's really sweet to see them together. Mamma is so much nicer to him than she used to be. More thoughtful for his aches and pains. And he is blissful about her. She even admitted to me that she might marry him rather than face a lonely old age. He was always an enchanting companion, but she wished to wait until I was married. Well, Kathee, that might be in a year's time when she thinks me old enough to marry Jean.

So it seems that financial misfortune, far from destroying the di Voccheronis, has brought them peace and a new kind of happiness. As for me – when I think of what lies in front of me tomorrow – I am the happiest girl in the world.

Renato, Mamma, and Bianca are all due in Newquay this afternoon. Coming on the Cornish Riviera. Poor darlings! They have had to learn to travel in trains, because they can't afford to hire a big car. But they don't seem to mind. Renato's last letter said that Mamma was quite looking forward to a spell in Cornwall and seeing 'poor Connie' again, after all these years. I bet they'll talk for hours about the old schooldays. It will be most amusing. After Renato and I have gone away Mamma and Bianca are moving here to stay a fortnight with Mummy and Daddy. It's heavenly in Mawgan Porth in June and the fresh sea air will do them both good after the heat and dust of Rome.

I haven't seen Renato for a month and I have

been home now since the end of April. He came over once and met me in London because he said he could not bear such a long separation. But oh, how wonderful to know that after tonight we won't have ever *to be separated again!*

Later.

Peter has just torn in with a telegram for me. He teased me before I opened it.

'Bet it's to say your Iti has changed his mind.'
I almost kicked the little horror.

'Don't you dare *call my Renato an Iti. He is as English as you are and I'll never let you come and stay with us in Milan if you don't behave!'*

Then he giggled and backed out of my bedroom, saying: 'Beg your pudding, Marchesa.' He said it three times, ending in a yelp of laughter and then fled back to the others and his picnic tea. He's a real boy. I love the little demon and would forgive him anything. I know he really is one of Renato's greatest admirers, too. In fact, Renato was a huge success with my whole family when he stayed with us six weeks ago. But I think the highest praise of all came from old Jake, our old fisherman, who afterwards said to me:

'He'm a very pleasant young gentleman you be a-marrying, Miss Kathy. He be all there and knows a thing or two "about catching lobsters".'

Well, that's a lot from Jake who always says no stranger knows anything.

349

I've just opened my wire. It was sent off from London this morning. It lies here on my desk. I look at it (having written the last page of my diary), it seems to have been a bit delayed, sent off before he left Paddington. The train is due in about an hour. Of course I shall meet it.

The telegram says:

I am on my way. Tomorrow is the Day of Days. I love you now and for ever. R.

Just that. But it's enough!

This Large Print Book, for people
who cannot read normal print,
is published under the auspices of

THE ULVERSCROFT FOUNDATION

... we hope you have enjoyed this book.
Please think for a moment about those
who have worse eyesight than you ...
and are unable to even read or enjoy
Large Print without great difficulty.

You can help them by sending a
donation, large or small, to:

**The Ulverscroft Foundation,
1, The Green, Bradgate Road,
Anstey, Leicestershire, LE7 7FU,
England.**
or request a copy of our brochure for
more details.

The Foundation will use all donations
to assist those people who are visually
impaired and need special attention
with medical research, diagnosis
and treatment.

Thank you very much for your help.